Seed Blood

A Kayne Sorenson Mystery

Thomas Paul Severino

Thomas Paul Severino

Seed Blood

A Kayne Sorenson Mystery

Thomas Paul Severino

Copyright © 2018 by Thomas Paul Severino

Pollywog Pond Communications, LLC

www.tomseverino.com

tomseverino100@gmail.com

Cover painting: *The Martyrs in the Catacombs* by Jules Eugène Lenepveu (1819 – 1898)

ISBN: 978-1-7322278-1-1

Seed Blood

Also by Thomas Paul Severino

The Kayne Sorenson Mysteries: The Quartet of Blood

Seed Blood

Tribal Blood

Stage Blood

Ancient Blood

The Kayne Sorenson Mysteries: The Quartet of Evil

The Evil Genius

The Shadow of Evil

The Pearl of Great Evil

The Evil League

The Kayne Sorenson Mysteries: The New Adventures

The Crystal Orb

The Flower of Gold

The Amazing Adventures of Rebecca Quinto

The Frozen Diva

The Lost Museum

The Last Maya

Thomas Paul Severino

Seed Blood

For Anton

Thomas Paul Severino

Seed Blood

Virtue, therefore, is not based upon dogma but dogma upon virtue, and it is not faith that creates martyrs but martyrs who create faith.

– Miguel de Unamuno

Thomas Paul Severino

Prologue

Soft weeping was the only sound in the dark open space. The young man lay naked and semi-conscious on the cell floor at the back of the large room. Wracked with intense pain, the captive groaned. His mind was flooded with hallucinations as he surrendered to their anesthetic and hypnotic power. These dark dreams dulled the pain from beatings and hunger. He no longer could differentiate between reality and the miasma of his mind movies. The whirling images moved back and forth in time.

Images of sailors gathered in the dark corners of his injured brain, crisp white uniforms, and shorn heads. His hallucinations overlapped from his training days and tours of duty--speeding boats casting for underwater demolition, divers for search and rescue, decks of large aircraft carriers launching helicopters into cloud-darkened skies.

He loved the Navy. Both his Dad and Grandpa served, each attaining officer status. A headline in his home newspaper, "High School Valedictorian to Serve His Country. Scholar-Athlete Continues Family Tradition," streamed through other disjointed remembrances of home.

Initial Entry Training at Naval Station Great Lakes, Illinois, was grueling. Still, he had the disciplined body and mind to get through it. He established himself as a platoon leader, admired by his battle buddies, and respected by his drill sergeant. He kept many personal secrets, but some eventually became public. Alone at graduation, he made himself think it did not matter.

An intense physical training regimen and a total psychological adjustment to combat behavior should have prepared him for his present ordeal, but his movements were confined. His captor met any resistance with armed, brutal force. Leg irons softly clanked in the silent, black warehouse as he moved. He did not hear the truck return to the parking lot as his body shifted on the cold cement.

America's Navy! The camaraderie of those initial months confirmed his devotion to his fellow warriors. He was a standout of bravery and courage. The young man saw himself through the visions that came now, training, going to class, and learning to be a dedicated sailor. Images of battle Stations aboard the USS Thrayer filled his jumbled thoughts.

In the beginning, his homosexuality held few concerns for some of his comrades in arms. Still, there were a few "phobes," including one asshole captain who began to call him out. Soon, there were the looks, insinuations of improper conduct, shunning, and hateful remarks that came before the fights.

"Hey, cocksucker, c'mere and do a bud a favor." Close-up of red, sneering faces of shipmates, his fists clenched unconsciously in his dreams. An angry captain glowering with rage, "Like to see all of you faggots out of this man's Navy."

He passed into a deeper sleep, but the visions stayed and continued to sweep him into a swamp of memories. He rolled on the cement floor. Stabs of pain from his broken ribs pierced his semi-comatose dreams.

Now, Mr. Rutzel, his eighth-grade swim coach, was teaching him to train tough. "Form is all-important, kid. The only way to make gains." He stood in front of a locker room mirror, flexing his muscles, no longer a skinny geekazoid but a new and improved muscled pup. *Bully this, fuckers!*

An image flashed by of a handsome young jock, his first crush, Jason Callaghan, a crazy hot pole vaulter. Jase sat directly in front of him in tenth-grade geometry class. He found himself so lost watching his buddy's young, muscled back and shoulders and the way his hairline came to a point at the nape of his muscular neck. Touch? No, be cool, Jared. Jase C... in his mind, his own All-American Boy. But it all got ugly when the guys began to talk. The fight and then, "Just stay away from me...."

"Jase!" He raised his heavy arms in his dream.

His outraged mother's scream ripped through his mind as the image of his angry high school dream boy vanished. Now, he was faced with his furiously angry parents reacting to what he called "The Reveal." Mother, crying and quoting scripture. She paced, wailing, "Get pastor Michaels to talk to him. I want him in that program, he mentioned. They guarantee a cure."

His father, red-faced and pounding the kitchen counter... "After all we've done for you, how can you disgrace us like this? The Navy will never allow it. You will never amount to anything. Get out of my house!"

This image morphed into a specter of his raging grandfather shaking his fist. "No member of my family, ever... do you hear me?... ever... It is against the laws of God, an abomination."

In his cage, the young sailor now curled into a fetal ball and cried, "Michael, where are you?" in his feverish sleep.

More swirling images. Fleet Week... dancing with Michael ... hot sex, followed by long talks into the night. Telling secrets, feeling safe. His dreams advanced and retreated like wind-blown pages of a diary frantically tumbling in his mind. Despite the cold, sweat covered his entire body.

Michael was speaking again. "That guy doesn't mean anything to me, Jared. It's just that sometimes you're not here when I need you. We should be together more. I guess it comes with your job. I thought it would work; I was wrong. I'm sorry."

Why is there so much pain?

The roll-up door to the warehouse chamber hit the ceiling 50 feet from the prisoner's cell. Street lamps in the parking lot backlit the hulking man in the baseball cap standing in the doorway. Overhead lights in caged, reflective housing began their charge-up, increasing illumination from a soft glow to bright white accompanied by a low, rasping hum. The big man rolled down the door and picked up a thick canvas bag.

Gripping the bars for support, the captive staggered to his feet as footsteps approached the cage. Over the seemingly endless hours, the boy was sure of one thing. Throughout the days and nights of brutal torture, he had clearly seen the face of his tormentor.

The young sailor knew he would die.

Thomas Paul Severino

Chapter One: The Mark Of Kayne

NICK SECHI'S JOURNAL

The tall man in the back of the classroom was "The Vampire Lestat." His appearance was haunting and strangely exotic.

Yes, I have a very active imagination. I am overly visual, but I swear to God – the spitting image of Ann Rice's regal antihero.

Now my cop training kicks in. The "suspect" stands 6'3", about 210 pounds, and, from the cut of his slacks and the French-cuffed, long-sleeved white shirt, he was very, very fit. I placed him in his early thirties and quickly made him out to be an executive of some sort.

Well-groomed, he was a natty dresser with flatteringly tailored clothes. He had thrown his dark blue, bold peak-lapel suitcoat on the student table next to his expensive, professional knapsack, loosening his wide-cut tie-- guessing J. Crew, with matching pocket square. Rolling up his sleeves, he revealed the strong arms of a gym rat. He wore his Fitbit tracker on his right wrist, the non-dominant hand. Therefore, he is lefthanded. He showed no rings and sported brown hipster shoes, which completed the outfit.

I stood in the back of the Florida Global University downtown graduate building's fifth-floor classroom, analyzing this fascinating fellow student. My new crush's white skin startlingly contrasted with his very straight, almost blue-black hair. He wore it closely cut on the sides and relatively long on top, sporting a very trendy "hard part" on the right. Ears were close to his head. He showed a widow's peak above a prominent forehead. High cheekbones, an aquiline nose, and a tightly cropped goatee suggested a northern European background. However, his almond-shaped eyes hint at the ancestral steppes of Central Asia – a mysterious Tartar lord – smoking hot.

My gaydar went into high gear. There is no doubt that Mr. Sexy plays on my team. He has the look of a man who takes excellent care of himself. His chest, back muscles, biceps, and even his nipples shifted with prominent definition beneath the close cut of his gleaming white, spread-collar shirt and dark blue gabardine slacks. The dude is also rockin' a very spectacular jock butt, from what I can see. VPL-- briefs, boxers, commando? This last is a partial observation because he only stood once to remove his jacket and sat down rather quickly, hunching over his laptop.

His movements were very poised and unobtrusive. Nevertheless, it is apparent he quietly emanates alpha energy in the room. Every student entering the class checked him out. He was aware of their interest but did not acknowledge it. Sometimes, hot people can be so cool about being attractive.

I struggled as I cruised the good-looking man, trying to keep my libido in check. I thought, *No, Nick boy, the last thing you need right now is an affair. Things at home are bad enough*. My Italian grandma used to warn about *essere colpito con il fulmine* – getting hit with the lightning bolt. The full meaning is falling in love or in lust with the power and suddenness of a blazing sky bolt. Happens to me all the time. This evening, I resigned myself to think with the big head instead of the little head.

Attempting to sublimate my extreme horniness, I concentrated on analyzing my subject's observable idiosyncrasies. The man in question seemed very comfortable in his skin. Long fingers glided over his laptop keys like a musician stroking a Stradivarius. He occasionally paused to speak to surrounding classmates. He ran his left hand through the pesky shock of black hair, which arches from the crown of his brow over his forehead and eyes on the right side. This movement is like a poker player's tell, unconscious and often repeated.

His smile was like the slash of a sword through his black goatee, flashing some dazzling pearlies, enhancing his strong jawline but disappearing instantly-- the very definition of a "killer smile." Sometimes, it seemed forced. It would appear that he does not smile regularly; it is not a natural response. Just what exactly would make him laugh, I wondered.

Are there extended vampiric canines on this Byronic beauty so strongly reminiscent of the undead? Despite my reservations, I decided to get nearer.

Yes, a closer observation confirmed he was a major hottie, but without bloodsucking equipment. I did my best cool jock swagger and dropped into a seat near him. My strong visual sense is getting hyper-engaged in what promises to be a fascinating course here at FGU. The glass high-rise is mere moments from my work, the Wilton Manors Police Department. I began to think I could enjoy this.

A bit reluctantly, I had decided to go back to school. Since my last case had been extremely violent and resulted in a temporary suspension from the force's patrol division, I had been fighting off a barrage of sleepless nights connected to my job. Consequently, I needed a distraction to offset some post-traumatic stress and the real possibility of getting fired or worse.

I hoped to use some time to begin my graduate degree in criminology with an emphasis in behavioral sciences as related to crime prevention and social control. Criminology 307-001: Biopsychosocial Crime, taught by Kayne J. Sorenson, Ph.D., would create some exciting evenings from the looks of the class members.

I hoped the prof would not be a dull, droning, old academic. After working a long shift, albeit currently chained to a desk because of my suspension, the last thing I needed to do was nap out in class two nights a week while an old codger droned on and on. Hoping to be reinstated as a beat cop but still smarting from the disciplinary actions of my captain, I decided to take this course to hone my craft as an up-and-coming young "crime-stopper." My Flash t-shirt might be a giveaway as to my aspirations to corral the "bad guys."

So, at the ripe old age of 26, it was back to school. A least these students were non-traditional, adult learners like the "Prince of Vampires" in the last row whom, try as I might, I could not resist. I decided he was a hot-shot lawyer with judgeship aspirations. Yes, long black robes offsetting his--- damn, are those eyes ice blue? Seriously? Judge Pretty also had the eyelashes of a drag queen. As unobtrusively as possible, I moved closer one more seat.

Fitbit tap. "So, how long are we supposed to wait for a late professor?" Lestat says to no one in particular.

"Ten minutes, right?" He was carefully but casually covering up an accent.

Cell phone check... back to the laptop. "Prof's twelve and a half minutes late." Sensing my staring, he lifted a look in my direction,

"Good evening, Officer." Not waiting for a response, he closed his computer and began packing up his gear.

Damn! Outed. So much for undercover. Wait, how...? And the dude is leaving without giving me his number? Shit!

I stopped him, "Excuse me. How did you guess I was a cop?"

That killer smile and a brief, piercing, Siberian Husky stare...

"I never guess, Mate."

Raising his voice, he announced to the group, "You know, anyone with half a brain can teach this class. Why I can teach this class. So why not have a go, eh?"

He picked up his jacket, slung his knapsack over one shoulder while standing, and approached the podium. The class got a complete view of his long, athletic legs and jock butt. He dropped his gear on the instructor's console as he flipped the media switch, firing up the overhead projector.

"Good evening, students. I am Kayne Sorenson. Let's get a start on it, shall we?"

The classroom monitor screen ignited:

CRIMINOLOGY 307-001: BIOPSYCHOSOCIAL CRIME

Kayne J. Sorenson, Ph.D.

Tuesdays and Thursdays, 6:00 PM-9:00 PM

Provocation: Are serial killers naturally born? Why don't psychopaths have empathy for their victims? Is a life of crime genetically hard-wired? The field of neurocriminology is an interdisciplinary, biosocial course that brings scientific data to these inquiries. This relatively new discipline combines social, clinical, and neurosciences research to help students and law enforcers better understand, predict, and prevent future crime.

Professor Sorenson's Office hours, professional contact information, academic portrait shot, jacket, tie, and specs came up on the overhead beside the course abstract.

OK. I adjust my imaginary fantasy image. The dude is not Lestat. Criminology 307-001 would be taught two nights a week by the handsome and daring Dr. Indiana Jones.

Oh, hell, yeah!

***

"Throughout this course, we will explore the biosocial basis of crime and violence, analyzing controversial neuroethical, legal, and philosophical issues surrounding neurocriminology. Our studies in Biopsychosocial Crime will reveal perspectives from essential research in psychology, neuroscience, criminology, sociology, law, business, public health, psychiatry, anthropology, neuroimaging, neuroendocrinology, forensics, and nutrition.

"Before half of you stand up to leave, you should note something significant. You do not need to have an extensive background in biology or psychology. Still, the basics of criminology are a must. This is a graduate course. If you are planning a leadership-level career in Criminology, Psychology, Nursing, Law Enforcement, or Forensics and are not afraid of hard work, you will benefit significantly from our work together."

"Rather than be imprisoned by the podium, Dr. Sorenson moved among his students, making eye contact while speaking with the warm authority of a passionate educator. Members of the group smiled, nodded, and appeared to be engaged as he illustrated his remarks with gestures and expressions boarding on the theatrical.

"To learn and assimilate this new science, you must be prepared to smash the idols that restrain your creativity and curiosity while being grounded by and accountable to fact. The criminal's mind is our stock in trade, and we will pursue the social deviant from many perspectives. Intersecting disciplines hold much knowledge for us in this regard.

"A few additional considerations, if you please. You must be ready to work steadfastly to acquire and benefit from the group's shared knowledge and experience. You must forget all your assumptions about crime, criminal motivation, and criminal profiles. Your first homework assignment is to read everything in the Holmesian Canon by Sir Arthur Conan Doyle. Finally, in this course, be prepared to approach murder, the murderer, and his victims in the dispassionate academic style of Dr. Hannibal Lector. I do not refer here solely to his notorious culinary arts."

This last remark brought laughter and probably eased the minds of a few of us, for whom the first 10 minutes of any class hold the potential for staying enrolled or dropping the course. I have a theory that one learns much when one likes the teacher and even more when a respectful love of the discipline connects scholars.

"At this time, I am supposed to take this attendance." He paused and closed the roll book. "Let's do this a bit differently."

Striding forward, Professor Sorenson addressed a sparkling-eyed African American woman in the row where he had been previously seated. "Good evening. You are from the Boston area, Swansea, I perceive. You work for the Broward County Schools. Am I correct, Ms. Brown? If I may, you should wear your gold hoop earrings more often. They are stunning."

Starting to walk away, he paused, took a step back, squinted slightly, and gestured, "A family heirloom, correct? Oh yes, and Angela, if I may call you Angela, placing your instrument on "stun" will prevent any additional calls from your friends or family during class time. Thank you."

Angela Brown's jaw dropped in astonishment; her right hand reached up to touch her faux diamond posts – not hoops. She appeared to be mystified. Finally, she and the rest of us checked that our cell phones were on silent.

The teacher moved on to a second student and conjured a similar profile, including the young man's technological expertise and his passion for a particular national baseball team. The Professor enlightened the group, "You have experience in social work administration." The student, Jonathan Yurick, stared openmouthed, seemingly likewise astounded by Professor Sorenson's uncanny deductions. His puzzled expression expressed disbelief at how the professor would know anything about him.

Dr. Sorenson continued profiling through eighteen students astonishing us with seemingly impossible to ascertain personal information. He was exact to the last detail, backgrounding everyone in the class with names, professions, family members, places of origin, and, often, unique personality traits. Each encounter created surprised looks and a few soft gasps but many smiles and nods. Then, he placed both hands on my table and looked directly at me.

Speaking to the class but staring good-naturedly at me, Dr. Sorenson said, "It would appear we have in our midst our own 'boots on the ground' in the field of local law enforcement. Class, may I introduce Officer Nicola Michael Sechi of the Wilton Manors Police Force. He holds a BA in Criminology and is a New York Police Academy graduate. He hails from the Bronx, one of six siblings, and his extended family in Milan, Italy, is very proud of him. A graduate of St. Raymond's High School in the Bronx, Officer Nick excels in athletics and, together with his friends, occasionally enjoys the legendary Italian American cuisine."

Smiles and "golf claps"-- hands softly applauding-- came from all around.

He continued, "Officer Sechi, we are grateful for your presence. Hopefully, you will provide much by contributing to the class based on your experience. We expect many of your expert insights. The group will surely benefit from your reputation as one of Wilton Manor's Finest."

Present circumstances notwithstanding, I thought – fuckin' deskbound.

Raising one hand to toss his hair from his forehead and crossing his arms, he struck the dramatic pose of a carnival mind reader. "Furthermore, any help I may provide regarding ongoing investigations will be happily provided with all due confidentiality and discretion."

I was speechless and slightly embarrassed. I hoped I was not blushing after being christened teacher's pet so early. I looked around, expecting smirks.

How could he have known I was hoping for some advice on a current case?

Spinning away to address the class, Kayne Sorenson raised and waved one hand. "Reactions, please, to my methods?"

My hand shot up.

Turning back, "Yes, Officer?"

"Sir, a conclusion, a question, and one observation."

"Please, proceed."

"Conclusion: Your profiling of each student is right out of TV's "Elementary" or the Rathbone-Bruce send-ups from Hollywood in the 1940s. I am suggesting, for example, "Sherlock Holmes and the Voice of Terror," et al. You were going for Holmes' statement, 'You see, but you do not observe, Watson,' to illustrate the power of accurate forensic observation. To do this, you had to quickly come up with some general personal details from overheard conversations, dress, and observable personal belongings.

"So, my question, Sir, is how you guessed the specifics-- names and things like cherished jewelry, fashion choices, and favorite ball clubs? These details are impossible to speculate. "

Striding back up the aisle, he announced, "As I mentioned when we met, Officer, I never guess."

He announced with a bit of bravado, "My dear students, the importance of comprehensive research cannot be overemphasized." Waving his cell phone, he added, "Detailed information on who you are is everywhere. Welcome to the Twenty-first Century." On the overhead, he pulled up the Facebook page of one student, Barbara Kolasa.

Next, the computer screen changed to Angela Brown's University student ID picture featuring lovely gold hoop earrings. He enlarged the screen.

"The jewelry is definitely of the '20s. As such, it features old gold with filigree; *ergo*, a family heirloom."

He nodded to the beaming Ms. Brown. "Your great-grandmother's?"

"Yes, Professor."

Next up was a photo of Jonathan Yurick wearing a distinctive blue and white ball cap complete with his favorite team logo.

The Professor looked at the surprised student and said, "Go Dodgers!"

Caroline Deal's LinkedIn picture was next. Her uniformed student ID portrait confirmed Dr. Sorenson's seemingly uncanny deduction that Lieutenant Deal was former USMC.

Seed Blood

Dr. Sorenson announced, using his best Holmesian camp, "This is not elementary. It is work. Research on your subjects is essential! The profiles and pages you see are only the starting point.

"Throughout our considerations in this course, I will continuously encourage you to observe and draw conclusions based on published research from a variety of sources and disciplines while discerning your gut reactions to crime in all its gruesome manifestations. However, be warned. It is essential to keep those emotions separate from the data on those psychopaths whom we will explore."

Bam! He had us. This course would be fun and challenging with the opportunity to expand our knowledge of what motivates the most notorious criminals and leads to their most heinous crimes.

I thought, *Yeah, I can always tape the soccer matches on Tuesday and Thursday nights and get my ass to class.*

Coincidentally, my Chief had recommended I meet Dr. Sorenson and seek his consultation on a case that was becoming very quickly notorious with the potential for some panic throughout South Florida.

What were those office hours, again?

"Officer Sechi, you indicated that you also had an observation. What would that be?"

"Well, my observation is that you are from Oz, Dr. Sorenson-- Australia. So, tell us please, how often does your 'Strine kick in?"

My hunky professor did his best to hide a double-take at my recognition of the Australian slang phenomenon. Still, his rare smile was infectious and a bit long-lasting this time. As he walked toward me, he fully unleashed his accent and said, "When I am back in Brizzie or knackered or off my face."

Translation: When I am back in Brisbane or tired or drunk.

Gracefully, he recovered from my rather snide one-upmanship in the art of deduction and said, "Now, let us begin our exploration of the criminal mind by considering...."

The screen changed to a picture of a notorious Floridian.

21

As he moved to the back of the classroom, Dr. Sorenson's now mildly accented voice announced to the class, "Theodore Robert Bundy was an American serial killer and necrophile. He kidnapped, raped, and robbed his victims. The monster here depicted assaulted and murdered numerous young women and girls during the 1970s and possibly earlier. Mr. Bundy will serve as the first of our 'natural born killers' for dissection. I am providing you with electronic research on him."

Without missing a stride, he placed something on my table while speaking softly, "And this will provide the answer to your earlier concern regarding my somewhat intimate knowledge of you."

I turned over the small "bar rag" periodical he had placed face down on my desk. I turned it over-- Hot Shots LGBTQ+, "First Responders in South Florida."

Cover boy – Wilton Manors Officer Nicola Sechi.

Chapter Two: Quarto
NICK SECHI'S JOURNAL

At only 26, I often amazed my friends at trivia games. A great lover of movies, Broadway shows, opera, music, and literature, I was a walking encyclopedia of gay arts culture. Since middle school, this very visual gay boy was making associations with film icons way beyond my years. Thanks to my mother's tutelage, I balanced my love of sports and the arts. A theater buff between sports seasons, I acted a bit through my college years and devoured theater lore. My sisters say I have the soul of a fabulous old gay man, describing people and situations in the movie of my mind.

So, it would not be surprising that my brain connected the woman standing in the back of the classroom with the iconic glamor star Chita Rivera-- totally "Aurora" in the musical *The Kiss of the Spider Woman*. I placed her in her mid-thirties, with black, bobbed hair, a real vintage appearance in her white, formfitting, cream-colored Anthony Vaccarello, setting off her café au lait completion. Highlighted by sensibly understated daytime jewelry, the stunning woman had a silver Gucci bag hung on a small-link shoulder chain to the left. She cocked one hip and stood on the opposite leg scrolling the screen of her mobile phone. The moderate slit in her dress would have inspired my cousin, Nolo, to fire off one of his signature remarks, "Girl's got legs that go from here to there and back again, cuz."

Exiting students eyed this Diva, but she took no notice as she was so focused on her phone. Without looking up, she ran a hand through her luxurious black hair. She moved up the now empty aisle with a dancer's grace to Dr. Sorenson, who packed up his bag while speaking to the last few students. She stood next to him, caught his eye, and winked with lashes slightly longer than his. After finishing with his final student, Kayne and Rebecca exchanged a chaste, triple-cheek kiss, European style. They were apparently very close.

Straight? Damn, need to get my gaydar checked— it might not be working. Reset?

As I turned to leave, I heard, "Officer Sechi, join us, please." Dr. Sorenson gestured me to the front of the room as I was about to be the last student out. He introduced this Chita look-alike."

"Rebecca Quinto, my student Nicola Sechi, Wilton Manors Police Department. Nick, this is my friend, Rebecca. You must never call her 'Becky' and expect to live."

"How nice to meet you, Officer Sechi. I have been reading about you. How is your partner, Officer Shahnawaz?" Rebecca extended her hand. Her pronunciation of Eshani's surname was perfect.

"You have been to Afghanistan, I perceive."

"I beg your pardon."

"Sorry. A line connected to Sherlock Holmes," I said as Dr. Sorenson smiled.

"A Study in Scarlet."

I shook her hand. "Please call me Nick, and thanks. It looks like Shan is going to make it. I visited the ICU right before coming to class. A bit more flexibility in my schedule lately as I am riding a desk these days."

I have a theory that beautiful people hang together. Up close, Ms. Quinto was as stunning as her boyfriend and just as charming. Dazzled twice in one night-- totally nutso!

"I am so glad she is out of danger." Pointing to Dr. Sorenson, she added, "We both have been following your case. So terrible for you. That young man and all."

Dr. Sorenson remarked, "Rebecca is the CEO and Head Curator of the Fritcher Museum of Art here in Ft. Lauderdale. In fact, I believe we made quite a splash here at the gala for her opening of 'The Treasures of the French Revolution.' Securing that collection from the French was quite a victory, my dear."

Rebecca smiled. "Kayne was the keynote at the accompanying symposium, *Murder and Torture in the Reign of Terror: A Psychological Analysis.* SRO, correct?

So, do vampires/Tartar warriors/underwear models blush? It would seem so.

Looking at Kayne, Rebecca asked, "Are we still going to get that drink, Darling?" Turning to me, she added, "Nick, you must join us."

Dr. Sorenson nodded, "Rippa, Mate! We are on our way to Quarto."

Quarto Bar was a seriously new hot spot a few blocks from the FGU building; martinis and eclectic music-- super chic.

I asked, "Student and his prof out drinking. No concerns?"

He answered, "No worries. Call it our first consulting meeting, perhaps?"

"I insist. You can be my date, Darling. And relax, Kayne never actually sleeps with any of his students until after they have passed his course."

I thought to myself, Bingo! Always trust your gaydar, baby.

"My love, you really must work on the propriety dimension of your very over-the-top personality." Dr. Sorenson joked sarcastically through somewhat clenched teeth and tossing back his forelock.

Too interested to be thoroughly appalled, I said, "I'm afraid I am a bit underdressed." I pulled on the center of the Flash logo to illustrate my relaxed look.

"Nonsense, Nick. Jeans and T-shirt – scorching, grunge style. One suggestion, Darling..." Rebecca's perfectly manicured fingers reached out to roll up the sleeves of my shirt above my biceps. "... show those magnificent guns, Officer."

Dr. Sorenson again shot his forelock and rolled his eyes at his friend's somewhat bold handling of the merchandise.

"Oh, and one more thing. Wear a tank top, sexy. With that chest, you're sure to get an 'A' in this course," Rebecca said in a stage whisper.

Turning the two of us toward the classroom door, Dr. Sorenson said with a bit of insistence, "Ohhkaay, you two... teacher needs his Hibiki. The next class is coming in. Nick, you look great for Quarto. You in? Great. We can walk."

***

As we stepped out on the street, Rebecca's mobile chirped. "Damn, I need to take this. Excuse me." She dropped a few steps behind, speaking softly.

I addressed the Professor, "Hibiki?"

"Seventeen-year-old Japanese whiskey. I did some consulting in Japan for the Imperial Family a few years ago regarding a bit of blackmail concerning an errant nephew. A rather interesting Minister of State introduced me to the drink. Superb. What are your spirits of choice?"

"Ever had a Negroni, Sir?"

We stopped at the crosswalk. Kayne checked that Rebecca wasn't talking and walking into traffic by gently taking hold of the back of her dress with two fingers near her neck. She looked up, came to a stop, and turned to smile a thank you for his concern while returning to her call.

Kayne took her arm as we crossed on the green and looked behind her to speak to me.

"Nick, it's 'Kayne,' like the Bible's first murder. Genesis? Only spelled differently. I even have the divine brand." He turned to me and lifted his floppy bang to reveal a scar just below his hairline on the right side of his forehead.

"Behold the Mark of Cain!"

With Rebecca now ahead of us, Kayne placed his hand on my shoulder. As if he could read my thoughts, he said, "I have no professional ethics concerns regarding having a drink together after class. I hope to offer you some critical advice on the missing sailor, *pro bono*, so there is no contractual obligation. Do you sing?"

"As a matter of fact, I do. All gay men sing and dance. It's in our genes."

Bending back a bit, he checked out my ass. "I can see that," he said, grabbing hold of the rather apparent double meaning.

Looking up, he mustered a super grin, ear to ear.

Seed Blood

"Dr. Sorenson, did you just check out my butt?" I stopped on the sidewalk and laughed.

Faking an abashed look, Kayne responded, "Come along, Officer, we will miss our set."

***

The city's newest hipster bar, Quarto, was the latest rage. It was a well-kept secret by locals with broad musical tastes. The lounge featured audience performance, but you needed to be accomplished— no karaoke. A memory for correct lyrics was as crucial as a well-trained voice.

January was the height of the tourist season. Still, Quarto had a very discriminating velvet rope line-up procedure restricting admission. The owner, Erasmo Vile, and his muscled bouncer culled the beautiful people to fill the interior with only the most gorgeous and talented clients. The impresario preferred returning guests who represented known fabulous talent. Sidewalk auditions were frequent. On nights when the Broward Center for the Performing Arts hosted a musical or an opera, Quarto was the place to be after the final curtain call. In December, a fantastic string quartet featuring four gorgeous and accomplished gay musicians did an after-hours show that continued the SRO tradition at the packed club.

Vile waved Rebecca forward and received triple-cheek kisses. Kayne and I followed a handsome maître d' who acknowledged my two companions and led us to a table close to the stage but private enough to have a conversation. It consisted of three u-shaped, aged Chesterfield sofas centered around a dark wood coffee table.

Kayne solicited, "The usual, my dear?"

Rebecca nodded as Kayne made his way quickly to the bar. She and I took our seats as our waiter came over. She smilingly waved him closer to say, "Good evening, Max." Rebecca did a kiss hello. "Kayne's hitting on the new bartender again."

"Ahh. Yes, Mr. Vile's new hire certainly gets a lot of attention."

"Easy to see why. So, Kayne will bring the first round, but check on us later, please, Darling."

Turning to me, she said, "I love this place. Kayne and I have been coming here for a while. Sorry about that phone call. Some trouble with our next exhibit. Are you naturally ginger, Nick?" She rolled her eyes provocatively, Mae West style.

Talk about a question out of left field. I responded, "Yep, my family is from Northern Italy. We are Milanese, red-headed, and fair. My dad was Napolitano, however. My sisters favor him, dark-eyed beauties."

"How many brothers and sisters do you have?"

"I'm the only boy, so five sisters." I counted off, "Portia, Olivia, Julia, Silvia, and Cleo."

"Nick's mother is Viola Sechi, Ph.D., professor of English Literature at NYU, a graduate of the University of Milan and Shakespearian scholar *assoluta*," announced the arriving Kayne, positioning three drinks on the table. He handed her his cell, "See?" He returned to the bar.

Rebecca scrolled through the browser on Kayne's phone— the professional profile of my mother, pictured with a bust of the Bard.

"Impressive. Hence your sisters' names, but I do not remember a 'Nicola' in Shakespeare."

"My Dad's name. Mom has three Yorkies. Care to guess?"

"Wait, wait, I can do this. OK, Hamlet, Macbeth, and Othello."

I made a loser game show buzzer noise as Kayne returned.

"Incorrect! Hint, they're all females."

Kayne gave Rebecca a give-it-another-try look. "Regan, Goneril, and... and..." he coaxed.

"Oh, Lear, yes... yes...Cordelia! How chic!"

I leaned back into the stuffed leather and spread my hands wide. "And an assortment of aunts, uncles, and cousins here in Florida, in 'The City' and back in 'the Old Country.' Warning: we all have very eccentric and notoriously stubborn personalities."

Rebecca grinned, "Goes with your red hair." She tousled me.

Kayne raised his glass in a mock toast. "Ah, families. Ya can't cook 'em. Ya can't eat 'em."

First sips, Rebecca leaned in to look at her friend while indicating the bar, "Well? Success?"

Kayne's most exceptional shit-eating grin so far. He removed his jacket, rolled up his shirtsleeves, and tossed a white cocktail square on the table-- phone number. The Divine Rebecca picked up the napkin, eyed the figure, and raised her eyebrows in mock admiration of his high-speed seduction.

"Such a slut."

"A purely professional relationship, my dear, for my paper on alcohol as a murder weapon. I need a somewhat professional and intense consult."

"Umm hum. Just remember Studly's name in the morning, Darling."

I realized that I had quickly involved myself with two beautiful and engaging people who were so close they shared all sorts of intimate secrets. I needed some backstory so as not to feel like a fifth wheel.

"So, how do you folks know each other?"

"Ms. Quinto and I met in Budapest about six years ago. I finished my studies and presented my dissertation in cultural and global criminology as part of a seminar at Eötvös Loránd University. After my presentation, I spent a few weeks absorbing the culture of Hungary."

Rebecca continued the story, "Yes, Darling." She patted his leg as one would assure a child and continued the story, "So, I managed to pull Kayne away from some gorgeous Hungarian men... I beg your pardon, the culture... right, the culture... and whisked him away to Rome. I needed some credibility to open significant doors at the Vatican. I had an idea for a grand exhibit here in Florida, and my gorgeous genius here knows everyone, Darling."

"Seriously? Impressive."

"There was a papal secretary who turned out to be very accommodating, I will admit. However, with my darling Rebecca here, I confess it was pretty much love at first sight," Kayne added, lifting a glass to his friend. "Though strictly platonic."

Rebecca pouted and commented, "I intend to create a blog on converting one's gay crush. The working title is *Forget It, Girls.*" She returned his toast with a laugh.

"We have many common interests, such as the arts, education, spirits...." Kayne gestured to Quarto's stage, "an eclectic taste in music and ...."

"Men-- beautiful, fit males. Darling, what was the name of that cavalryman I rescued you from in Budapest?" She looked at me and said, "A beautiful Hussar, curly blond hair...." Turning to Kayne, "And this oversexed genius was about to create an international scandal. Nick, I'm talking, running down the Danube Promenade with his slacks in his hand, calling me on his cell, his military lover in hot pursuit."

Kayne looked embarrassed but a bit wistful, "Ádám as in 'made in the image and likeness of God' – a divine beauty." He sighed, "Genesis again, Nick boy. Trouble was the lad was starkers most of the time." He made a circling finger to the side of his head motion. "Hungarians are so intense. It's all that Hapsburgs-rule-the-world blood and imperial inbreeding."

He turned to Rebecca and chided, "My dear, please remember I value your confidences. Besides, that was the old Kayne." He sat up in an attempt to regain his dignity and sipped his Hibiki.

"Umm, humm. I see, and this is the new and improved Kayne Sorenson 2.0, or is it 6.0? I am going to guess at least 8.5. So many upgrades. I've stopped counting."

She exchanged a loving touch with her best bud.

I followed Rebecca's gaze back to the bar to see the tall, muscled studly tossing drinks into glasses and mesmerizing the customers in an impossibly tight tank top-- the infamous Gints.

Pulling me back into the mix, Kayne ignored her and motioned to my glass.

"So, what do you think?"

"Familiar but different. What is it?"

Seed Blood

He sipped his Hibiki on the rocks and smiled.

"It is a Negroni, but my Samson made it with scotch, the house's best scotch, to be exact."

"May I?" Rebecca asked.

I offered. La Divina sipped and made an icky face.

"You boys and your whiskey. I thought the gays only drank vodka."

She pronounced the "v" as a "w" - such a Romanov wannabe.

"Try this, Handsome. This is a real girl's drink."

Before I could ask, Kayne piped up, "It's a 'Marie Laveau,' named after the notorious voodoo queen. Discovered when we were in some very questionable Parisian dives last spring. Our Rebecca positively inhales them... drinks almost nothing else. Absinthe base and poisonously delicious."

They both smiled.

"And Gints serves them with this." He placed a Tarot card face down between Rebecca and me. He flicked it over to reveal "The Lovers."

Rebecca exploded in laughter, "Oh Kayne, that was so meant for you, Darling. He should have put his phone number on that."

Her cocktail tasted very exotic-- orange and honey and the smooth licorice of the wormwood. Still, I liked my new fav, Scotch Negroni.

Chapter Three: How Will I Know

Hadji Murad could look like any one of many legendary Hollywood actresses, including Bette Davis, Lucille Ball, Carol Channing, and Ethel Merman, in a vintage, moth-eaten way. In the 70s, her Claire Trevor, alcohol-soaked rendition of "Moaning Low" from *Key Largo,* brought down the house two shows a night at the old Tropics Restaurant and Show Bar at the southern end of Wilton Drive. In fact, her drag name, Gaye Dawn, was an homage to Ms. Trevor's Oscar-winning role in that film.

Tonight, she was pissed off from the feathers in her wig to the gaff that hid her "candy."

"Fuckin' ignorant low-lives!"

She burst through the door of the Drag Queen's dressing room at Masque Bar in a fury. Her post-performance outburst upset four Styrofoam heads and their exotic wig occupants belonging to the three other Divas who shared the cramped space cobbled together by the management from a janitor's room. She dumped two armfuls of glittered costumes on the chair of her minuscule make-up station, almost hitting her head on the overhead pipes that served as apparel racks.

"Bitch, watch what you are doing there. Mohka ain't got time for no comb out before her next set." Picking up one of the fallen hairpieces, the performer shook it at her fellow queen, saying, "This shit ain't cheap, doll."

Mohka Mirage was pushed by the enraged artiste to rescue a few more of the jumbled wigs, tiaras, exotic headgear, and a few crushed bustiers. Miss Gaye was slamming and swearing with no attempt at calming down.

"No appreciation of vintage beauty! Fuckin' none! Florida red-necked mother fuckers! It's this assimilationist shit. Time was when gays knew what and who made them fabulous. Not this metrosexual bullshit!"

She waved a hairbrush, "I've been in this business for close to fifty years, bitches. These sexually fluid assholes can kiss my entire ass! It was like a funeral parlor out there, and I was the fuckin' corpse!"

As she undressed, she tossed parts of her last costume change onto the makeshift rack in a fury while reaching for her blood-red, dragon-embroidered dressing gown. The pieces of her discarded previous costumes cascaded to the floor.

"Somebody's tip jar empty again, girl?" Helluva Bottom Carter, the third room occupant, leaned close to the mirror. She held her sequined Cat Woman eyeglasses before her heavy-lashed eyes as she deftly added glitter gloss to her chocolate-red lips. Her wig, a mass of dirty blond curls that hit just above her shoulders with its signature headband and bow, sat on its foam head at a safe distance from the tempestuous Ms. Dawn. Cockeyed on the mirror was a picture of Whitney Houston in the same get-up the drag queen was attempting to imitate.

Turning to Gaye, she continued, "Sista, I been telling you for years you need modern material. These bitches don't know half the folks you been doing out there. Queen, Bette Midler is a fuckin' grandmother. No one knows who they are or who you are anymore."

"She is right, Hadji baby," said Mohka. They even forgetting Whiney, just sayin'. Face it, girl, your audience left years ago."

Her face was a mask of anger and frustration. Hadji growled and brandished a wooden hanger at her sister queens.

"Now, you bitches listen to me. My ladies are goddamn classics. Do you hear what I am saying? E-fuckin'-ternal! And I am damn good at making it real – have been for a long time. These fucks just don't know beauty when they see it. Six quick changes in 50 minutes. Shit! Who else? I ask you, who else can do that? Nobody in this business like Miss Dawn and her classic divas. Nobody! Lip-synching disasters coming around here with their pirated CDs. My public hears my voice. My voice! And I am talking mother-fucking Julliard!"

This last sentence was apparently standard Gaye-- picked up by Mohka and Helluva so that all three said together, "... mother-fucking Julliard." Miss Dawn did indeed need new lines.

Gaye straightened up, took a deep breath, and dropped into her chair, taking stock of her drooping face and its blurring makeup.

"Fuck me! Looks like someone erased my face!"

Her sagging reflection stared at her two fellow entertainers.

She let out a long sigh and raised a tissue to repair her makeup. "Babies, my ladies have been inside me a long time now. I can't let 'em go. Do you understand?" She lit a cigarette and blew the smoke Margo Channing style.

Helluva was now entirely in drag as Whitney Huston, ready to crush "How Will I Know?" on stage. She stood behind the senior member of the cast and gently massaged her tense shoulders. They eyed themselves and each other in the mirror, eight of the twelve bulbs on its frame still working.

Hadji sighed mournfully to her friend, "What happens when they say you're done, Mo? Where do old drag queens go to die?" Her sad eyes revealed a worn and tired soul.

Mohka joined her sister queens in the mirror shot. She crooned sincerely, "Just relax, Gaye. One more show tonight, and you can sleep all day tomorrow."

The dressing room door slammed open again, cheers roaring in from the house. This time, a duplicate of Pink strode into the cramped and cluttered room. Her platinum blond hair was short on the sides and styled in three cannoli roll curls on the top of her head. Gold hoop earrings splashed on the planes of her face as the youthful drag queen in a short orange shirt-dress and white, strapped heels danced in the minute space, clutching wads of cash and upsetting wigs on fake heads for the second time.

"They fuckin' loved me!"

Chapter Four: Fantasy
NICK SECHI'S JOURNAL

Quarto crowd's applause started before the last notes of the K.D Lang ballad, "Miss Chatelaine," faded. The appreciative audience continued their acclaim as a beaming young blonde woman stepped down from the stage, shyly acknowledging her fans.

We continued to sip drinks and share conversation when our erstwhile waiter, Max, returned to our table. As he arrived, the dazzling cone of a pin spot from the club's ceiling suddenly nailed the attractive server. Simultaneously, the first chords of what could only be Puccini soared over the club's sound system. Still holding his empty drink tray, Max turned to face the club patrons and began in an astonishing tenor to perform the signature aria from *Turandot*, the sensual and lush "Nessun Dorma."

The famous love song to the beautiful Chinese princess carried by an emotion-filled, opera-trained voice soared across the lounge, transfixing the audience and stopping all conversation. Rebecca reached across the couch to take Kayne's hand with eyes glistening, responding to one of the most exquisite pieces of romantic music. The passion of the legendary prince, overwhelmed by unrequited love and a desperate hope to possess the ice princess, filled Max's rich vocals.

When he reached the timpani-pounding finale of victory, *"All'alba vincerò. Vincerò, vincerò,"* the audience rose as one person for a thunderous, sustained ovation. Kayne stood to take Max in a bear hug and double-cheek kiss. With an impresario-like, dramatically raised hand, he presented Max over and over to the applauding club patrons. Still holding his drink tray, the waiter bowed and smiled like a grand opera tenor.

I could not hear their conversation, but as they stepped apart, Max was gesturing to Kayne with each hand as if to say, "Your turn, *Professore*," while waving on the encouraging cheers from the crowd. The audience began clapping in rhythm, shouting Kayne's name until he bounded up on the stage and took the mic.

The DJ cued up the voluptuous opening notes of Lloyd Webber's "The Music of the Night" from *Phantom*. Within a single spot, my criminology professor crushed that song, singing in a well-trained first tenor with all the passion demanded by the lyric. He embodied the tortured beauty of a soul in prison and the craving for an unattainable love.

I was transfixed. The lock of Kayne's hair that fell over his forehead seemed to transform his visage into the disfigured musical genius who lives in a secret lair beneath Paris' 1890s Palais Garnier. As the song concluded, Kayne fell to one knee and reached out to the audience, conveying the monster's desperate longing for his Christine in a grand display of musical seduction and desire.

Hardly a man or a woman in the audience could not connect with the pathos held in one single voice that night. Throughout the final cords of the song, the audience went wild for Dr. Sorenson's performance. One particular, muscled-up Latvian bartender whistled, shouted at the Professor, "Bravo, *Pasniedzējs!*" and joined in the audience's chant of "Kayne! Kayne! Kayne!" A myriad of cell phones flashed.

The singer smiled and bowed classically with one hand modestly held at his chest, acknowledging his fans. He whirled on stage and stretched out one hand to our table. Rebecca stood and runway-walked forward to join him under the spotlights. The audience cheered. Apparently, my "Lestat" and "Chita" were club favorites.

She unbuttoned his dazzling white shirt a few more buttons, and the audience yelled their approval. This time, the music bounced with a familiar 50s rock n' roll beat, transforming Rebecca and Kayne into the iconic Sandy and Tony from Ridell High.

Mimicking the made-over, gum-popping heroine in the final sequence of "Grease," Rebecca opened the number by stabbing Kayne with one perfectly manicured index finger and responding to Kayne's best goofy Travolta, "Sandy, you look so different!" with her hip Newton-John, "Tell me about it, stud."

She pantomimed, dropping and stepping on a cigarette.

Music vamped up with a rollicking "You're the One That I Want." Kayne popped his collar, fake slicked a dove-tail in an Elvis meme, swivel-hipping his rockin' ass. Rebecca gyrated with a few seductive dance moves even Ann Margaret would envy. The performance ended with Kayne lying adoringly, face-up on the floor as Rebecca planted one stiletto-heeled Manolo Blahnik suede pump on his gorgeous chest.

I was amazed at their overwhelming talent. The love that they had for what they were doing emanated from them out into the audience. "This shit is amazing fun," they seemed to be saying.

The Hipsters and Baby Boomers were yelling, "More! More!" I bounced up to the stage with their cocktails. As Kayne took his drink, he said to me over the din, "Don't go away, Nick." Nevertheless, I managed a quick retreat.

Kayne stepped over to say a few words to the DJ, and Rebecca stepped forward into the spotlight. Her solo was "Somewhere" from *Westside Story,* resulting in yet another fantastic performance, ending with her reaching up into the spotlight.

As the applause subsided, Rebecca hooded her eyes with her free hand. She said into the mic, "We need that breathtaking, redheaded police officer up here, right now, and I need that bartender hottie to make us another round. Gints, Darling!"

I was blushing down to my socks as I was pushed up onto the stage. Laughing uproariously, my costars walked to the back of the stage with a show-us-what-you-got-boy expression as the DJ handed me a mic and nodded at my requested selection. As I turned to the crowd, Rebecca lifted my t-shirt and flashed them my abs.

More applause, and I remember thinking, *Just watch this, boys and girls!*

I walked forward into the spotlight and asked Max to join me, and turned to invite "Tony" and "Sandy" into the quartet. A brief huddle, a series of nods, and then the first descending crescendos of Morricone's "Nella Fantasia" filled the room like an exotic perfume.

I knew the lyrics by heart. The hymn is a family wedding favorite, full of the sunshine-filled hopes of the Italian people. Max and Kayne knew the lines also. Rebecca pulled them up on the DJ's mobile phone.

Stumbling a bit at first, we soon blended verses worthy of an Italian boy quartet in an anthem evoking universal peace and love. Intricate harmonies began fitting together, and the song's unique counterpoint throughout the verses of the second stanza surprisingly materialized. The stunning music rose to the rafters with passionate lyrics of hope for all humankind raised to a musical apogee until a decrescendo softly ended the performance.

No one moved for a few seconds. Then, as the audience cheered enthusiastically, Gints appeared in front of the stage with a tray of four drinks. Before we could do another act together, my phone vibrated in my jeans pocket. I pulled it out and looked at the display, recognizing my Captain's name, Robert Mays. Shit! This call was about Shan.

Something most important had happened.

Chapter Five: Marcellinus

NICK SECHI'S JOURNAL

As I left the stage, Kayne took off with a raucous rendition of "Sweet Child O' Mine." The audience transformed from opera and Broadway aficionados to hard rockers with an appetite for destruction. I could tell by their faces as I exited to the street that they were in love with the singer.

Without listening to the message from Captain Mays, I hit the call-back feature.

"Mays. Is that you, Nick?"

"Yes, Sir. Is Shan OK, Sir"

"Affirmative. Officer Shahnawaz remains in stable condition as of the last report of 20 minutes ago. She hasn't awakened yet."

I let out a long breath of air as I stood in the lobby of "Quarto." I handed a passing staffer my unfinished drink.

"Officer Sechi, were you able to connect with Dr. Sorenson as I requested?"

"Yes, Sir. In fact, I am in the process of briefing him about the missing sailor now."

"Well, it sounds like it's a pretty lively discussion, Officer, considering the background noise."

I moved to the sidewalk outside the club. "Well, actually, Sir, we haven't really talked about the full details of the case yet, but...."

Captain Mays interrupted, "Nick, we've got a floater. I need to see you and Dr. Sorenson STAT. What is your current location?"

"We are downtown at Quarto, 300 block of SW 2nd Street, near the Museum of Science and Discovery."

"Oh yeah, that geeky music place. Hold on a moment."

In ten seconds, he was back on the call. Captain Mays indicated that he was sending a squad car to pick us both up. He would have more to say when we arrived at the scene. Looking up the street, I noticed a police car making a U-turn and heading to the curb in front of Quarto.

I waved to the officers in the front seat of the cruiser, helped up one finger in a "hold-on-dudes" gesture, and dashed back into the club.

Most of the audience was standing and applauding Rebecca and Kayne as they descended from the stage, heading back to our table.

"Nick, has something happened?" Kayne asked, seeing my expression.

"Yes, as a matter of fact, I just got a call from my Captain. I wonder if you would do me the favor of accompanying me to meet with the chief right now?" While I had directed this question at Kayne, Rebecca announced, "I'm so coming along."

Kayne pulled out a wad of bills just as Erasmo Vile approached the table to congratulate us on our performances.

"Please, Dr. Sorenson, *devo insistere*." He protested, "Please put that money away. You have again astounded my customers. You have, as they say in America, brought the house down. On behalf of Quarto, we are indeed most grateful. Just promise me you will provide us with many encores."

Kayne pressed four twenties into the hands of the propitious Vill and said, "For Max and Gints.' The owner nodded.

We hurriedly apologized for our hasty departure and left the club. Jumping into the backseat of the waiting squad car, the driver put on the roof flashers and the siren as we headed out to meet Captain Mays.

***

Port of the Everglades, one of the top three cruise ports globally, is also among the most active containerized cargo ports in the United States and South Florida's leading seaport for petroleum products such as oil, gasoline, and jet fuel. The US Navy has a station at the Port.

A fog was rolling off the ocean, bringing with it the strong smell of the sea as we arrived at the cargo terminal yard on Pier 31. A crime scene area had been cordoned off with lights and yellow police tape at the water's edge. The landside of the pier was crawling with law enforcement from two municipalities searching for evidence. A small police craft used searchlights in the channel for the same purpose. As we approached, two marine divers seated on the edge of the boat gently splashed backward into the inky waters of the harbor, switching on their underwater beams. Naval and Coast Guard personnel joined detectives gathered near a blanket-covered corpse recently fished out of the waters of the Atlantic Intracostal Waterway.

"Robert, so good to see you again." As Rebecca alighted from the police car, Captain Mays took her hand in a cordial greeting.

With a look of genuine respect, Mays shook hands with Dr. Sorenson, "Thank you for allowing me to interrupt your evening, Doctor. As always, I appreciate any help you can give us." He lowered his voice and added, "Frankly, the FBI and Navy investigators have been more of a hindrance than help up to now."

"Happy to be of service again, Chief Mays. Officer Sechi briefed us on the facts known by your office regarding the disappearance of Petty Officer Second Class Jared Christiansen. I believe he said the young man has been missing since November 26th. Last seen on Wilton Drive in the Manors."

"Yes, Doctor. He failed to unite back with his squad after three days of R and R here in South Florida."

Captain Mays moved closer to his colleagues and continued, "Dr. Sorenson, Ms. Quinto, may I introduce Special Agent Mary Chaffee of the FBI and Captain Anthony Rota of the US Navy Judge Advocate General's Office in Jacksonville. I believe you both know Sheriff Dian Crawford of the Ft. Lauderdale Police Department and Annmarie Owens, Lauderdale's Chief Medical Examiner. Folks, I have asked Officer Nick Sechi from my jurisdiction to serve as my duty officer investigating the case."

Addressing the group, Mays went on to say, "As you may know, Dr. Sorenson has helped both our police departments before with some difficult cases. He and Ms. Quinto, who, by the way, is a very recent graduate of the FBI Citizen's Academy, have agreed to be a part of the investigation as advisors in an unofficial capacity."

My new friends acknowledged the introductions by exchanging handshakes with warm greetings for the Sheriff and CME. I nodded to the two government officers who had become colleagues since the report of the disappearance of the young sailor at the beginning of December.

Captain Mays continued "Officer Sechi knows of the missing person's case, which he has shared previously. Sheriff Crawford will attempt to fill you in on the details of our present situation. Right this way, please."

As we moved away from the parked vehicles and down the pier, Mays, Crawford, and Rota walked with Kayne filling in more details of the case and the newly discovered body. Annmarie Owens fell back to walk with me while Rebecca and Mary Chaffee seemed to know each other.

"How's the Museum, Rebecca?"

Rebecca managed a genuine smile, "Hey, Mary. Good to see you again. I am feeling a bit like the Mayor of Crazy Town these days. The new exhibit has some huge problems, mostly in the vein of community relations. I don't mean to sound macabre, but helping with this case is a much-needed diversion. Being an objective outsider with all these professionals is fine with me. Most times, we see details differently." She gestured to the group as we approached the mist-haloed lights of the crime scene at the end of the pier.

"How are you doing, Nick?" CME Owens said with a note of concern.

"Oh, office-bound these days, as you know, Annmarie. Bored spitless, to be honest."

"And Shan?"

"She's holding her own. I saw her just before my class with Dr. Sorenson, so that would be about 5:00 PM. She has remained in the ICU since they removed the bullet. They induced a coma to support healing, so she is not completely out of it yet. It's wait-and-see time. I expect the next few days will bring some critical decisions by her doctors as to what to do next."

"You know I cannot comment on your Internal Affairs investigation, but I just want you to know that I'm unofficially available. If you ever need somebody to confide with, please get in touch. It all sounds very stressful and depressing."

"Yeah, thanks. I may give you a call for a coffee sometime. Wondering when I'll stop reliving the shooting and seeing that kid's face." I stopped for a moment to contain a sudden, unexpected rise of emotions.

Most of the detectives working the crime scene were well off to the side at the water's edge, where they had fished the body out of the channel. The corpse was under a blue blanket near the center of the pier. A lone detective with an evidence camera stood next to the body, waiting for the approaching senior officers.

Annmarie Owens provided the members of our party with rubber gloves as we rejoined the group. She, Kayne, and I put them on. With a gesture from the Ft. Lauderdale Sheriff, the detective guarding the body carefully removed the covering from the deceased, took up the forensic camera, and began photographing the body lying face up at our feet.

Sheriff Crawford addressed the group, "The Port's night security spotted the body of the deceased. It was floating approximately thirty feet from the western end of this loading pier at 11:37 PM EST, snagged on a fishing buoy. Ft. Lauderdale police were immediately dispatched, and they removed the corpse from the water. Per our collaboration on missing person cases, I contacted Chief Mays of Wilton Manors, PD."

As the photographer stepped back, Kayne moved closer to me as I knelt next to the deceased. At the request of Sheriff Crawford, the Examiner turned on the voice recorder, spoke a few opening case identifiers, and handed it to Dr. Sorenson, who began with, "Observations, please, Officer Sechi."

"The victim appears to be a male in his mid to late twenties, approximately 5'11', weighing between 185 and 195 pounds. His head is shaved military style. There is a tattoo of a naval insignia on the outside of his right bicep. He is wearing torn, ragged jeans and is bare-chested and bare-footed. The left leg of his pants is almost completely ripped off at mid-thigh. Handcuffs hold the dead man's wrists in front of his torso. The upper body and visible extremities show a bluish-grey skin coloration.

Seaweed and small branches suggesting entanglement in the water plants of the harbor wrap the body. The area between the folded arms of the victim and the upper torso is where the debris is concentrated.

The body shows slight bruising along the soft tissues of the torso-- arms and legs. Broken bones, three of which break the skin on the left side of the body, include four ribs, the collarbone, and the upper left arm. There is some extensive injury to the face, including severe bruising to the eyes and what appears to be a break in the nose and another in the jaw on the right side."

The sight of the semi-naked, battered boy was devastating. Even for seasoned law enforcement, the appearance of the boy's body was a bit overwhelming. Each of the onlookers shifted uneasily. This kid had taken a savage beating.

Kayne carefully opened the victim's mouth and stooped to smell the open cavity. He said to me, "There is significant froth emanating from the nose and mouth." I repeated what he said for the recorder.

He took the dead boy's hands, examining the nails, palms, and backs of the hands. Skin shredding appeared on the knuckles. The skin tears on the palms of the hands were also extensive. He spoke a bit more loudly, "The dermis on the palms and soles is tight, showing little signs of loosening. All of the victim's nails are broken."

Using a penknife, extracted the remaining dirt under three broken nails. Kayne also removed a tiny portion of the boy's hair. The attending officer provided an evidence envelope for the material and handed it to Dr. Sorenson. I palpated the circular bruises on the thighs and shoulders.

Pointing, I added, "There are deep gashes in the flesh on the ankles and wrists suggesting heavy, sharp restraints."

I started to ask that the body be turned over. Still, Kayne stopped me, pointing to the remaining detritus of seaweed and branches that had lodged between the boy's folded arms. The entanglement obscured the torso from the collarbone to the lower thighs and was held in place by his locked arms. I had carefully parted the materials during my examination. Believing that he wanted me to continue a closer, unobscured observation of the chest and upper abdomen, I carefully picked away the rest of the seaweed, placing them near the body.

Kayne put his hand on my shoulder. "Stop."

Seed Blood

The body was left with one single branch of what looked like a green date palm branch-- distinctly out of place among the marine flora. The stalk had been cut cleanly with a knife. A few coils of hemp tied the stem to the crossed forearms.

"What is it, Dr. Sorenson?" said the JAG officer.

Turning to face Captain Rota while standing and removing his rubber gloves, Kayne said, "It is a message, Officer Rota. The killer is speaking to us."

He pointed to the corpse holding the palm.

"And I can assure you there will be more."

Thomas Paul Severino

Chapter Six: Miss Dawn

Hadji Murad thought to herself as she left the club, how goddam tired she was. The final show of the evening featured all the drag performers on three stages as the male strippers walked along the bar, making their last contacts of the evening. Hadji realized that the audience's response to her was just as miserable as her first show. As she exited the stage with the finale ensemble, she swiped an open bottle of scotch from a passing barback.

Taking her time to remove her makeup and change into street clothes, she poured the scotch into a dirty water glass and threw it back. Mohka, Helluva, and Dani McQueen, aka Pink, tiptoed around the fading star, soaking in booze and self-pity. By the time the dressing room was empty, 45 minutes later, the bottle of scotch was "a dead soldier."

"You OK to drive, Sugar? How 'bout you let this doll take you home?"

"Mohka, when the day comes that I need help from you, I'll be hanging up my tap shoes permanently. Leave me the fuck alone."

She was the last to leave, pushing out through the panic bar of the door at the rear of Masque Bar with her oversized handbag and rolling luggage. Her tattered costumes needed a few alterations before returning to the club in three days. All in all, she was steady on her feet. She had learned to hold her liquor a long, long time ago.

Maybe those "biotches" were right, she thought as she crossed the dark parking lot to the back section where management required performers and staff to park. The act could use a few updates.

"Fuck, I am too tired to think about a rewrite," she said aloud to herself. Where do old drag queens go to die?

She awkwardly shifted her belongings to finger-wave a goodbye to Scott Le, the club manager, as he turned out of the parking lot ahead of her. In the juggling, she dropped a scarf that was trailing from the handle of her handbag and her car keys.

Pausing to retrieve it, she lost control of the bag and the grip of her rolling luggage. Her belongings were scattered over the asphalt. As she turned, she was astonished to see a tall man directly behind her, one hand behind his back, stooping for the scarf and keys.

"Please allow me to assist you, Miss Dawn."

Chapter Seven: Fever Dream
Nick Sechi's Journal

Blood was pooling quickly from the two dead bodies on the floor, black in the night-soaked room. Stepping carefully, guns drawn, shadows swirling in the cramped living room... flashlight beams crisscrossing in the dark... old, battered furniture overturned and thrown in confusing heaps as if the whole place were lifted, shaken, and set down. Outside, a rush of night rain bombards the tin, leaking roof, sounding like the report of an automatic rifle.

The apparition of a homeless man in a wheelchair flickers in a mirror on a wall streaked with water. Voices invade the gloom and echo from the wet walls, scarred with peeling wallpaper.

"Remember your training, officer."

"Check the corners."

"Behold the vengeance of the Lord!"

Outside, lightning rakes the night sky, causing the broken windows to flash white. The cripple's American flag grows larger and then bursts into flames, morphing into a blazing cross. The wraith erupts in maniacal laughter, spinning the wheelchair in circles. He raises his voice with intensity, "It's time to bring all to the Great Reckoning." The specter vanishes.

The female officer was on point. The male signals to flip down night vision... light and dark... fluorescent, green-black soup. She weaves back and forth as they move to the back of the house. Speaking into her mic, "Officer requests backup. You have our position." She kneels and continues, "We have two bodies requiring immediate medical assistance." The other officer stands above and scans the room.

A death's head flickers across a cracked and peeling ceiling. A voice screams, "Make a silent approach. Look for cover," The last phrase is drawn out like a death wail.

Electronic squawking noises at shoulder level—bumping and erratic movement from the back hallway. Someone is in the backroom and is moving around. The policewoman signals and the duo sets up, one to each side of an open door next to a filthy kitchen. The broken, wooden Venetian blinds rattle in smashed windows in a howling night wind. The room pitches and blazes with images of horror—insanely flashing lights and psychotically creeping shadows.

Movement. A dark figure comes forward out of the shadows.

"Halt, Police! Put the gun down and get on the floor!"

The sound of a midnight train roars. The sound fills the room and then suddenly stops. Outside, the wind picks up, rattling broken shutters. The old woman on the floor opens her eyes suddenly and begins to scream, "Watch the hands!"

Rushing... metal clattering to the floor. The policewoman is in a headlock, her hajib falling to the floor... killer and officer are struggling in a red-and-black inferno.

Shots! Shots! Shots!

The policeman's chest explodes. Falling....

From above, a demon and a police officer struggle in raging, hellish lights... "Say goodbye, fucking pig!" His head presses close to hers. Gun barrel to her temple.

Two more shots and relentless, ear-splitting shrieking.

Mine.

***

The ravaged-animal screaming continued as I sat up in my sweat-soaked bed. My naked torso was covered in a feverish flop sweat. My partner, Hudson, grabbed me and called my name over and over, shaking my shoulders to rouse me from the horror. Trembling, I fought for consciousness. Although I usually sleep very soundly, since the incident, this recurring dream, filled with insane fits of anger and violence, more than once had tossed one or both of us to the floor.

When will it stop?

Seed Blood

I apologized to Hud as I staggered through the bedroom to the sliding doors and out onto the patio. I was still hyperventilating, my mind filled with anguish.

"Mother fucker!" I yelled into the early morning.

I could feel the terror begin to slip away. "Sorry, Kiddo. Go back to sleep. I'm fine," I called into the bedroom as I stepped outside.

Dawn was about an hour away, and the rosy skies over Wilton Manors were slowly erasing the night silhouettes of the trees surrounding the pool. High in the branches, wild green parrots had responded to my screams with raucous chatter. The colors of dawn in paradise returned, the pool turning from sable grey to azure blue.

I dove into the still surface, sounding deep as a rush of January's ice-cold waters encased my feverish body shocking me back to reality like getting butt fucked by lightning. I began swimming my laps-- escaping, running, leaving, trying to forget.

About 40 minutes later, Hudson Ch'en, in his Calvin Kline tighty-whities and sandals, slid back the patio door, balancing a tray. He brought out my coffee, his tea, my cell phone, his tablet, and our Sun Sentinel newspaper. I mounted the pool steps. The full morning light was crisp and brightening as if to sear away the terrifying shadows of my recent nightmare. Chouko, my black and white Akita, bounded out behind Hud, nearly upsetting his tray before he could safely place it on the patio table.

Opening my mouth to apologize again for yet another violent night, Hud handed me a towel and interrupted me.

"Nick, I am going to repeat it. Take some time off. You are in very rough shape. You have had practically no sleep since the shooting, and those nightmares seem to come every night."

I stared at the light dancing on the disturbed waters of the pool, echoing the movements of my final laps and exit from the deep end. I absentmindedly rubbed a hand over the bruises on my upper torso, settling into a patio chair.

Chouko patrolled the perimeter of the yard, checking the back wall and side fences for evidence of critter intrusion -- squirrel, opossum, raccoon, iguana, and pausing to water a hibiscus. He came back to us and sat at attention next to me. Hudson reached for the tray on the table, handed me my coffee, and sat next to me. It was my turn to talk.

"I have to stay connected, Hud. If I sit around all day, I'll obsess about that kid, those bodies, and Shan in that awful room. It only gets worse when I just sit around. Besides, we found that missing Navy guy last night. Mays wants me in on the investigation big time."

"Nick, you may have PTSD. You were shot three times in the chest and watched as your partner took a bullet to the head. Thank God for Kevlar or you...."

He couldn't finish his thought.

Chouko nuzzled my naked lap.

"Chouko, Īe."

I gently pushed him off and did a genital-adjust.

I looked Hud in the eyes, "And I shot and killed a 17-year-old."

"He was a killer, Nick. His own family. Shan, and you could be dead if you didn't stop him."

I turned to look at my lover and took his hand. The Akita Prince, his name in Japanese dialect, means "butterfly child," settled into a crouch at my feet. Chouko was a gift from my father when I graduated from the Police Academy. My dad was a Japanophile and thought it would be great to have a pup who responded to commands in Japanese. A Rosetta Stone language program came with my Beautiful Butterfly.

The dog was on alert, as usual. This morning, Chouko was scrutinizing the top of the 9-foot wall that separated the back of my property from the rear of a lush city park. The wall was a favorite runway for cats, squirrels, and raccoons, all the foresworn enemies of the honorable Chouko-san, a K-9 warrior who lived in the house with the pool.

"I'm coming out of it, sexy man. I am." I reached over and rubbed Hud's muscular thigh. The image of a rising phoenix wound from his upper leg, disappearing up and back through his briefs and peeking through the waistband at the back. He was unresponsive.

I attempted to change the subject a bit. "My criminology class and my professor, Dr. Sorenson, are both amazing. The dude is brilliant. He specializes in psychopathic crime. After class Last night, we went to that performance bar, Quarto. You know how I get when I sing-- so fuckin dope. Helps me forget everything."

"You did that Il Divo song, and you cried. Am I right? You are such a dreamer, Nick."

He tousled my wet hair and cuffed me like I was a 5-year old.

Stirring his tea, he said, "You came in after 2:00 AM. Must have been quite a performance."

I looked back at the pool and said nothing. Then, I turned to Hud. "They pulled that poor sailor up at the Port. Someone beat that Navy kid badly, Hud. Fuckin' savage."

"Yeah, I saw." He pulled up the news feed on his tablet and showed me the press report from Port Everglades, just seven hours old. It read,

A body suspected to be missing Petty Officer Second Class Jared Christiansen, 22, a native of Lehi, Utah, last seen December 15 in Wilton Manors, was recovered from the Intracostal Waterway at the Port of the Everglades. A spokesperson representing the investigating team of the Navy, the FBI, and the police departments from Ft. Lauderdale and Wilton Manors said that developments in the case would be forthcoming following notification of the family and an autopsy of the deceased. Sheriff Dian Crawford of the Ft. Lauderdale Police Department will release a complete report later today. Police from both municipalities are calling for all persons with any information on the missing Christensen to come forward.

"There's a monster out there, Hud. I want to help bring him in before he kills again."

"Again?"

"Yeah, Kayne, that is Dr. Sorenson, thinks we got a repeater on our hands. Mays has him consulting, and Crawford has used him before. In South Florida, a thing like this cuts the balls off the tourist industry, especially during 'The Season.' Snowbirds and serial killers – a dangerous combination."

"Are you seriously thinking you are in any shape emotionally to take on a serial killer case, Nick?"

Hudson returned to scrolling through his tablet. I checked my phone for overnight messages, news feeds, and emails.

"To be honest, Internal Affairs says, 'no,' but Mays wants me to be the liaison with Dr. Sorenson. I'll be fine. I have to work, Hud. And it appears that Captain Mays believes this is important in my ability to move forward."

"Nick, does Mays believe that, or did you convince him?"

I didn't answer, trying to avoid his gaze.

"Just as I thought," he responded.

The morning sun had risen over the eastern back wall of our yard, and the sight of Hud, bathed in its light, reminded me of how in love I had been with this man when we met. Tall, gym-toned, and "hottern hell," he was my remarkable Asian beauty.

Hud had been a significant catch eleven months ago when mutual friends introduced us at a party. We both were recently single and the chemistry, in and out of the bedroom, was epic. He moved in last June but kept his chichi condo in the trendy Las Olas neighborhood of Ft. Lauderdale.

Hud boasted that his bloodlines were ancient Manchu from the region between Northern China and the Russian Far East. "I am not Chinese. My family is Manchurian. There is a difference." He claimed warrior ancestors in the armies of the Qing Dynasty, the last rulers of China before the formation of the Republic in 1912.

Hudson currently serves as the Executive Director of the Preston Foundation, the most important private family foundation in the state and the seventh-largest in the country. His low-key style added to his professional presence in a way that drew respect from colleagues and the community. The Foundation was rarely interested in fame or publicity surrounding its philanthropy. Hudson Ch'en personified institutional discretion, dedicated leadership, and a quiet sense of community engagement.

My reserved warrior overlord snapped his tablet shut and returned to the conversation. "Nick, I am very concerned. You know how I dislike your work because of the danger and the high public profile. You're dancing on the edge of the volcano and obsessed as shit. Nothing new, I will admit, but, as I have said before, I do not like this at all. It's not good for you or us."

Translation: Our lovemaking had taken a significant nosedive, and it was my fault.

"And watch yourself with this Sorenson guy, total bad reputation. I remember him from the Museum Gala last year. Just how many guys was he dating at the time?"

"I think he most probably escorted the Museum's CEO, Rebecca Quinto. You know her from the upcoming exhibit. Your Foundation is the title sponsor, right? Maybe he just likes a man posse."

Hud responded with dripping sarcasm, "Yes, the beautiful people entourage. Ultracool and unforgettable. Apparently, a rule-breaker, also. Out drinking with his students. Look, I have to get to work."

He began to gather up the tray, leaving me the coffee, the phone, and the Akita. He stood to go, giving me a disdainful look.

"I was also very late last night because I stopped at ICU to see Shan again after we finished at the pier."

"Anything new?"

"I just looked through the glass wall in the ICU. She's still unconscious."

"You know, Nick. It would be nice sometime to have a conversation that was not about your work."

Hud gave me a long stare and continued to the house.

"Put that towel on, Officer Naked." He shot over his shoulder. "The pool boy will jump your hot bod in a lust frenzy. Today is his day – for the pool, I mean."

As he slid the patio door closed, he added, "And please tell your mother and sisters to leave me out of the family text message group. Such a fuckin' bother. Phone alerts are going off constantly. I can do without."

I checked my phone. I saw the message string. Jesus, fifteen since yesterday. I typed a response to my family, mother, and sisters, reaffirming my recovery from the shooting without a comprehensive reading of their copious chat bubbles filled with cutesy emojis.

I stopped at my sister Portia's entry of this morning: *Say, brother, how is this Dr. Sorenson? Crazy hot! Get me a date, and I will come down to FL ASAP. LOL.*

She attached an online photo of a shirtless Kayne in kickboxing gloves with the cutline, "Australian University Professor or Martial Arts Pro." She had read the reports of the Navy's case online and Googled my professor.

I thumb-typed, "Sorry, Por, he sings in my choir."

Not waiting for a response, I started to get up from my chair. Work time. I'd hit the gym later.

My phone chirped with a new message.

Ready for the autopsy, Officer Sechi? On your way? – KJS

Chapter Eight: Crown

"I'm telling you, I have no idea where that bitch is. I called. No answer. I went by that rat hole she lives in. No car was parked in the driveway. Gone. I'm telling you, I don't like it one bit."

Helluva Bottom Carter looked at her boss over her own reflection in her make-up mirror. She slammed down a mascara brush.

"Shit girl, when you gonna replace these dead lightbulbs anyway? This doll needs to see her natural beauty as she enhances it, you know what I'm sayin'?"

Cha Cha Rosette paced the small area between the dressing tables. As bad an act as Gaye Dawn had become, she filled the bill. When Cha Cha bought the club ten years ago, Hadji came with it like the furniture. She remembered how Hadji at first resisted the changes Cha Cha had made. She made herself the new Star Headliner, and Hadji had to take a "featuring" spot. Six years later, when Cha Cha retired, Hadji continued with her "Hollywood Revue." The club owner did not have the heart to tell the old queen that she was show business roadkill.

"Who saw her last on Sunday?" Cha Cha asked in a voice that mixed frustration, anger, and a slight bit of fear.

Inca Peru, aka Pink, spoke up, "That would be Scott. He closed, and Gaye was still packing up when I left."

"Go get him for me, Baby."

Inca went into the club, brushing past the bustling Mohka Mirage.

"Sorry, I'm late, Cha Cha-- boyfriend trouble." Looking from her boss to her drag partner, Mohka added, "What's going on, queens?"

Ms. Bottom Carter answered while applying impossibly long false eyelashes, "It's Hadji. She's gone."

"Help me, Jesus. Whaddya mean gone? Like ran away? Committed 'The Big S?' Quit the business? What?"

Mohka looked around, "Shit, that sixty-seven-year-old diva don't know nothing but drag and no way she offed herself. Most likely, she is sleeping one off. She was glued to a bottle of scotch the last time I saw her. I bet she went on a bender."

Shrugging, she started to remove her street clothes and put on the makeup for her first number.

"Where, Mo? Where she sleeping? Her car's gone. Gone." Helluva shook her head in consternation.

Inca returned with Scott Le, who confirmed that Hadji was the last to leave the parking lot after he locked up on Sunday. "She was getting to her car as I left. I thought I saw someone else in the lot at the time. I figured it was one of the homeless guys that live in the bushes on the back side of the parking lot."

"Now, you hold on right there," Cha Cha said, pointing and glaring at Scott. "Do you have the balls to look at me and say you left a sixty-seven-year-old drag queen in the parking lot with some strange guy at 4:00 AM? Are you fuckin' nuts?"

"Boss, it was one of those homeless guys. They're totally harmless."

"Harmless, my ass. And now Gaye is missing. You are one sorry-ass manager, Le. Fuckin' shit for brains."

Scott cringed and looked at the floor. No one spoke for about five minutes.

Cha Cha pointed to the youngest queen, "Inca, call up that doll friend of yours. What's her name? That light-skinned girl-- does Shakira."

"Venus Noire. That girl is smoking, Boss. You won't be sorry." Inca grabbed her cell and ran from the room.

"Fuck! I got a show to fill. Business is business. Scott, get your scrawny Asian ass out there and outta my sight. Manage something, for shit's sake."

Cha Cha Rosette stormed to the dressing room door.

Seed Blood

Helluva Bottom Carter stopped her boss, saying, "Miss Cha, what are you gonna do about Gaye? Something about this shit ain't right. The way she was feeling after her last show on Sunday and all."

Cha Cha turned around. "I'll tell you what I am gonna do. I am gonna go see that sexy ginger cop at Wilton Manors PD. What's his name? Him." She pointed at the picture of a shirtless Officer Nick Sechi cut from "Hot Shots Magazine" that was pasted on Mohka Mirage's mirror. "He shot that black boy a bit ago. He owes us one."

"Nah, uh, Miss Thang, Officer Stud Man is my next husband. Hands off." Mohka pressed her fan pic with a pair of beautifully manicured nails, making sure it did not fall off the mirror. She purred over the photo of Officer Nicola Sechi.

She continued, "We both goin.' Not only is that old queen missing, but she absconded with my property. I am a victim of a crime!"

"What?" asked Helluva. "What did Hadji steal from you?"

"Only my best drag trophy from the Ms. Florida at Large Pageant. My crown."

***

She would never regain consciousness.

He made sure that the fabric gag and the duct tape stifled her cries. In the end, she succumbed to the beating after the first blows. He was surprised that she was so pliant, seeming to welcome what they both knew would be the end of her. She embraced her death with regal resignation. There was blood running from open wounds and pooling on the floor.

He took her body down from the cross and dressed her in one of her most outlandish costumes and wigs, preparing her for her last appearance. He began zipping her up in the body bag, stopped and removed a tiara from her rolling valise, and added it to the encased corpse.

Hoisting the body bag into his arms, he carried her to his waiting SUV.

Thomas Paul Severino

Chapter Nine: Guiltless

NICK SECHI'S JOURNAL

Angela Brown stood at the front of the class, summarizing the research on the psychology of psychopaths done by our student group in Dr. Sorenson's class. Two of our fellow students, Jonathan Yurich and Michele Aimes, assisted her. Our portion of the class assignment to compile the characteristics of serial murderers consisted of a comparison of the differences between psychotics and psychopaths.

As Angela reported our findings, Kayne tapped the keys of his laptop, adding our report to the previously presented results of three other groups in the class. Notes with his embellishments appeared on the overhead monitor.

The classroom had an eerie feel to it. The only illumination was the media projector hanging from the ceiling, whose stream of light hit the screen at the front of the classroom. The sides and back of the room remained in almost complete darkness. Within the beam's periphery, a combination of light and dark played across the speaker. The illumination and the ghoulish topic of discussion for the last hour increased the evening's sense of the macabre.

After completing our report, Ms. Brown sat down. Kayne stepped into the projector's beam, which overshot his handsome features and cast him in chilling relief – Hitchcock-esque and most assuredly staged for effect.

"And so, we have seen this evening that psychotics and psychopaths, both capable of the most heinous crimes, have traits in common. Such as...."

He pointed to Jonathan Yurich, who was initially unresponsive, possibly tired from his day job. He had contributed very little to the previous discussion in our group. He now seemed to resist the professor's attempt to coax an answer from him. He stared at Kayne from the dark. With a low and rather shy voice, he said, "It is like she said." He pointed to the notes on the screen.

A hand shot up to catch the teacher's challenge. Kayne turned from Jonathan to acknowledge the student volunteering the answer.

"Blunted emotions – lack of guilt or remorse."

"Yes, which is acutely stronger in the psychopath."

He changed the display to present a quote. "I don't feel guilty for anything. I feel sorry for people who feel guilt."

Indicating the quote on the screen over his shoulder, he raised his eyebrows and said, "Who?"

Liesl Morelli, a forensic science technician, called out, "Ted Bundy."

"Yes. Bundy was active in the 1970s, when he kidnapped, raped, and murdered many women, twelve of whom he decapitated. Death by electric chair in 1989. Thank you, Ms. Morelli."

He turned back to the class, "What else have you heard this evening?" Looking around. "Where are my psychopaths?"

A petite woman in the back of the class spoke up. "Psychopaths show a lot of superficial charm. They are also distinguished by pathological lying, impulsivity, and unrealistic life goals."

"Well said, Ms. Neary. What else, please?' He pointed, "Mr. Wallner ...."

Steve Wallner glanced at his notes. He spoke up, "Early behavioral problems and a feeling of being above the law. Data shows evidence of a chemical imbalance."

The Professor responded, "Precisely, Mr. Wallner. True psychopaths believe there is nothing wrong with them. We will address the brain chemistry factor shortly."

Kayne's display bulleted the discussed characteristics in this first round of summation. Looking around the class, he continued, "This is a very comprehensive list, thank you. Now for the traits of psychotic patients ...."

Three students in tandem provided the next set of bullets on the screen: delusions, hallucinations, loss of interest in regular activity, lack of personal hygiene, paranoia, confusion, and violence toward self and others.

Seed Blood

"Students, what else should a criminologist know about the topic we have explored this evening?"

Kayne stepped to the podium and edited the electronic display as class members shot out responses.

"There is a little over a three-percent chance that a psychotic disorder will remain throughout one's lifetime."

"The age when adults are at higher risk for psychotic disorders is between the years of 30 to 40, Professor."

After a pause, a familiar voice spoke up from the darkest part of the back of the class. "Almost all serial killers throughout history were male."

The group turned to follow the source of the comment. Kayne smiled. "Class, someone who needs no introduction, my good friend Ms. Rebecca Quinto, a remarkable woman."

I could tell in the dark Rebecca was smiling slyly.

***

"Dr. Sorenson," Rebecca said with mock formality. "Please summarize the findings of the autopsy on poor Jared Christiansen. I am so dying to know, Kayne Darling."

We dined at "Parakalo," a Greek bistro on Wilton Drive. Despite being well into a plate of saganaki with tomatoes and lemons, our waiter, George, added dishes of tzatziki, stuffed grape leaves, grilled octopus, and spanakopita.

The City of Wilton Manors, minutes from downtown Ft. Lauderdale, lies to the north and east, surrounded by the waterways that empty into the Intracostal on their way to the Atlantic. "The Island City" combines Old Florida domiciles, sparkling new homes, and very bohemian tourist venues. The Manors boasts of one of the largest, per capita, LGBT communities on the planet. Wilton Drive is famous for trendy shopping, fantastic food, and exotic clubs. On weekends, the nightlife draws thousands, especially during "The Season" or the Wilton Manors Stonewall Pride Fest in June.

"Drink your Velvet Dynamite, my love. I would defer to my protégé, young Nick, but this is hardly a topic for dinner."

He deeply "nosed" his glass of "Black Sheep," his ice-blue eyes deepening against the smoky ruby of the Syrah. In an aside to me, he said, "Are you getting the fig and plum aromas? Silky smooth." I imitated his caressing of the wine and nodded. I clinked his glass with mine.

"Then let's get a bit more white-boy wasted and discuss." She held up her nearly empty glass to our passing waiter.

"I adore Greek men, Darling." Kayne glanced at George's butt and nodded in assent. A slow Bouzouki started up near the rear of the restaurant. The soft, enchanting strains floated across the dance floor to entice the diners and add a captivating layer to the food, the wine, and the liquor.

Before responding to Rebecca's request, I checked my phone for a message from Hudson. Although we lived only a few blocks away, he was unable to join us. He was still pissed at me, I guessed.

"The identity of the corpse was confirmed. It was the body of Navy Chief Petty Officer Jared Christensen. The coroner's report will indicate death by drowning. Time of death is estimated to be anywhere from 24 hours before they discovered the body. Although his injuries consisted of smashed internal organs and some broken bones, there is evidence that the boy was alive when placed into the water and thus drowned. He did not die because of the extensive trauma sustained by the beatings before being placed into the harbor."

I looked at Kayne, who requested, "Please continue in detail, officer, regarding your conclusion as to the cause of death, etc."

"The frothing in the respiratory tract, the weight of the lungs, and the excessive bleeding when the coroner opened the torso, these are associated with disambiguation—respiratory impairment from submersion in liquid. Remarkably, the body continued to bleed despite the earlier time of death."

Kayne interrupted to explain, "Gravity pulls the body fluid to the dorsal side post-mortem, except in the case of drowning where there is an excess of fluid throughout, hence the blood. Continue, Nick."

"The toxicology report will tell if there were poisons or drugs in the system. It should be completed tomorrow. I would guess that it will come up negative. We observed no punctures in the usual places of intravenous injection. The stomach contents, or lack thereof, suggest that the victim was allowed very little to eat during his ordeal.

"Officer Christiansen was most likely unconscious when placed in the water, but because of his near-fatal beatings, he was unable to survive. Every major organ was compromised by acute and severe trauma, according to the autopsy. The fractures were in bones lying close to the skin."

"I am confused. You indicated that the boy was pretty mashed up inside. Yet, I understand the external bruising was not that traumatic – skin breaks and ruptures, the sort of thing associated with blunt force. How does that happen?" Rebecca asked.

Before I could answer, George returned to the table with our entrees. A shout of "*Opa!*" came from another table, and eight customers moved to join the band on the dance floor. They took their white napkins.

As we tucked into our orzo paella, I said, "To be honest, Rebecca, I am not sure. There were some anomalies revealed by the ultraviolet that we want to further investigate. Also, the results of any of the nail scrapings that survived immersion may tell us something."

"What is also puzzling," added Kayne, who gestured with his fork. "How did the killer get into the port with the body? Security at Port Everglades is extremely comprehensive. The evidence of the nail scrapings and the species plants tied around the torso suggests contact with materials not found in the Port or the waters off the pier. The salinity of the water in the lungs was significantly lower than that of the Intracostal."

Rebecca jumped on it. "He put the body in the water, and it drifted."

Kayne faced her, touched their glasses, and said, "Damn, you're one smart shelia!" Then, more seriously, he added, "I had the opportunity to analyze the currents, the wind, and tidal flow in the Intracostal last night. By my calculations, the body was put into the water somewhere north of the Port, most likely around the 17th Street Bridge. Water plants there correspond to those snagged on the body. The freshwater from the incoming rivers results in a lower salinity of the water in the lungs. I would estimate that occurred approximately 24 hours prior."

More revelry from the dance floor. The crowd was jumping for a Thursday. A familiar muscled beauty trailing two attractive companions burst through the revelers. He came up behind Kayne, encircling him in a hug.

"I recognize those guns anywhere. Mmm, mmm…" Kayne went with the hug, pulled into the embrace, and joked, "Who says the Latvians are cold-blooded? How are you, Gints?"

The muscled beauty whispered into Kayne's left ear and bit the lobe softly. Raising his head, he introduced Kostas and Davin. Standing, Rebecca received the latter gorgeousness with outstretched arms.

"My sexy centaur, when did you get back from Crete, Darling?"

Davin spoke softly between two cheek kisses. They are intimates, obviously. I had dated Kostas over a year ago, just before Hud. We exchanged similar pleasantries. I must admit, as low as my libido was since the shooting, "K-Boy" felt great in my arms.

George arrived with a tray of six full shot glasses and a tall bottle. "Ouzo, my friends, compliments of the management." Kostas led us in the first of three toasts, "*Se néous fílous kai palioús.* To new friends and old."

Rebecca's phone chirped. She looked at the notification but did not answer. "My board chair… probably wanting to know how my meeting with the Archbishop went. The man is such a dolt."

"Your chair or His Excellency?" Kayne asked, still wrapped in some Gints lovin'.

"Which do you think?" Rebecca smirked and rolled her eyes.

As the music swelled, propelling circling dancers on the floor behind us, Gints looked around at the six of us with large brown eyes and said one word. It was an invitation. "*Kalamatianós.*"

"Yes!" said Rebecca. She started to slip her phone into Kayne's man bag, saying, "Darling, if we are going to dance, I do not want to be disturbed, so… Oh, my God!"

As she opened the bag and looked inside, she stopped, squealed, and slowly withdrew a skimpy, white article of men's underclothing from her friend's satchel. The group paused to stare open-mouthed at the gleaming white man-thong dangling between her fingers. Rebecca snickered at Kayne. "Oh, Darling, don't you love when the sleepovers leave behind a stunning memento?"

Gints squeezed Kayne's traps gently, saying, "Good, you bring it. It is favorite."

Davin and Kostas slapped Gints' back and high-fived. Winking at his roaring buds, Gints gestured at his once-lost thong and added, "This one very lucky for Gints."

The eminent Dr. Sorenson, looking like a small boy with his hand caught in the cookie jar, gently removed the discovered souvenir from Rebecca's fingers and placed it between his teeth. He did his signature hair sweep and, as they say in Australia, "grinned like a shot fox."

Davin and Kostas exchanged remarks in Greek. My jaw-dropping gape morphed into an ear-to-ear, leering smile. Gints gently removed the thong from between Kayne's teeth and kissed him. Tossing white cloth napkins to his buds, he announced, "Come, we dance!"

Rebecca and I took the offered ends of the napkins provided by our respective partners. Kayne took up the other end of Gints' undergear, holding it aloft with his sexy partner. Wobbling a bit, the hunky professor said to the muscle boy through a heavy Aussie accent, "You're stoking my old fella, Mate."

Shouts of *"Opa!"* filled Parakalo as we joined in the hypnotic swirl of music and circling dancers.

Kalamatianós!

Thomas Paul Severino

Chapter Ten: Citrus
Nick Sechi's Journal

The homeless child reminded me of a character from Theodore Dreiser's Sister Carrie. Of indeterminate sex and very dirty, I figured the street denizen to be anywhere from fifteen to twenty-five. The early January morning air caused the person to pull a bulky sweater closer to the body. It was well before dawn. The three of us huddled near a trendy arts district in Ft. Lauderdale cobbled together from what was once a collection of small warehouses and storage garages-- urban shabby chic.

"Nick, this is Mikey. She is my friend and helps with details of street life and some of the nightly goings-on, as it were."

Mikey did not smile but glanced through half-closed lids like a grungy elf. She pointed at me. "You're that cop. I seen you lotsa times. Shot a gangsta a bit ago. Took a couple off that baddie, I hear."

I nodded and touched my chest unconsciously. Neither Kayne nor I had been home after our bistro debauch with the Greeks. Rebecca had left with Davin just as Kayne received a text from Mikey. We left Gints and Kostas propped up at the bar, promising continued revelries at an undetermined date and time.

"Listen, Doc, let's make this quick. I don't want anyone to see me with a cop if possible." Mikey continued in a whisper, "What you're looking for is Number 221 just down that row and next to the dark blue dumpster. "Hell Boy said he heard some strange late-night doings coming outta there last week, but he was afraid to say something to anybody. Same thing late last night, too."

Mikey rubbed the snot from her nose onto her sleeve and shivered a bit, continuing to look around as if expecting trouble. "I sorta opened it for ya, Doc. Yeah, don't ask."

"Did you go inside?"

"Fuck no. Oh, sorry. Hell said there was bad shit in that place, awful moaning and the ultra-vicious." She rubbed her head and shook it like a wet pup.

"When are the dumpsters emptied here, Mikey?"

"Mondays, Doc. So, tomorrow."

"Good work, my girl." A pause, and then said, "How are the other Shadows, Mikey? Any problems?"

"The Peeler ran off again, but she'll be back. She ages out in June. Think she is looking for other accommodations when her foster care ends. Hell Boy is sneaking out on the Claypools a bit too much if you ask me. I seen him out way late."

"Please let him know that I want to see him. Hey, you clean, Mikey?"

"Fuck yes, Doc." She pushed the sleeves of her sweater up, baring each arm. No new tracks. "No more of that shit. I'm virtuous and staying that way. A promise is a promise."

"How about the education? You talk to that guy?"

"Yes, on that too. The College will help me get my GED and get into a certificate program by the fall. I owe you big time on that one, Doc."

"Good, we need to talk about school clothes then, but we have some time. I have a friend who would love to help you become super stylish as you embark on your college years. She would be a great mentor, Mikey."

The young woman looked at the ground and considered the offer. She raised her head slowly and said, "I'd like that. Time to get some class."

He gave her a wad of cash, pointed to her chest, and said, "Share that with the other Shadows. And Mikey, Covenant House, now. You get to the shelter. You need to eat."

"Hate that fuckin' place. Oh, 'scuse me."

She looked from Kayne to me. In her mind, her cussing was a step backward in her attempts to be more refined.

"Overcrowded as shit."

"I need you and the others healthy and straight, Mickey. Do it."

"Ahhh... OK. Catch ya later, Doc. Lemme know what else comes up. Same way to contact, OK? Stays secret. And thanks for this."

She pocketed the cash.

Mikey gave Kayne some elaborate secret handshake and faded into the shadows amongst the clutter of the dark alley behind us. We turned and walked to the unit nearest the blue dumpster. A broken padlock hung in the hasp of the closed overhead garage door.

"So much for prints on that," I said.

Removing my flashlight, I held Kayne's as he took out a handkerchief and raised the door. We slowly entered the maw of the dark interior.

***

The light switch did not work. The power to the unit was off. We stood at the threshold, our light beams playing over the pitch-black space. The empty enclosure was roughly sixty feet wide by one hundred feet deep. The back of the area was partitioned off as a barred lockup. The cell's door hung ajar. I called the station for backup.

"OK, we do not have much time. Give me your mobile and show me the soles of your shoes, Nick." I complied, and Kayne snapped each raised foot. He handed it back to me and lifted each of his feet as I did the same for his shoes." He retook my phone.

"We want to identify all footprints in the dust and make sure we are discounting ours."

As we moved into the room, he murmured, "Touch nothing."

Kayne hit the floor like a bloodhound on the scent at least eight times to photograph disturbances in the dust on the concrete floor as we moved to the back cell. More than once, he actually smelled and tasted the floor dirt. The odor of rotting fruit pervaded the scene. Kayne gathered dirt and dust in small envelopes, which he stowed in his man bag. He photographed footprints on the floor.

Lashed to the outside of the cell was the X-shaped St. Andrew's Cross. On a heap of rags lying just outside the cell door, the light revealed several fronds of a date palm and a coil of hemp. A torn, bloodied muscle shirt lay on the debris. Kayne sniffed and tasted a corner of the ripped fabric. He began examining tiny bits of light extracted from the rubble.

73

Easing around the open cell door, we ran our flashlights over the enclosed space. Scratches marked the walls and floor of the cage. Leg irons hung, crusted in blood, hung from a hook on one of the crossbars of the cage. Crumpled on the floor was a matching set of manacles. There was blood on the back wall, the bars, and the floor. My cell phone camera flashed as Kayne recorded elements of the scene and took samples.

Outside, three police SUVs pulled close to the open door. The investigative team began to unload equipment and personnel. Mays and Crawford pulled up in separate cruisers with members of the government entourage. Two other vehicles brought members of the press.

Realizing that the virgin crime scene was about to be trashed by an army of intruders, Kayne and I looked around the cell for any last essential clues.

"Nick, over here."

Still using my phone, Kayne flashed on the back corner of the cell. The wall scratches and the blood were heaviest here. About eight inches from the floor, the claw marks and blood created an unusual graffito-- intersecting arches, traced in blood.

***

Outside Number 221, Kayne handed me my phone. The alley, the street, and the open storage chamber swarmed with police. Sheriff Crawford and Chief Mays were in a cluster with the Navy and the FBI representatives. Kayne and I enjoyed the distance from the flurry of activity as the sun rose to illuminate the rows of warehouses. Lack of sleep was beginning to take its toll. I leaned against the nearest upright object.

"The autopsy showed no evidence that the young navy man was a smoker. There were no cigarette remains in the chamber or outside. Yet, the t-shirt reeked of nicotine."

"He spent the night at a bar."

"The only place where such smoke concentration would correspond. And considering the other traces found on the shirt, a place where dancing is featured, close quarters and hot enough to produce sweat."

"Could be any one of a number in this town."

74

Kayne scrolled through the pictures on my phone.

"Also, it would appear that our killer wears Timberland work boots and spends some time down by the Middle River in Wilton Manors, the South Fork, east side. The clay of that color is found only on that shore. An abundance of ferrous oxide from a chemical plant that once stood there. This sample of vegetation embedded in the mud comes from a weed that favors that spot, *Asclepias curassavica*, tropical milkweed."

Pulling up a shot of the floor, he said, "Nick, look at this."

The picture was of widely spaced footprints in the fine dust on the storage unit floor. In places, they were interrupted by something that had been dragged through. Here and there, glitter winked in the light of the phone's flash. Kayne handed me a plastic evidence envelope. In it were three silver sequins.

"This doesn't make much sense regarding the naval officer. What do you make of it?"

Without waiting for an answer, he handed me back the phone.

"Please be so kind as to forward me those pictures from your mobile. We will have found more accurate information from this fresh crime scene than anything your colleagues may find."

I stretched and yawned in the morning light. "Can I buy you coffee, Professor?" I said a bit sleepily. "The Vienna Cafe on Thirteenth should just be opening."

"God, yes! But we have one last task, my friend." He nodded to the dumpster against which I was leaning.

He stopped to select a small piece of lumber lying nearby and flipped over the lid. The bang caused some of the investigators to turn in our direction. Standing on a wooden crate, Kayne shined his light into the heap of garbage that filled half of the dumpster.

"There." He pointed with the stick. "The instruments of torture perpetrated on the unfortunate Officer Christiansen."

I reached into the foul container and extracted the object to which Dr. Sorenson pointed – a net bag of oranges.

75

Thomas Paul Severino

Chapter Eleven: Vienna

NICK SECHI'S JOURNAL

At the Vienna, I texted Hudson, explaining my failure to come home last night after class. I received a one-word response. *Whatever*. I anticipated another round of ultimatums when I got back.

"I hesitate to call Rebecca," Kayne said, looking at his watch. "I am sure she and her Greek god are well into the morning-after-the-night-before or round seven as it is more commonly known."

I smiled. "And your Gints?"

Kayne looked wistfully into his flat white and stirred.

"Officer Sechi, although this subject of our conversation is highly unprofessional, let me say that boy shags like a Baltic pagan warlord."

To emphasize the last part of his comment, he tapped the table in time with the previous three words.

Kayne looked up and swept back his forelock. His smug expression turned into a slight smile. Before I could tease him, he pointed at me. He added, "We continue to be in the consulting part of our relationship, remember. Let me point out that it would be a breach of proprieties for me to ask about your past with one very hot lad, the overly attentive young Kostas."

He arched an eyebrow, and his blue eyes twinkled. I said nothing, just blushed.

Shaking my head, I changed the subject, "Oranges, professor." We had pulled out three bags of very mashed citrus. "Tell me."

Kayne leaned back and looked up at the ceiling while speaking.

"They are indeed the instruments of torture used by the killer to beat the young Naval Officer to unconsciousness before drowning him in brackish water. There is a forensic myth that beating a person with a bag of oranges will pulverize the internal organs without any external bruising."

77

He looked at me and continued. "It is a mistaken notion. There are, in fact, external marks. Despite the hard body sported by the young sailor, you saw the round indentations on soft tissue. Review the marks, and you will see a faint impression of the net bag in each of the circles, as well as the dimpled skin of the fruit. Observe." He pulled up a closeup of the upper abdomen of the body on the pier on his phone.

Kayne continued, "The site of concussion will show a minimum of the victim's blood, hence a closed wound and little breaking of the skin. Actual trauma depends on where the killer hit him and how hard the oranges were at the time. Most importantly, how long the oranges stayed on the impact site after the hit. The blood we found was from the mouth, the lacerated ankles and wrists, and the rectum."

He raised and clenched his fists, "The damage of the impact corresponds to the physics of boxing. It's not the actual strike but the combination of the impact and surface area of the glove that causes trauma – a knockout. In reality, the arms are more important in boxing than the fists. The arm carries the glove and keeps it in the same spot. If you get enough inertia behind a bag of oranges or anything for that matter, you could cause pain and destruction internally with minor edema at the surface."

Kayne concluded, "Because the weapon absorbs the initial impact, i.e., the oranges, there are fewer broken surface vessels. However, there is major obliteration to associated organs and bones, ribs, jaw, etc., which lie near the surface. Overall, Officer Christensen received some damage to external blood vessels, but the fatal damage was internal."

I considered his analysis and added, "The killer is a strong male and is left-handed. The victim's right side received the heaviest beating."

"Excellent, Nick."

"But what about the palm branches?"

"To answer that, Officer, we need to go to church."

Before I could ask for an explanation, we were interrupted by the appearance of two very excited individuals. The manager of Café Vienna, Janet Sousa, was accompanied by an unwashed and raggedly little boy. I couldn't say what was more worn, the child himself or the disheveled backpack he dragged behind him. Ms. Sousa pulled him forward by the frayed collar of his ragged, oversized sports jacket. Patrons turned from their breakfasts as the two shuffled in the crowded eatery.

"Oy, keep your bleedin' hands offa me, ya prozzy. Naff off!"

The exasperated Janet bent nose to nose with the urchin and said, "I told you not to set foot in here, you little thief." Turning to Kayne, she continued, "He's a pickpocket and steals my food. Claims he's your friend. Please tame this creature, Dr. Kayne. I got a business to run and customers to protect." Recognizing me, she added, "Hey Nick, this street rat belongs in juvenile hall. Do us all a favor and arrest his no-good ass."

She released the boy into our custody, but the child broke loose from Kayne's grasp. He hit a ninja pose, confronting his adversary. Kayne rose and gathered the feisty hellion by the shoulders, pulling him away from a frustrated Janet before the boy could take a few swings at her.

"Jackie, stand down, bud. Let's take this outside. Janet, I will need another breakfast sandwich, a large OJ and two chicken salad sandwiches to go, two apples, and a large Gatorade. We three will be on the patio."

"Chips, I suppose."

"Yes, my lovely. Make it three bags--the ones with sea salt and vinegar." He smiled a gorgeous and charming flash of teeth.

Pouting, the devil child marched between Kayne and me as we relocated to the patio of the café. He looked over the remains of our breakfast with large, brown eyes.

"Nick, may I introduce another of my associates, Mr. John Cochran Dawkins, Esquire, of Perth, Australia, and Ft. Lauderdale, Florida."

"Beach," The child snarled, puffed out his chest, and tugged at the lapels of his jacket. "Ft. Lauderdale Beach, the swanky north end."

Kayne resumed his seat and corrected his intro with a hidden smile, "I beg your pardon. Of Perth and Ft. Lauderdale Beach. Jackie, this is Officer Nick Sechi of the Wilton Manors Police Department."

"Looks like a poofter, Boss."

"And an extremely handsome and intelligent, one at that, my lad. Let me see the best of your professional training, Mr. Dawkins. I want you to do me proud despite the allegations about your illegal activities here at Café Vienna."

"Please to meetcher, Off Sir. Name's 'Hell Boy' on the streets. At your service, Sir." The young boy stretched up to his best height, pushed out his chest again, offered me a very grimy hand in a fingerless glove, and bowed slightly. He was tatters and patches with spiky brown and green hair and very much on the puny side.

I switched us to a fist pump and said, "How's it going, bud? So, what's it like being one of the Shadows?"

"It's a rippa, Mate. I'm happy as a cat licking shit off a thistle."

Kayne interrupted his pint-sized assistant. "Jack lay off the 'Strine. Only proper English, if you please, Sir. Remember, you are my field agent, and Officer Sechi is an essential member of local law enforcement."

Hell Boy did a brief slouch and stared at the floor.

"Sorry, Boss. It is quite fine, Sir, working wif the Professor here. And the Boss gives us each a cell phone to report in. Us Shadows have special powers like superheroes."

I looked at Kayne with a smile.

"S'right. Take me, for example. I knowed life on the city streets since I was four. And lookit me, Mate. I am small and able to slip in and slip out where blokes can't see like shit through a pig's arse. I am especially good at hiding, a cinch in situations when the Big Bad is nearby. I gets to hear rumors that you won't while you are out on your investigations. Ear hustling, we calls it. Ya know?"

He went on, "My bestie, Mickey, is good too but not as good as me. She is fun to hang out wif. And she's a jackaroo of a climber, bleedin' Sherpa, to say the truf. Excellent good at the B and E."

At the mention of breaking and entering, Kayne did a sharp inhale.

Turning to look at him, Hell Boy said, "Wot?" he raised one hand to cover his mouth and smacked his forehead with the other.

"Ohh! Sorry I cussed, Sir."

"Here you are, Dr. Sorenson."

A server arrived with a large sack of takeout and an array of breakfast food and drink. Conspicuously added to the tray was an unordered cinnamon bun. It caused our little pickpocket's eyes to bug out.

"Hands, Jackie."

The boy held up two dirty paws and frowned.

"Go on. Wash up and do not abuse the patrons in the process."

As the mite rushed back inside the café, squeezing between a leaving couple to hit the men's room, Kayne turned to me and said, "He's fifteen and looks twelve. Abandoned when he was four back in AU. Arrived here as a ten-year-old. Human trafficking – a real horror show, Nick. Children's Services and INS cannot contain the lad. He is an accomplished escape artist. Ran away six times and counting.

"I met him last summer and got him into the group. A bright little bug, perceptive, avid reader, and entirely self-taught. I am working on getting him legal, but that is a morass of bureaucracy. I am hoping that the Shadows will provide some training and discipline and get him to a place where he will agree to more structure in his life."

Kayne placed the takeout sack in Hell Boy's backpack, but not without inspecting the boy's collection of items. He put his uneaten bagel, bacon, and cheese on the food tray next to the other sandwich.

In a flash, Hell Boy was back, seated at the table, eyes big as saucers and holding up his hands for inspection.

"The cinnamon bun shall be last, Boyo."

"Ahh, geez, Boss. Not like I will lose me appetite if I have sweets first." Without further argument, he removed his jacket and dove at the food and drink.

I asked the boy between bites of his food. "Mr. Dawkins, tell us about Warehouse 221 if you can."

Hell Boy looked up from his feast with a wary look and said, "Bad shit going on there, Off Sir. The Big Bad. Think it was fighting or some such. Maybe a bit of how's yer father. Dunno. Hard to say."

I looked at Kayne quizzically. He explained, "Sexual intercourse."

"Righto, sexin' up. Anyway, pressed my ear to the door, but just got talk and like hollering, ya know? No way to see inside. Checked for holes and cracks ever where."

Kayne asked, "Jackie, did you see anyone coming and going?"

"Yeah, Boss, ya see, I was squeezed in behind a dumpster and some pallets in the alley, and I saw the creepo. Big chav. Took his cap off at one point. Berk's got hair like a bush pig's arse."

That one I got.

"Tossed somptin' in the dumpster, but Hell Boy ain't no diver. Yuk!"

Kayne faced his buddy and spoke clearly, "Jackie, remember our rule to make sure you are well away from potential danger. You crossed the line with this one – too close to danger. Please put into action our safeguards for protecting field agents. Stay well away and always have an escape plan. Just in case things go cockeyed."

"I hear you, Boss. Haven't been back there since. Scary bugger, that one."

Kayne slipped some cash into the front of the backpack between the pages of a very beaten-up book. "Agent Dawkins, have you maintained our agreed-upon relationship with the Claypools?"

The boy now faked all innocence as he said, "Oh, yeah, Boss. They're cool. But they are talking about a real school for the Hell Boy. Sucks major. Plus, we're negotiatin' on my street time."

"Might need to change up some of your responsibilities, Bud. I sure could use a well-schooled partner with a lot of training and respectability. You know, really go after the Big Bads. Like a police officer or a private detective."

"Ever hear of the Police Academy, Jack?" I offered. "Real intense superhero training and looking for recruits."

"Yeah. You know I got what it takes for that gig." He mugged toughness and threw a double biceps shot with his skinny arms.

I answered with a one-arm flex. Hell Boy reached over. "Damn, I need to bulk up, I'm guessin'."

Kayne smiled. "Gotta finish school, bud. Schools have great fitness programs. Let's plan it out."

"Ok, Boss. Just text me." He began to gather up his belongings.

"One more thing, Jack."

"Boss, I know what you are going to ask, and the answer is, 'No.' He looked over at me and then back to Kayne with an expression of shame. "Not sellin'. Stopped totally like we talked."

Oh, shit. I gulped.

"Good. Stick to our agreement. Dismissed, Agent Dawkins."

"Aye, Sir." He mock-saluted us both, grabbed up his backpack, and dashed.

***

"Kayne, I have so many issues with that boy. A minor, a thief, an illegal, and a pusher? He needs to be off the street for his own good. I need to arrange for an official visit to the Claypool family with Children's Services. I would not be doing my job if I did not make sure that Jack was receiving adequate services and protection."

Kayne heaved a deep sigh, "Nick, he has been up before the magistrates numerous times. As I said, he unbelievably escapes incarceration every time. Jackie resists strict intervention. So many of the street kids age out of foster care. Then there is nothing for them. Mickey is a good example."

He leaned close to me and continued, "John Cochran Dawkins is gay, very ornery, and small. In a prison for juveniles, he would be dead within two months. Right now, the Claypools are an alternative foster care option. Professional Counselors, but yes, operating outside the system.

"We are working with Jackie to get him more and more stabilized and agreeable to some normative behavior, but it takes time. The Shadows team provides structure. It's a group of urchins who fall through the cracks and are in danger of being completely lost. Inevitably, Jackie must be reminded of the rules now and again.

"I'm sure you can understand his immigration status is a real problem, but we have some compassionate folks in high places. However, as you know, that is changing. So, what happens, that boy gets shipped back to Western Australia?"

"Kayne, you know I can't accept that, and neither will Mays. The only thing the Captain knows is doing things by the freaking book – following established procedures, especially with any shit in which I am involved. A foster care situation that allows this child to be on the streets is not beneficial for Jackie. What about the drugs?"

Kayne stopped and looked far off for a bit. He turned back, made direct eye contact, and continued.

"No, Nick, Hell Boy was not selling drugs. I'm very sad to say that the child was selling his body for the flesh peddlers, Nick. As I said, the human trafficking situation here is a heinous crime. Jack was a victim with horrible consequences."

I thought I detected a tear in the eyes of my Professor. Kayne looked off into nowhere a took a long pause before he continued.

"If he takes his meds, the virus will remain undetectable."

Just then, in a wild rush, the boy reappeared and ran into Kayne's arms and gave him a big kiss. "I forgot to say thanks for the food and everything, Boss."

In a flash, he ran out of the café.

Chapter Twelve: Fire
NICK SECHI'S JOURNAL

"Jesus, not again!"

I pounded my desk. My PC screen had turned completely black and was unresponsive to any pressed key. I could not even turn it off. Tech support at the department sucked. Nevertheless, I punched their number on my desk phone.

Before I could complete the call, the screen turned on, and the image of a heart monitor coursed across the screen. Against a blood-red background, a green line, traveling left to right, mimicked the diastolic and systolic contractions of the human heart. Quickly, I brought my phone up to the computer and hit "camera," " video," and "record." A heavily modified voice came over my desktop speakers.

"Good morning, Officer Sechi. I am aware that you have discovered my *tormentis cubiculum*. However, rest assured, I will not be deterred. Sin for sin. Officer Christiansen refused to serve. He was powerful but, alas, *passus est*. His precious death will not be in vain. Hear me and heed me. More will take the palm and wear the crown. Do not prevent what must be. *Deo gratias*."

The heartbeats flatlined. My picture from the cover of Hot Shots engulfed in yellow and red flames expanded on the screen before it went black. After a minute, my computer came on as if nothing had happened.

The other occupant of my office stood pale-faced and stunned at what we both witnessed on my desktop.

"Holy shit!" He was shaking at what he saw.

I hammered at the keys in every combination I knew to recall the recording, but to no avail. The message was gone. I made two calls. The first was to police tech support, and the other to my Chief. Tech support responded immediately. A techie was dispatched. Chief Mays' assistant indicated that the Chief was in a meeting with Internal Affairs. She would let him know that I urgently needed to see him.

As the technology officer, Cathy Wayne, stepped through the door, I told her of the hack. She reacted with one word, "Impossible," and commandeered my desk.

I turned to my guest and suggested that we grab some coffee at Barista Boys, about a block away.

Michael Crowley had been dating Jared Christiansen for about eight months. Their relationship was pretty much long-distance. Jared spent most of that time at sea, but he stayed with Michael when he returned to port. During their time together, Michael realized Jared's unhappiness with recent developments in his military life.

Michael was also running for Mayor of Wilton Manors, a campaign fraught with the vicious hatred of the current American political scene. His inclusion message was stomped on by his leading opponent, the Reverend Cale Norton. Pastor Norton's flock was taking the position that the hamlet of Wilton Manors needed to purge itself of "sin and debauchery." The implication was that only a straight man of sterling religious values could make the Manors a God-fearing American city again. As we settled into a table at the back of the cafe, Michael was anything but focused on his campaign. All of his public persona gave way to that of a man dealing with a profound personal tragedy.

He explained, "Jared was sick and tired of the homophobia he encountered and quite outspoken about it. Really got into it with one captain, I think it was. A few times, when he got drunk, he would start yelling and telling everyone about how fucked he thought the Navy was. Last month, he had just about all he could take. Something about derogatory remarks spray-painted on his locker. Despite some assurances from the top brass, he was furious. Said he never wanted to go back."

He wrung his hands and continued, "Jay was a great guy, kind and beautiful. You know we actually have...." He stopped. "... had the same birthday. How weird is that? He used to say it was fate."

Attempting to compose himself, he continued, "Jay loved the Navy, mostly. Wanted to be a career man in the military. Thought it would go a long way to overcome the discrimination and hatred he found growing up.

I felt a bit sorry for him, you know? He was a strong guy, but he was all alone in the world. Yeah, he had family back in Utah, but they disowned him when he came out. Jesus people, ya know? Mormons. Didn't even come to his graduation from the Naval Academy. I bet they won't claim the body."

He was right. My brief conversation with Jared's father resulted in his telling me he was the Navy's responsibility. They wanted nothing to do with him. I heard his mother sobbing in the background when I called to express my sympathy and test the waters regarding some questions I had.

"Michael, what took you so long to come forward?"

"I've been out of town. My family is in Hawaii, and my mom is awfully sick. I flew out just before Thanksgiving to see her. I let Jay stay at my place here in the Manors. He was due to report back to his ship in Jacksonville on December 27.

"We discussed for a long time what would happen if he went AWOL. When I went to Hawaii, he promised me he would return to Jacksonville and press for some critical advocacy from his superiors. Then I lost contact. I left messages starting around Christmas Eve until his voicemailbox was full. I thought it might have something to do with maneuvers or some shit. Then, when I got back yesterday, I found out he had been missing and was discovered dead."

"Any idea of his activities after you left for Hawaii?"

Michael Crowley held up three fingers and counted off. "Quads Gym, Metropolitan Bar — he loved to dance and cruise the leather bar, Prowl. Jay rocked the grunge scene. Nothing extreme, you know, just some rough consensual fun."

He sipped his coffee, trying to compose himself. I felt sad for this young man. The death of his lover was a hell of a lot to deal with. His affection for his dear friend was tangible. Michael continued, "Will the Navy take him, Officer Sechi? For burial, I mean."

"Yes, Michael, They will contact the family. I will put you in touch with JAG Captain Rota. He will let you know the details of the internment. Rota is a good man."

He paused and looked at the floor. "I can't believe he's dead and, in that horrible way... tortured and drowned."

87

I thought: *Someone went to a lot of trouble to kill a gay guy.* Strange.

He covered his face with his hands and began to sob deeply, his whole body shaking. I put my hand on his shoulder, but words would not come. As his crying continued, he looked up at me. His face was a mask of grief and anger. He was trembling with fury as he spoke.

"Get that fucker, Officer. Make him pay for what he did."

Chapter Thirteen: Sweat

Nick Sechi's Journal

Robert Mays stared at my cell phone.

"Have Officer Wayne download this clip and scrub your phone. I will make sure that Dr. Sorenson views this evidence, but we need to keep it out of the ether – off the web."

He placed a copy of the latest South Florida Gay News on the desk between us.

The headline screamed, "Palm Killer: Murder in South Florida."

He tapped the front-page picture of Officer Christensen and said, "Not good for this town. Height of the tourist season, Nick. Ft. Lauderdale's Pride Celebration in February for the Snow Birds, the Mayoral race, the Boat Show, and the new opening at the Art Museum. Pressure is massive for us to catch this guy from city, county, state, and federal."

"We will get him, Sir. Part of his pathology is that he wants to be stopped – found out. In this, his behavior is contradictory. He prides himself on outmaneuvering the police yet leaves many clues to bring about his capture. Dr. Sorenson says psychotic killers want the gnawing addiction to murder to stop."

"And a bit of cat and mouse. It appears from this message that you are the bait, Officer. How do you feel about that?"

"I say bring it. Very capable of dealing with this, Sir."

He turned, stood up, and walked to the window. Removing a handkerchief, he wiped his brow.

"I wish I was that confident, Nick. Internal Affairs is on my ass to rein you in-- get you suspended from the force. I don't know how long they will wait for Officer Shahnawaz to recover for their decision on the shooting and your status in the Department. If she ever does wake up."

Dead silence. I tried to contain my anxiety. "Chief, if the Palm Killer is using me as his point of contact, I can't leave now. I need to be in on the investigation. Besides, the connection to Dr. Sorenson is critical. What I am learning from him is and will continue to be an important resource for the force."

"Just be careful, Officer, and play by the rules at all times. No hotshot maneuvers." He nodded to the door.

I thought that his last comment was a bit rough.

***

Hudson's head was thrown back in passionate ecstasy, every muscle tense, one arm behind his head. His naked, sweat-soaked body straddled my thighs as he rode, edging his hard manhood. The lights from the park's sports field piercing the darkness of our bedroom through the patio doors opposite the bed illuminated the sweat sheen on his muscled body. On my back beneath him, I ran my hands over his wet thighs, abs, and pecs, coaxing his climax with hot verbal encouragement. He was panting and close. I was disappointingly flaccid between his legs.

As he reached a very powerful orgasm, he looked down at me and slowed his rocking. Rolling off to his side of the bed and turning away from me, he said, "Would have been nice if you at least stayed hard, Nick."

Looking at his glistening back and shoulders, I said nothing as his breathing slowed. I knew he was staring at the wall.

I rose and went into the bathroom to wash the remains of our sweat and his semen from my face, abs, and chest. We had disturbed the dog, which was unusual.

"Go to sleep, Chou." He usually found our sex play boring, but tonight, he was restless, staring out at the yard and whining.

As I returned to bed, I reached out to touch Hudson-- a bit apologetically, but he was unresponsive. It seems like I was apologizing a lot these days. I knew he was not asleep.

Withdrawing my hand, I turned over to my edge of the bed, remembering the fantasy that got me hard at the beginning of our lovemaking. In my mind, I had imagined two naked men, positioned precisely as Hud and I were, sexing up like savages. The glistening body of the rider stretched, raising an arm to sweep his black hair back off his forehead and out of his eyes. His muscled companion lifted his hips beneath him with fiery intensity, thrusting up and into him with such brute force that each impalement made his partner cry out.

On the floor, next to the bed, was a white thong.

Thomas Paul Severino

Chapter Fourteen: Catherine

Sally Holt loved the fact that people always said she resembled Uma Thurman. She took care of herself and dressed to kill as a senior vice president of a major Florida investment firm headquartered in downtown Ft. Lauderdale. Single but in a three-year relationship, she shared her eighteenth-floor condo at River Edge with her latest boy toy, Alexsander Leoniewski, six years her junior.

"Sasha" hated mornings, so Sally's daily predawn runs were jealously guarded private times. She started out on the south shore Riverwalk of the city's New River, directly outside her condo building. Crossing to the north side at the Andrews Avenue Bridge, Sally headed east to Las Olas Boulevard. From there, she ran all the way to the beach. The return trip rounded out her daily run at six miles.

As she started out, Sally looked at the city's skyline, known as the "Venice of America," glistening in the slowly arriving dawn. Its glass towers and streetlamps reflected the gentle chop of the inky river. The Dixie Queen Riverboat, docked directly across from her, gently rocked against the pylons. It was a significant tourist attraction, busily churning along the shorelines of the New River and taking in the architectural sights and wildlife of this beautiful city. Its rear paddlewheel, twin smokestacks, and classic showboat design were a visitor's icon of carefree vacation days with a touch of a bygone era.

Sally wondered if the vessel was recently out of commission for maintenance. The side of the paddlewheel facing her across the river was shrouded under canvas for repairs. The runner had one of her premonitions and decided to get a closer look, crossing the river at Third Avenue rather than going one block further to Andrews.

As she approached the land side of the boat, the partially covered side of the stern wheel was now facing away from her. Looking through the spokes and paddles, Sally saw a curious silhouette. A passing yacht created a more extensive than legal wake, causing the docked riverboat to rock and lose its canvas shroud.

Other runners on the south shore began to scream, yell, and point. Sally looked through the spokes and saw the body.

Chapter Fifteen: Portiuncula

NICK SECHI'S JOURNAL

The Broward Center for the Performing Arts commanded the north shore of the New River at the west end of the Ft. Lauderdale Riverwalk. Since it opened in the 1980s, the Center has always been the place to see and be seen amid its quality fine arts performances and cultural gatherings. The trendy bistro, Audra's, served an impossibly delicious three-martini lunch, and a trio of late arrivals shared a table overlooking the river. The last vestiges of police officers, cruisers, and police boats gathered near the cordoned-off dock of the River Queen and dominated their view to the east.

The atmosphere was somber as we attempted to make sense of the tragic discovery. Kayne was nursing a "Churchill," and Rebecca had a "Marie Laveau" before her. I was not drinking.

Kayne gestured with his martini to the down-river crime scene.

"The identity of the victim is hardly a problem. Hadji Murad, aka Gay Dawn, has been a drag fixture in South Florida since the early seventies. She was a multi-pageant titleholder and *demimonde* star of the first order, albeit a fading star. She had also been an outspoken advocate of rights for transgender people." His gesture was also a toast to the unfortunately deceased entertainer.

Rebecca said, "Same guy?"

"No doubt," I said. "The victim was beaten to death. Similar bruising pattern. Evidence from the warehouse shows that the killer held and tortured the second victim there, also. Traces of her costume and makeup were among the evidence found at Warehouse 221 among the debris — the glitter and sequins."

"Drowned?" Rebecca asked.

"No," Kayne responded. "No sign of submersion before death. The autopsy will show similar massive organ trauma to the young sailor's. In her case, because of her age and poor health, the beatings were fewer, less intense, and just enough to result in her unfortunate death."

I added, "And then there is the killer's signature."

"The palm?"

"The palm."

Rebecca took a sip of her drink and commented, "So very, very sad. What bizarre staging of the body-- stretched out on the paddlewheel, in all her drag finery, including that huge tiara."

"Yes," said Kayne. "The crown. Interesting."

The three of us remained silent for a few minutes in tribute to the unfortunate Hadji Murad. I noticed that each of us seemed to have no appetite but went through the motions of ordering light.

"Nick, you don't look so good. Buck up, Darling. You'll get this monster. You have the best of help." She nodded to Kayne.

I wanted to respond that my melancholy had to do with a combination of domestic issues and the tragic death of yet another innocent victim of Broward County's new killer. But I said nothing.

Rebecca leaned forward and said, "OK, my loves, this is all very tragic, and I do not mean to make light of any of it. Consequently, we need to get reinvigorated about catching this monster."

She reached across the table and touched my hand.

"What you need, handsome," Rebecca looked at me. "Is hot, monkey sex and lots of it. I have always found fun and restoration in the ways of the flesh, Darling." She smiled broadly, not realizing how ironic her comments were in my situation.

Kayne now turned his undivided attention to his beautiful friend.

"Also intending no disrespect to the late Hadji Murad, I feel compelled to address your activities since Parakalo. I will conclude that your returning Cretan god lived up to the proportions of the priapic myth you referred to last night?"

Doing her best Blanche DuBois, Rebecca said, "Why Doctor Sorenson, whatever do you mean, Sir?"

"If you bat those eyelashes with any more force, Ms. Coquette, the breeze will clear the table."

Despite myself, I smiled.

Rebecca raised her arms, aping a 40s tragic movie queen. "Ah, Davin, Davin, my raging centaur, I do adore your incredible lovemaking and your god-like endowment."

"Oh, brother!" Kayne exclaimed. "Well, he is confirmed as quite the stud. You know he, um, gets around."

Kayne intoned the opening lyrics of *Just a Gigolo*.

"Yes, I understand Mary Chaffee is a mutual friend." Her eyes twinkled as she continued, "My dear, this boy is way too much for one person. Literally. Sharing his extraordinary... um... talents is to be expected."

"I thought Mary was bi," Kayne said.

Rebecca looked down at her drink, shifting uncomfortably.

"Why, yes. I believe she is."

Kayne shot me a knowing look.

"My dear, we must get you another drink," he said. "Nick, there is nothing quite like the candor of a friend bathing in afterglow following a night of unbridled...."

"Doc, we need to discuss the killer's video message," I said with an edge of urgency in my voice, trying to change the subject. "Mays had you preview it, yes?"

Kayne arched an eyebrow at my outburst and turned serious. "Quite right, Nick. Returning to the discovery of the second body, the killer is screaming for attention. His recording in English and Latin is filled with code. Let's finish up here and head on over to the Portiuncula Center. Brother Fintan has agreed to see us at two forty-five. I believe he will help us to dissect the killer's message. We can reconnoiter before heading to Masque Bar tonight to talk with colleagues of the recently deceased."

I remained silent for the rest of the lunch, pushing my food around on my plate. My ruminations about Shan, Hud, Jared, and Hadji so dominated my thoughts that I all but ignored my companions' banter. Their attempt to snap me out of my dark funk was unsuccessful.

As if reciting a line, Rebecca said, "Kayne Darling, just what goes into a Churchill?"

Hoping I would at least smile, Kayne imitated the legendary British First Lord of the Admiralty, "Fill a glass with gin. Look at the vermouth. Drink the gin."

***

Brother Fintan O'Connor was a member of the Catholic monastic order, which staffed The Portiuncula Center in Wilton Manors. In 1987, this all-volunteer effort was founded to feed those rejected by society and dying alone of complications from HIV/AIDS. With advances in treatment over recent decades, the Center expanded its programs to include wrap-around services for the sick and indigent.

"Yes, Doctor Sorenson, I have the book right here. It is a bit old and tattered, you see. The Church continues to revise the calendar, so saints come and go, I am afraid." The little Brother resembled a Hobbit as he opened a rather big, illustrated book to its introductory pages.

He drew one finger over the introductory page as he read, "The Roman Martyrology is an official liturgical text of the Catholic Church. The accounts of the martyrdom of the saints are believed to coincide with the facts of history. Monks read the entries at the liturgy, but, as time went on, they switched the readings to accompany the main meal of the day in seminaries and monasteries."

Brother Fintan turned the pages of the book. Illustrations of the saints in the throes of death appeared in lurid color and striking detail along with the texts.

"Please tell us more about the ritual connected to the reading, Brother," Kayne requested.

"Each reading began with the date and the phase of the moon for that day. The text of the saint's life is read and ends with the response, *Pretiosa in conspectu Domini mors Sanctorum eius.*"

Kayne translated, "Precious in the sight of the Lord is the death of His Saints."

Seed Blood

"Perfect, Dr. Sorenson." Brother Fintan returned to the opening pages of the Martyrologium Romanum.

The Friar noted, "The liturgical year in the Roman Church begins with the First Sunday of Advent, four weeks before Christmas. Here are the saints celebrated at the beginning of the cycle."

Kayne stopped the brother at the entry of November 25. The page depicted St. Catherine of Alexandra. In her right hand was a palm branch.

Above her head was a golden crown. Behind her were the spokes, rim, and hub of a gigantic wheel.

Thomas Paul Severino

Chapter Sixteen: Hack

Before returning to my office, Chief Mays summoned Kayne and me to a team meeting at the Ft. Lauderdale Police Department. On the way back downtown, I checked in. The tech department scrubbed my work cell phone, but they could not recover the killer's video message from my PC. They impounded the device with hopes that further investigation would discover the source and means of hacking. Detectives entered the video message from the killer on my phone into evidence as part of the Christiansen murder case. The cybersecurity breach put the City's Police Department at risk. The latest patches and safeguards were loaded up to prevent further entry and exit of classified information.

In addition to local law enforcement, FBI agents led by Mary Chaffee and members of the US Navy Jag settled into chairs in the large conference room to hear Sheriff Crawford. She introduced those representing each agency and reminded the team that Chief Mays had called a press conference at 4:30 that afternoon. The purpose of the meeting was to update the greater community on the facts of what had quickly become a very high-profile case.

"I'd like to begin by stating that facts surrounding the recent double murders have put us in the position of searching for and attempting to stop a serial killer."

Those gathers responded audibly to the startling announcement.

Kayne had been insistent with the leadership team before the briefing. "Only two murders, but look at the two similarities of M.O., the killer's messaged threats and the signature staging of both victims. This small series of killings is merely the beginning of a well-planned killing spree."

The Sheriff continued, "During this briefing, we will lay out the reasons for this classification of these bizarre killings. Our inquiry focuses on uncovering motives and possible suspects and developing theories on where he will strike again. Both police departments have added more personnel to the team. Also, the FBI will be involved in the investigation as we endeavor to apprehend the murderer."

She nodded to Special Agent Mary Chaffee and stepped away from the podium. One of the policemen from Ft. Lauderdale turned to me and said, "Terrific, these guys. Remember how the Feds botched the Cunanan investigation in '97? Hope they do better with this one."

I was five at the time of the infamous rampage that resulted in the murder of Gianni Versace in Miami. Still, I was familiar with the case from the readings assigned in class. I said nothing, confident that the Bureau had gone through some significant changes in the last 20 years.

Mary took the microphone and began a rundown of the timeline from the disappearance of the young Petty Officer three weeks ago to the results of the recent autopsy on Hadji Murad. Her intent was to provide the group with a detailed background for the search for a psychopath.

She called up a map of Broward County on the overhead computer screen.

"We believe that the center of criminal activity, specifically, the abduction of the victims, appears to be Wilton Manors while the torture, murder, disposal, and display of the bodies occur in Ft. Lauderdale." Using a laser pointer, she marked locations in Wilton Manors and the two sites in Ft. Lauderdale, Port Everglades, and the downtown New River, where the bodies were found.

Rebecca entered the back of the briefing room wearing a special ID badge. She silently acknowledged the speaker, who returned a nod of approval. I thought, Sometimes, it's who you know that gets you where you need to be.

Agent Chaffee continued, "Before going further, I would like to acknowledge the assistance of Kayne Sorenson, Ph.D., for his work on this investigation. Dr. Sorenson is one of the leading criminologists in the nation. He is a resident of South Florida, where he teaches psycho-criminology – the research-based theories behind the behavior of psychotic criminals. An author and lecturer, he has done consulting work for Law Enforcement worldwide."

Gesturing to Kayne, she said, "Doctor, please share with us your perspectives on the case."

102

Seed Blood

As Kayne moved to the podium, I felt the curious looks of several members of local law enforcement from both cities again. As an out gay police officer, I had grown accustomed to the looks. My position on the inquiry team was questionable, given my status with the high-profile Internal Affairs investigation. As inconspicuously as I could, I moved to the back of the room. I stood next to Rebecca, who squeezed my hand reassuringly.

Kayne's laptop fed the investigation's most current information to the large conference room's monitor. Slides of text, pictures of the two victims, and images of saints from the Roman Martyrology moved across the broad overhead monitor.

"Good afternoon. Officers, evidence from the warehouse, and the two bodies indicate that we are looking for a left-handed, white male with brown hair, height of approximately 6'2", and weighing somewhere between 200 to 215 pounds. Our killer is a man who is highly aggressive and robust. He can overcome a trained soldier-athlete and can lift a considerable weight.

"He would appear to be methodical and disciplined. The torture and murder of his victims are systematic and pre-conceived. He works quickly and with precision. However, he leaves behind clues and signatures that will allow us to bring him to justice, provided we can out-think him.

"The killer is a product of conservative religious upbringing, probably Roman Catholic. He may currently be, or at some time had been, a member of a Christian religious order or sect. He is most likely from the region around Ocala, Florida, or has recently spent time there."

A slide showing two bags of oranges and a coil of hemp rope came up on the screen.

"We have traced these instruments of his torture scenario to the groves in Central Florida. There is no doubt that the killer bludgeoned the victims, one to unconsciousness and the other to death.

"While it is true that Florida growers ship these oranges everywhere, the organic components of this hemp are rarely found anywhere outside a twenty-mile radius of this monastery outside Ocala. The Friars make it from natural materials grown on the property. They use it for baling hay and binding chords of wood and equipment bundles. The result is a chord with high tensile strength. This abbey, St. Anselmo's, established the Portiuncula Center in Wilton Manors to care for the sick."

He changed the slide from the Central Florida monastery to show the pages of a large, illuminated book.

"This is the Roman Martyrology, in Latin, *Martyrologium Romanum*. It is part of the Catholic Liturgy. It provides an extensive list of the saints recognized by the Church and contains descriptions of their torture and death. The present Martyrology contains approximately 7,000 saints venerated by the Church. Their cult is officially recognized and proposed to the faithful as models worthy of imitation."

He stopped the slides at a painting of a Roman soldier holding a palm branch in both hands clasped before him. Kayne read the description of the saint.

"The young man Marcellinus… being enrolled among the new soldiers and refusing to serve, was beaten almost to death and for a long time kept in prison. Being finally cast into the sea, he finished his martyrdom and is venerated on January 4th."

The following slide was Jared Christiansen's cadaver on the pier with the date palm branch clasped against his torso.

Kayne paused and then switched the view – Warehouse 221's stark interior showing the cage, manacles, and St. Andrew's Cross. He then showed a split image of Officer Christensen and St. Marcellinus.

The display changed again, and the Professor continued,

"Please consider St Catherine of Alexandria, condemned by the Romans in the Fourth Century of the Common Era. At her execution, she was bound, spread-eagled, and broken on a saltire, a cross consisting of two wooden beams nailed in an "X" shape. Her executioners then displayed her mangled body on a giant wheel. I draw your attention to the palm and crown, symbols in the Church of the victory of martyrdom."

"The corpse of the unfortunate Hadji Murad spread across the paddlewheel spokes of the River Queen was the next image. The killer fastened her elaborate gown and cape to the wood in a way that suggested the flowing garments and wings of a heavenly being. Her head sagged slightly to the right beneath an elaborate crown. Her outstretched right arm held an attached palm branch.

He continued, "The murders and staging of Officer Christiansen and Ms. Murad put the killer in the class of serial murders that seeks to inspire fear and panic in the community. He is not a spontaneous murderer choosing random victims. He has carefully created a theater of death, transfixing, and horrifying all onlookers."

Kayne paused a moment to allow the image to emotionally impact the group. His repeated use of the victims' names was meant to remind the investigators that the dead were people and, as such, demanded dignified treatment and swift justice.

"The killer is highly skilled in computer and internet technology. Bypassing the most sophisticated firewalls, he has decided to communicate to us through Officer Nicola Sechi of the Wilton Manors Police Department. Earlier this morning, the Officer received this message from the killer sent to his office computer."

The following display was again a split-screen. The murderer's video on my phone played next to a printed transcript of the killer's message. In the script, Kayne highlighted six relevant passages and proceeded to offer commentary on them.

"*Tormentis cubiculum,* Latin for 'torture chamber,' refers to the discovery of Warehouse 221 with those instruments and structures that resulted in the beating of Officer Christensen and the torture and death of Ms. Murad. Unfortunately, our efforts were too late to prevent the second murder.

"Please notice, 'Sin for sin' goes to motive. This phrase is more psychological rather than evidential. The killer is obsessed with what he believes is the great sinfulness of his victims. The motivation may include homophobia, considering both were gay. We are looking at classifying these murders as hate crimes."

Kayne circled the second "sin" above us on the screen using a laser pen.

"With the mention of a double transgression, I believe the killer not only despises his acts of murder but suffers from a psychotic sense of self-loathing, typical in most homophobes. The killer, I would suggest, is a severely repressed gay man, as is the case with most homophobes.

"This statement, 'Officer Christiansen refused to serve,' has connections to the life of St. Marcellinus and is corroborated by Officer Christensen's friend, Michael Crawford. Officer Christiansen was feeling discriminated against in his military profession and had discussed with Mr. Crawford his desire to resign from the Navy. I would suggest that the unfortunate sailor mentioned his dissatisfaction with his career to others in his circle and may have inadvertently included the killer in such a conversation."

Captain Rota of US Navy JAG interrupted, "Professor Sorenson, relative to that point, I want to assure the group that the US Navy Judge Advocate's Office is interviewing Officer Christiansen's naval colleagues regarding any prejudicial treatment— hazing, bullying, that sort of thing. We are attempting to determine if there is any connection between any such behavior and the young man's murder. So far, we have no suspects within his Navy squad."

"Thank you, Captain."

Kayne returned to his cryptological analysis of the killer's message.

"*Passus est*. The term is Latin for 'he suffered.' It occurs in the accounts of the death of the martyrs and is the killer's affirmation of the brutal treatment of his victims. While the killer acknowledges Jared Christiansen and Hadji Murad were tortured, he shows no remorse and implies that the result was redemptive.

"In the prayerful readings of the life and death of the Martyrs, the assembly would repeat this verse, *Pretiosa in conspectu Domini mors Sanctorum eius* or, in English, 'Precious in the sight of the Lord is the death of his saints.' Again, the killer is stating religious motivation for his deeds."

Kayne turned to the display of the video message's transcription and circled the killer's use of the word "precious" in reference to his victims' deaths. He allowed the point to sink in before continuing.

"Note also that the message contains a challenge. 'More will be given the palm and forced to wear the crown.' The killer has a taste for it and carefully plans his victims' demise."

106

Again, Kayne circled a line in the message.

"Finally, the phrase, *Deo gratias.* Translated as 'Thanks be to God.' This liturgical phrase connects the killer and the killings to the method of execution by which the saints of the Church died in the first four centuries of Christian history. For four hundred years, the Church considered saints to be only the murdered members of the faithful-- killed because they refused to deny the faith."

Returning the screen to the screensaver, Kayne addressed the audience. "I will take your questions now."

Team members asked for clarifications of some of Kayne's conclusions. In response, he referred to evidence gathered from the bodies and materials collected at the warehouse, as well as his vast knowledge of criminal psychopathology.

Anxious to discuss a capture plan, a detective with the Wilton Manors Police asked, "Dr. Sorenson, if the killer is using that book to plot out his murders, how likely are we to be able to use it to predict his next move?"

Kayne responded, "Please allow me to clarify. I do not imply that the killer is using the calendar of the saints in the Martyrology to plot his murders. While the feast of St. Marcellinus is January 4th, St. Catherine's feast day is November 25. The murder seems to be organized but selective regarding whose death to imitate. The feast days of the martyrs do not matter to him. He prefers to kill in the manner of those saints with the grisliest details of martyrdom.

"Therefore, regarding your question as to prediction, I would say that it is highly improbable, but detailed research may prove fruitful. To do that, we must reside in the sick mind of the psychopath, matching history with available venues and methods of torture and death that may be employed. The killer knows this book and uses it as a manual for death. That being said, please keep in mind the texts include more than 7,000 saints."

Kayne tapped his copy of The Martyrology as he continued.

"Rather than predict his next move, the connection between the murder's activities and the saints provides a context for his crimes and therefore reinforces clues to his identity – who is he?. Again, the religious fanaticism of the mind of the psychopath we seek needs to be understood if we are to plan a course that will lead to his capture. Keep in mind, please, this man wants us to stop him, so understanding the nature of his psychosis is vital to ending his rampage."

"So, where do we look for this guy?"

"Regarding his next move. We know he strikes marginalized people. He hunts them in Wilton Manors, one of the largest LGBTQ communities in the country. His pursuits are in isolated spots near nightclubs and bars. We need to pay very close attention to his communication with his chosen mouthpiece, Officer Sechi. The killer is telling us where next to find him.

He seeks out the solitary, most likely the conflicted and lost. He ingratiates himself with the victims and overpowers them. Considering the fitness of the Naval Officer, most likely, alcohol is involved in the capture. The blood alcohol levels of Officer Christiansen and the entertainer, Ms. Hadji, were high. He needs them to be cooperative... passive. I advise you to keep the bars and clubs under extensive observation."

"How about public venues?"

"While the night is his cover, and he needs the darkness to obscure his operations, he is acting with more boldness and craves a public viewing of his victims. However, he stages with stealth. I suggest you step up surveillance during the night and early morning hours at places where the public gathers."

I raised my hand from the back of the room, and Kayne acknowledged me. The gathering turned to look at me as I spoke.

"Professor, the killer has access to a boat big enough to move a body and the materials needed to stage his victims. We have officers working on waterfronts and questioning marine businesses who may have seen something."

"Excellent, Officer. Thank you."

Kayne began to gather up his materials and added, "Please remember the Roman Empire perpetrated the suffering and death that characterized the Apostolic Age of the Church. It was a bloody propaganda device called 'Bread and Circuses' to showcase the might of Rome. Regardless of his ability to blend in, the killer craves the spectacle of public display. He finds it empowering and affirming of his superiority."

As the Q and A came to an end, Mary Chaffee stepped forward to close the meeting.

"Thank you, Dr. Sorenson. Officers and colleagues, please remember the details of this investigation are classified. Sharing detailed information on this case, particularly the killer's methods, will inhibit our investigation and his capture. I am distributing case talking points, which will be delivered to the press this afternoon. Please, no varying in your comments."

Before she could dismiss the group, the large overhead computer screen exploded in light and sound. The tech support officer jumped to the console to investigate the interruption. Strains of Gregorian Chant filled the conference room over an image of the dead Haji Murad, which enlarged to a close-up. From her place on the wheel, the eyes of the deceased moved grotesquely, looking to heaven for her expected salvation.

The music continued over the next image, a close-up of the face of the unconscious Jared Christiansen. Similarly, a generated image opened and then moved the victim's eyes most pitifully. The men and women in the room reacted with revulsion, anxiety, and confusion.

Kayne spoke loudly to the techie, "This is a message from the killer. Do not attempt to stop it."

Cathy Wayne, jumping to the computer and moving aside her colleague, tried desperately to track the source of the feed. Her efforts appeared to be futile. The keyboard was frozen.

A lurid video replaced the dissolving image on the screen. Two naked men, glistening with sweat, coupled on a bed in the dark. One was straddling the upper thighs of his partner, who was lying on his back beneath him. The young man on top was masturbating, body arched, and head thrown back in passion. A phoenix tattoo coursed across the left thigh and gluteal muscle to the lower back of the upper man, shimmering in sweat and moving in and out of the light. The hacker had digitally added a laurel crown to his beautiful head. The man on his back in the bed held his partner by the hips while raising his lower body to meet his

109

movements. Flames engulfed the couple, and words burned across the image.

Sin for Sin

The image moved into a close-up. Despite the darkness in the room, dim light through the windows rendered the men identifiable.

Rebecca grabbed my arm as the group turned to look at me incredulously as I stood paralyzed with shock.

"Holy shit!"

Chapter Seventeen: Hud

NICK SECHI'S JOURNAL

I raced from the room, punching in Hud's cell phone on my speed dial-- voice mail. I switched to his office number. His assistant said he was in a meeting. Again, I did not leave a message.

Hud, you and I have a stalker, and he is a serial killer. It's not the kind of thing you want to leave on a recording. I drove to the Foundation.

"Hey, Nick. What's going on?" I walked into the offices of the Preston Foundation as Hud was leaving a staff meeting in the conference room. I was visibly agitated. He motioned me into his office. Behind his desk hung a banner of a Manchurian warrior on horseback.

"Hud, something terrible...."

"Excuse me, Mr. Ch'en. I have Mr. Preston, Sr. on Line 1 for you."

Before I could say anything, Hud stopped me by holding up an index finger and stabbing his office phone to bring his Board Chair on speaker.

"Good morning, Mr. Preston. How may I help you?"

"Hudson, what am I seeing? What the hell is this?" Thomas Mitchell Preston was highly agitated. "I want an immediate explanation, Mr. Ch'en and you'd better have a good one."

"Mr. Preston, I am not quite sure of what you are talking about." Confused, Hud looked at me and around the room.

"I just emailed you the URL that is all over the internet. Pull it up."

"Hud, wait..." I said, reaching to take his hand from the keyboard. I missed, and he clicked on the link.

The killer's lurid message appeared on the screen.

Horrified, Hud mouthed to me, "Have you seen this?"

I slowly and gravely nodded as the last part came on the screen, Hud's tattoo clearly showing on his sweating left thigh and gluteal.

"Holy shit!" Hud jumped from his chair and looked in a panic at me for an explanation. I said nothing.

"Mr. Ch'en, this clip has gone viral. Social media has identified you and your partner. Local news is carrying a somewhat digitalized version of this filth. You are aware of both the behavior clause in your contract and the Preston Foundation's aversion to public attention as part of our corporate culture. As of this moment, your position at the Foundation is under review by the board's Executive Committee. Have you anything to say?"

I put my head down on my folded arms on Hud's desk. I could not look at him.

Quickly, gathering his wits, Hudson responded with remarkable courage.

"Mr. Preston, this clip is the result of an invasion of privacy. It was obviously taken without my knowledge or Nick's, either. It appears to be part of the police investigation into the Palm Murders here in Broward County, most likely pirated and distributed."

"Well, I don't have to tell you I do not like this, especially with the opening of the new exhibit at the Art Gallery for which we are the title sponsor. The Preston Foundation prides itself on doing good without calling attention to ourselves as well as having the highest moral expectations of our staff."

The brief silence that followed was unendurable. I looked up at Hud with a pleading expression. Preston came back on the line.

"Until you hear back from me, you are to remain at your post. Get in contact with Karl Holt, my public relations expert, and discuss how the Foundation will handle the press on this. There will be a significantly damaging public reaction to this sordid tape. I am sickened to think that the Archbishop may resign from our board because of this incident. Goodbye, Mr. Ch'en."

***

Hud didn't say anything for a long time. When the call ended, he stared at me in a disconcerting way. The lines on his office phone lit up. His cell phone rang like a screaming child. Looking at it, he turned the device off, and at the same time, he waved away his intruding assistant, saying, "James, get my lawyer on the line ASAP. Then I need to speak to Karl Holt. I believe you have his number. And no other calls, James."

"Yes, Mr. Ch'en."

Hud folded his hands on his desk and looked at me.

I took a deep breath, pointed to the desktop's screen, and started to explain.

"What you saw was a message from a serial killer who has brutally killed two gays in Broward County. For some reason, he has singled me out for communication with the public about his murders. This first part of the video includes his first two victims and is meant to inspire fear in the city. Kayne says that these messages are a cry to be caught and...."

Hud slammed the flat of his hand on the desk between us. His rage was overpowering, but he fought to control his next words.

"I don't give a fuck about what Kayne says." He pointed to the screen and added furiously, "That was us! Nick that is private, and now it's out there for everyone in the entire world to see!"

"Hud, wait, I...." Despite his attempt to restrain his outburst, his voice became louder, "We were fucking!"

He hyperventilated. He turned to the window, seeking control over his emotions, probably thinking if he stopped looking at me, he would calm down a bit. I said nothing.

Hud turned back and said in a coldly smooth voice, "Technically, we were not fucking since you have been incapable of sustaining a hard-on for a considerable time. At least with me, anyway. "

His last statement was full of accusations and shaming.

"Hud, please, I'm sorry...."

"No, Nick," He looked directly at me and continued, "I've had just about all the apologies I can stand. We both know there must be some major changes in this relationship. It has been clear for some time."

I reached for his hand like a falling man, but Hud pulled away from my touch.

"I'll repeat it. Your job has always come first. I take a mere second, and sometimes I think third place. You see yourself as a one-person crime-stopper. You risk your life every fucking day. Do you hero types ever stop to consider how those who love you feel? Waiting at home, waiting to hear if you're dead. Shot three times in the chest.... "

He pointed to my chest bruises from the standoff with the druggie. I unconsciously rubbed my shirt and let him talk.

"Do you know what that feels like? Do you?" He paused. Continuing, he said, "And you fucking superheroes always put your partners at risk."

My turn to get loud. I flushed with anger and exploded. "Fuck you. Hud, you are way outta line here. I did the right thing. Shan is alive because of me."

"Are you so sure about that, Nick? You realize she may not make it or end up...."

This last comment was said very gently. Nevertheless, I covered my ears and screamed.

Silence, then, "I keep thinking that it could be me someday." He pointed to the computer screen.

"I will keep you safe, always. That's a promise."

He cocked his head, looking at me. "Really? How's that going so far? Huh? I'd say I am in the killer's gunsight right now. Oh yeah, and does 'safe' include jobless?"

His anger was rising again. "For once, just once, put yourself in my place. That feeling that the rest of us feel is like death, and it's getting closer. It makes me want to do anything to make that fear go away."

"Hud, I love you."

Now, more slowly and quietly, "Yeah, I know you do. That's why this is so difficult. In some ways, this video out there is not the point. People have a short memory. But you and I have come to a critical impasse in our relationship."

Jesus, make it stop! I knew what was coming. At some level, I knew for a while what was going to happen. The signs were there, the silences, the distance, the bickering. As he looked up at me, my insides began to feel like they were being burnt by fire.

"Hud, I will do anything. I'll change. I swear..."

He held up one hand to silence me. Slowly, he spoke the next sentence.

"Nick, I've been seeing Roy again."

My first reaction to mentioning his ex's name was another furious rage. I felt my face reddening and my fists clenching. I started to rise from my chair, furious.

Slowly and at that moment, I admitted to myself that I had known this for some time. I had mentally and emotionally blocked the truth. Staring at the reality of our relationship, I felt like this revelation had pulverized me to numbness. The anger went out of me like a deep and painful exhalation. Now, I felt utterly lost.

"Nick, Roy makes me feel things that I've needed to feel for a long time."

I narrowed my gaze. As cold as ice, I said, "Got it. Roy fucks you to hell and back. And he fucks you a lot," I bitterly added as I felt the rage returning.

Hud waited and said very quietly, "Yeah, he does."

We said nothing for a long time. I felt Hud looking at me but could not meet his gaze. I wanted to explode and argue, but the words would not come. I sputtered like a drowning man.

"Hud, wait... we can..."

"Mr. Ch'en, Wesley Nealon, Esq. on line 4."

Hud shook his head and turned away to take the call.

"Goodbye, Nick. Take care of yourself."

***

As I left the Foundation, I passed the staff gathered around a large flat screen in the reception area to view the press conference coverage on the Palm Killer.

"... identified as Hudson Ch'en, President and Executive Director of the Thomas M. Preston Foundation headquartered here in Ft. Lauderdale and

Wilton Manors Police Officer, Nicola Sechi. Officer Sechi is currently being investigated for the shooting death of a teenager in....”

I picked up a heavy paperweight from the reception desk and heaved it at the image of the reporter.

“We interrupt this broadcast....” I yelled as the TV hit the floor and broke into pieces.

Chapter Eighteen: Catharsis
NICK SECHI'S JOURNAL

"No, Nick, this is not coming from IA. This recommendation is coming from me, your commanding officer. It's my call. I need you to take time off– six months, even a year. Stick with the criminology courses and come back to us with some fancy graduate diploma. By that time, this mess with the video will be ancient history."

I felt I was watching the destruction of my personal and professional life from outside my body. This nightmare was surgically cutting away significant portions of my life. I was experiencing an emotional bloodletting brought on by the machinations of the Palm Killer. He had a tortuous hold on my guts.

"Captain Mays, Officer Sechi is the conduit of forthcoming information from the killer himself. In addition to his having to extricate himself personally from this highly emotional case, a suspension would most likely place him at even more risk in addition to putting the investigation in jeopardy and resulting in the death of more of our citizens."

Mays looked at Kayne, "Dr. Sorenson, while I appreciate your insight in this, I...."

"Bob, hear me out. Nick's work on the case is exemplary. He has an excellent eye for details at the crime scene. He can provide critical insights into the psychopathology of the killer. We can catch this guy, but he wants Nick. So, we protect one of our own and coax the killer out of hiding. We need to keep him active. Not only is he the killer's mouthpiece, but he is also an excellent cop. Bob, this is how we will catch the killer."

"You are asking me to put the life of one of my officers as bait...."

I snapped out of my funk of self-pity and said with a bit of surliness, "Sir, we do that every day. It is how a cop is a cop."

"Get serious, Officer. The last thing I need now is some fucked up heroics meant to lure a maniac into custody. You take too many risks."

I felt shame and anger at the same time.

Kayne interrupted with a balanced, logical argument. "Agreed. So sanely and methodically, we proceed. Mays, we have the best minds available on this thing regarding law enforcement – the FBI, the Armed Services, and the police departments of two municipalities. We can devise a plan to stop this guy while ensuring our officers are safe. Sure, it will be a risk, but an intelligent one."

Mays looked from Kayne to me and back again.

"Besides, he is my protégé. Not only will he remain safely under my tutelage, but I can also keep him focused on where in this community our killer is hiding."

Now, I was feeling very patronized. Jesus!

Mays leveled his gaze at me. "Officer, I would say that many are watching you, but that is a rather ludicrous comment at this point, given the recent video. Listen carefully to me. By the fucking book in everything you do, no exception. I don't want a hotshot. I want a responsible cop. Catching this killer has to be done without you falling apart mentally...." He looked away. "Or worse."

He looked from me to Kayne. And said forcefully, "Are we clear here, Officer?"

I raised my gaze to meet that of my commanding officer.

"Crystal, Sir."

As we turned to leave, Mays picked up a call. He held up one finger and stopped our exit. Putting down the receiver, the Captain looked at me with exasperation.

"You are paying for that T.V. monitor, Officer Sechi."

***

Outside the Wilton Manors Police Department, the street lights were coming on. Members of the press filled the sidewalk and the reception area.

Mother Fucker!

Gay porn cop and the serial killer – what news! And right here in your average, sleepy, gayer-than-gay community.

Rebecca stood within the plexiglass enclosure adjacent to the reception area. The mob of reporters pointed and erupted, "There he is!"

"Officer Sechi!"

"Hey, Nick! Look over here."

"Can you answer a few questions, Officer?'

Cameras flashed, and video cams swung our way. Rebecca steered Kayne and me to the area to the rear of the elevators. She took us down a corridor that ended in a door to the enclosed parking lot for squad cars and other police vehicles. The far end of this area led out through a gate to the Wilton Manors City Hall public parking lot.

We stopped to catch our breath. Rebecca took a closer look at me and pulled me in for a sincere hug. She could feel the emotional weight within me.

Pushing me back and holding me at arm's length, she said, "Relax, Darling. It's the Twenty-First Century. Who hasn't had a sex tape gone viral?" She winked, hoping to get a smile.

Kayne, drinking from a water bottle, did a percussive spit take. She clapped him on the back a few times and continued, "Why, look at Kim Kardashian. She ends up impossibly famous; she has a hot piece of man and a clothing line or some such. No? Or is that …?" Rebecca waved a hand in an "anyway" gesture, not wishing to slam a political figure.

I did not react but numbly stood on the pavement, looking at them as if I had trouble processing what was happening. I felt like I was disappearing, falling into a deep hole.

After considering my face, Rebecca said in a soft, earnest voice, "Jesus, honey, you got it bad. Don't you? Did your man take it that badly? Aww, I'm so sorry."

I looked at the parking lot beneath us and felt the hot tears coming, choking my breathing.

Kayne took us both by the arms and pulled us around the corner of the building, further away from any possible public eye and hidden eyes. Releasing Rebecca, he pulled me into his strong arms in a hug. With one hand, he pushed my head over his shoulder and against his cheek. As I sobbed, I slowly raised my limp arms and held on to Kayne as if to a life preserver. Rebecca ran a hand over my heaving back as I wept.

I had lost Hud. It was like he had been taken from me.

"Oh, Nick Darling, I don't know what to say."

Kayne said nothing as I cried against him. We stayed like that for a long time. I could feel the horror, sadness, and sense of loss leave my body as cleansing tears began to subside. He released me, stepped back, and handed me his handkerchief.

With a hand beneath my chin, he said to me softly, "Nick, it is very evident that this hurts a great deal now, and you have no reason in the world to believe what I am about to say. However, I assure you, Hudson and you will be fine given time."

I looked at him as I used his handkerchief to wipe my eyes, face, and nose. I heard what he said but had trouble interiorizing his clear and intelligent reasoning. It was like feeling the ground go out from under me. I was broken-hearted, ashamed, angry, and embarrassed.

No, I cannot fix this.

Rebecca allowed us a few moments and then leaned in, attempting to lighten the mood a bit. She tilted her head onto his bicep and said, "Kayne, when did you become such a daddy?"

Her quip had the effect of lifting the mood a bit. Without raising my head, I looked at Kayne. I moved one hand from his firm shoulder to wipe my slobber from his Tom Ford jacket. I pressed the other to his chest. *This dude is as solid as Gibraltar, and he felt safe and dependable.* He placed his hand on mine, holding my gaze in an ineffable connection.

Slowly trying to break what was becoming a bit awkward, I looked at the wet handkerchief in my free hand and offered the snot-soaked linen back to him. Kayne stopped and looked at my face, blinked, and then overacted being profoundly appalled.

"Oh no, no, no... you keep it. Oh, my stars, no!" hands up and fluttering like a stereotyped femme fatale who has just seen a mouse. Kayne pirouetted with one hand over his mouth — so butch and so nelly at the same time.

Rebecca and I stared open-mouthed. Then, we both started to laugh in a rush of cathartic, maniacal hilarity. I could not stop until hot tears again ran down my cheeks. They both watched as I slowly gained control of my hysteria.

"Jesus, you OK, Darling?"

I nodded and wiped my face again.

Now, very butch, Kayne looked me in the eyes. "Come on, Officer. We have work to do." He thumped my chest and then threw an arm around my shoulders and steered us both toward the emptying parking lot.

"On the contrary," Rebecca challenged. "We need to get this adorable man beauty laid, and I am talking the shag of the century — up against the wall, headboard-banging nasty." Her eyes went to my crotch and then back to my face. "And this time for real."

Following her gaze and doing his best Victor Frankenstein, Kayne clowned, "It's alive! It's alive!

Thomas Paul Severino

Chapter Nineteen: Metropolitan

The porn star was drunk, drunk as a skunk.

He and his posse had hit Metropolitan Bar around 9:45 PM for "Fur Fridays." By that time, the older bears had gone home to watch The Wheel, or Jeopardy, and to hit the sack. Younger hotties commandeered the dance floor and the club's four bars. The music changed to a more contemporary house mix.

Back in Ft. Lauderdale from LA, he had the weekend free. Filming on the new production began on Tuesday. He was supposed to meet four of his costars at the club and spend Friday night, Saturday, and Sunday sexing up-- rehearsal. This was not a subscription-based video-on-demand creation of a steamy hookup.

"This is art, you sexy slut, in the traditional sense. A plot, a real porn prince, nailing your ass. Could be an indie crossover, boyfriend-- high class as fuck..."

His producer went on to explain that the chemistry for the new film had to be correct. Making porn was a complicated business. Writers and directors had to choreograph very intimate moves and camera angles. Partners had to arrive on the set after a day of sexual abstinence, comfortable with each other's bodies and erotic movements.

He alternated dancing with just about all the guys in the company's entourage, drinking-- Tito's, cranberry, and lime, and making out with two of the other porn stars. The guy he was most attracted to was not in the group from the production company. He had his eye on another patron, a hot boy definitely looking for a studly for the night.

The porn star got the beautiful boy in the club's dark corners. Sweaty T-shirt dangling from the waistband of his tight jeans, the hustler made out like a bandit, and the young man responded, frisky and insistent. Two cocktails and one hot-assed boy were a combination for some major sex play, now and well into the long night.

He felt a powerful slap on his back and thought, *Security. How many security guards have I blown from here to California to get out of some club altercation like this? Oh, well.*

He turned, expecting a routine he knew well.

A man with the body of a linebacker snarled, "It's really important now that you take your hands off my husband, whore."

The porn star had removed his hands from their mission of exploration beneath the seat of the boy's pants and felt them clench into fists as he hit his stance.

"What did you call me?"

The angry, muscled bull responded to the "throw down" challenge by raising a set of cement-block fists at the ends of a pair of very impressive arms. He bellowed, "I called you a whore, Asshole. I've seen your videos."

Reflexes obscured by alcohol, the porn star missed his one and only shot. His opponent's roundhouse landed him on his ass.

Now, security arrived. The groggy young man was escorted out a rear door of the club on a lower level. His handlers were three fit guards who seemed to have no interest in some compensatory man-on-man sexin'. They left him sitting in a heap in the darkened alley behind Metropolitan. The club door opened a second time, and his wadded-up t-shirt followed him into the alley, hitting him squarely in the chest. He was drunk, surly, and his jaw hurt like hell.

Something's not right, he thought. He had never felt this drunk after only two drinks. Where were his fucking buddies anyway?

Damon Santos felt two hands, one under each of his armpits. Turning to face his champion, he thought that the man who now lifted him to his feet had earlier been talking to "make out boy," but he could not be sure. The man was well built and wore a hoody, baseball cap, black jeans, and work boots. He seemed very familiar, but Damon's mind was cloudy. Supporting most of the porn star's weight, the big man helped him stagger down the alley to a waiting SUV.

Realizing a bit of what he thought was happening, the porn star addressed his rescuer softly as they walked, "So, I charge $400 an hour, and there is a two-hour minimum. Sleepover is a cool two grand. Ahh... if you cum; it's an extra $100. If... if... if I cum; it's an additional $300. Cash or credit on my website...."

124

Seed Blood

The porn star slurred his escort service price list with unclear speech and a lolling head.

His prospective client, loading the slumping porn star into the passenger's side of the SUV, spoke to him in a deep voice.

"Please allow me to assist you, Mr. Santos."

Thomas Paul Severino

Chapter Twenty: Red Light

NICK SECHI'S JOURNAL

I took off my shoes and socks, removed my uniform shirt, and hopped out of my convertible without opening the door. I left the car running. Behind me, Rebecca pulled her Tesla behind the Mustang. She and Kayne got out and watched me as I hopped barefooted from the trunk of the car to the first branch of a black walnut tree that stood close to the wall at the far end of the park.

Climbing, I stepped from the tree to the top of the wall. I reached out to a branch about 5 feet from the top of the wall. I had pocketed a pair of wire cutters from my glove box and worked them back and forth to extract an object the size of a tennis ball from the tree branch.

Mother fucker!

I held the object aloft like a kid who caught a fly ball in Yankee stadium and called out, "It rained pretty hard last night and this morning, Professor. No fingerprints." I tossed the object to Kayne, who was standing at the foot of the tree below. Kayne moved back to allow me to climb down.

"Wait."

Kayne turned and looked back as I balanced on the top of the wall. I used the tree for balance and carefully removed my uniform pants.

In a stage whisper, Rebecca said, "Nothing changes one's outlook better than a good cry in the arms of a strong, sexy man. Take it from one who knows, Darling."

Kayne cocked an eyebrow and nodded up at me, replying, "Or a strenuous piece of detective work accompanied by an acrobatic strip."

I left my jock on, balled up my pants, and sent them sailing down into the backseat of the Mustang like I was making a foul shot.

"Darling, hasn't this town seen enough of your hot ass for one evening?" Rebecca shrieked with laughter.

I turned dramatically and dove off the opposite side of the wall. A loud splash followed my disappearance.

Rebecca, open-mouthed, spun around to stare at Kayne.

Kayne rolled his eyes and pointed in the direction I had gone. "His house... with pool... I hope."

Holding up the black ball, he said, "Captial! The killer's camera. Follow me, my dear."

***

I picked up the gate remote from the patio table and pressed "unlock." Entering the yard behind Rebecca, Kayne tossed me my keys while placing my uniform, shoes, and socks on the patio table. He set the spherical camera on top of the pile.

Surveying the yard, Rebecca twirled and said, "Beautiful, Darling. Just beautiful." Pointing to the distance between the back perimeter wall and the pool, she said, "Whoa, that was quite a dive. Don't tell me, Ft. Lauderdale High School dive team. "

Walking to the house, I corrected her, "St. Raymond's High School, Da Bronx. Soccer, lacrosse, and swimming. Also spent a college summer training in Montreal with Cirque du Soleil. Long story." Waving at the wall, I added, "Easy peasy. Good thing the deep end is on that side."

I unlocked the patio doors to the Florida room, and Chouko bounded out. "This is my Beautiful Butterfly, my Chouko," I proudly introduced humans and canine.

"The Butterfly" bolted out of the house at full gallop, running straight at Kayne and Rebecca. I clapped my hands and gave the dog a signal, shouting, *"Chūi, Chouko!"*

The dog stopped dead still and sat inches away from Kayne. The strangers in the yard put him on alert. Not a muscle moved. However, there was an almost imperceptible twitch of Chouko's left ear as he stared directly at the Professor. Kayne remained astonishingly calm.

Standing rigidly still, Rebecca managed to get out, "Hmmm, is every male in this house smoking hot and hung?"

Realizing I was standing in a white jock, the pouch transparent from my swim, I dropped my hands to cover my crotch, saying, "Oh, shit," and dove into the house for a towel.

Still hiding my privates, I stuck my head out and said, "Do not move."

Transfixed by Chouko's gaze, Kayne remarked, "Uncut... very nice."

"The boy or the dog?"

Nodding toward my rapid exit, Kayne said, "The one who still has his balls."

***

Quickly, I returned to the yard in a pair of jeans and blue tennis shoes. I rolled on my favorite bar tank top. With a command in Japanese accompanied by a hand signal, I released my prisoners from the guard dog's paralyzing vigilance.

The Akita nuzzled the two visitors. Rebecca went down on one knee to show some love by scratching his neck and back. Chouko had a new friend and wagged his curled tail in appreciation.

"The night of the ah... of the camera," I said, "Chouko was barking and whining in the house."

I pointed up to the now-empty branch of the walnut tree. I took up the camera and inspected it for a small red-light display.

Handing it to Kayne, I said, "My Butterfly is extremely sensitive to even the slightest changes in his environment."

Turning the camera, Kayne said, "Remotely operated, I'll wager. Let's see if the tech savants at the Bureau can trace the feed. Perhaps a digital fingerprint."

Kayne walked closer to the patio lights and continued examining the instrument. He did a "Sorenson hair swoop," walked back to join us, and remarked, "This baby is a pretty sophisticated device. I hope she can tell us something important."

Rebecca took the camera from his hand and said, "Come on, boys. We need a bit of diversion with our work. I speak of the one and only 'Masque

Bar' home to the hottest male strippers and most exotic queens in South Florida. And I am not just speaking of the performers."

She looked at me and said, "How about some Friday night gay bar couture, Darling?"

Mimicking a pair of fashionistas, Kayne and I walked in a circle around Rebecca as if deciding how to turn a turnip into Cinderella or, in this case, just the opposite.

In our quest to make a fabulous statement for divine decadence, I pointed at Rebecca's lower body. I said to my partner in fashion, "Hud's skinny jeans will work if he hasn't taken them. Twenty-eight inches at the waist?"

"Ohhh, a belt, Darling, or they will fall right to the ground."

Channeling a celebrity judge on Ru Paul's Drag Race, Kayne continued the mockery. "I think we can keep the shoes, don't you? Fierce!"

Rebecca began to unbutton. She looked at me and gestured to Kayne. "Fine, Donatella, but what about tall and muscled-up here?"

I mimicked the birth of a scathingly brilliant idea. "What do you say we go with a 'Hustla Ball' look for him? You know, the aging escort trying for a comeback."

Kayne said, "Hold on, you two. While I assured Captain Mays that we would keep our Nick boy, ah... shall we say, engaged...." He added, "We want to be in the audience at Masque, not on the stage."

With an expression of fake consternation, Rebecca joked, "Umm humm... yep... right... I so forgot. Modesty from a man who carries around his latest trick's G-string."

She and I howled. Kayne knit his eyebrows and frowned.

Gesturing to the house, Rebecca spoke to her new best friend, "Lead the way, Chouko, Darling."

Chapter Twenty-One: Masque

NICK SECHI'S JOURNAL

"Buy a fella a drink, Handsome?"

The young man in the Nasty Pig jockstrap and matching red and black high socks spoke lustily into the nape of my neck. Turning on my barstool, I slipped a bill into the hot stripper's waistband and took a pull on my Michelob Ultra. In appreciation, the beauty went into the standard pattern of small talk-- *Where ya from? Come here often? Blah, blah, blah*.

I was polite and friendly in my responses, my police training and natural affability coming to the fore. It did not take long for the dancer to recognize this late-night man stud from today's news broadcasts and social media. Digitalization of the clip hadn't blurred the faces of the performers, just our privates.

He pointed. "You're, you're... Oh, hell yeah, cowboy, I'd ride you any day of the week." He placed one hand on my lap. "So, you up for a dance, Officer Sexy?" He nodded to the private lap dance area. Slapping his jock-strapped, bubble butt, the beauty added, "Make you feel terrific, hot man. Name's Sam, by the way."

Behind the back curtain, strippers provided seated, willing customers with some sizzling body friction in curtained-off privacy. Usually, a huge bouncer oversaw the purchased services and prevented the customers from touching the lap dancers. They took cash or credit. Rates were by the minute.

I politely declined but allowed the sexy lad a kiss as he moved away.

"Lemme know if you change your mind, Muscles."

On the main stage, beneath a memorial portrait of the late Hadji Murad, Helluva Bottom Carter, in Diana Ross drag, announced the management's newest male discovery from the United Arab Emirates, "... the one and only, Farad."

The oiled-up Omar Sharif look-alike, circa *Lawrence of Arabia*, was dressed in black, from a sheer ankle-length *keffiyeh* to boots trimmed in gold. There was a curved gold dagger sheathed at the edge of his spectacular thong-trapped hips. He carried a whip.

As he seductively stripped to exotic music, Rebecca was enthralled. "Don't hold me back, fellas. I'm going in."

Kayne got up as rough trade, was staring up at the groin of a stripper who straddled his drink, standing on the bar and gyrating provocatively. He held up a folded twenty between the first two fingers of his left hand. The dancer went down on one knee to allow Kayne to slip the bill into his G-string.

"Please tell your boss I would like to speak to her about the late Gaye Dawn."

Five minutes later, the young stripper returned and led the way to Cha Cha Rosette's table in the club's corner, separated by a beaded curtain. She gestured for Kayne, me, and the very distracted Rebecca to join her and Mohka Mirage.

Gesturing with an unlit Marlborough Light, the club owner said to Kayne's stripper, "Junior, tell Scott to get his sorry ass back here, and then you get your hot butt back up on that bar and make us some cash." The semi-naked boy went back into the show bar. Kayne picked up Cha Cha's lighter and fired up her cigarette.

"Thanks, baby."

She pointed to me. "You, I know. Getting quite a name for yourself in this town, I see, Officer." Mohka purred in her seat next to me. She placed a hand on my forearm, moved closer to me, and smiled.

"You, baby." She turned and pointed at Rebecca. "Look at those damn shoes. Manolo Blahniks, Fuckin' BB's! Are you aware that they are created as a fashion tribute to the legendary French siren, Brigitte Bardot? In a blond wig, with those tits, you'd be the spitting image…."

She trailed off but quickly came back, "Your bad self needs to be up there on my stage. I know you can sing and dance. We need to talk contract, girl."

Mohka interrupted, "Um, Cha, this doll's a straight woman."

"And a damn hot one, too. But who asked you, Mo? You better take your hands off that hot boy and go out there and work up some rent money."

With a touch of a cocoa-brown pout, Mohka Mirage stood, adjusted her bust, and made a rather regal exit, but not without giving me a peck on the cheek. "I'll see you later, baby."

"Not telling me something I don't know. 'Sides, this is the twenty-first century." Ms. Rosette turned back to Rebecca. "Everyone's doing drag. Gay, straight, whatever."

Pointing to her new discovery, she added. "This club needs an 'Adele.' Ash blond wig, glam glam, the whole deal."

Rebecca smiled and sang the opening lyrics of the mega star's break-out anthem, "Skyfall."

Cha Cha smiled and said, "Presenting Club Masque's newest discovery...."

"While I appreciate your offer, Ms. Rosette. I am afraid I must decline. But, the way things are going at the museum with this new exhibit, I may be looking at career change soon."

"Call me Cha Cha, baby. Think it over. You are always welcome here at my club."

"Thank you, Cha Cha."

Finally, turning to Kayne, she said. "And... who the hell are you?"

Taking in Kayne's body and the sexy cut of his cobbled-together hustler outfit-- sleeveless T, knee-ripped jeans, she continued before he could answer, "They don't get much hotter than all this." Pointing through the beads to the male strippers, she asked, "Always a market for older, fit guys. Fuckin' ass of death on you too. Own a G-string, baby?"

Both Rebecca and I exploded. She did a spit take of her Hpnotiq and cognac. I snort-dripped my beer in a fit of laughter. Kayne remained stoic, peering at us through hooded eyes.

Cha Cha was bewildered. She looked around the table and said, "What's so funny?"

"Nothing, my Darling, nothing at all." More laughter at Kayne's expense.

Cha Cha turned back to Kayne. "I am serious, blue eyes. Skinny-assed millennium boys aren't everyone's cup of tea. Some of my guests pay big for a hot daddy with shoulders and pecs like Atlas. Got you some serious arms, too. New Talent Night is Sundays – audition. Hear what I say?"

Hardly able to sputter out a sentence, Rebecca hit a fake-serious expression and commented, "Use the white thong, Kayne. But make sure you've sent it to the laundry beforehand."

I tried not to disrespect my professor, but this was too funny. Rebecca and I were mopping up but still giggling.

Acting like the soul of sobriety, Kayne attempted to rescue the dignity of the conversation. "Miss Rosette, please excuse the Philistine conduct of my associates. The incongruence of their jocularity can be legendary at times."

"Handsome, I do not know what the fuck you just said. But I gotta tell you and Jesus that I do like a man rockin' a body of sin and a mind of hot, badass intelligence – getting this doll all…."

"I apologize for the behavior of my friends, Ms. Rosette."

"Cha Cha, baby."

"I beg your pardon, Cha Cha. It's a rather long and boring story."

Kayne continued, "I am Kayne Sorenson, and I am a professor of psychopathology. I am serving as a consultant to the police, through Office Sechi, as well as to the FBI to track down the killer of Navy Officer Christiansen and Ms. Hadji Murad."

The mention of her former employee transformed the club owner from a brashly sexual Eartha Kit into a somewhat subdued leader of her little troupe of entertainers. She said nothing but looked away with deep sadness.

"What he did to her… my, my, my… beaten to death… so savage," she said, shaking her head and looking away. She fought back the tears as she turned to Kayne.

"Hadji had no family. No one. I pulled some strings. They owe my fine ass, downtown, I mean. Anyway, they released the body to me. We cremated her."

Cha Cha Rosette wiped away a stray tear and thought a bit before she said, "She was a person, Mr. Kayne, first and foremost a person, a good person. What kind of diseased mind does that to someone like Hadji or to anyone?"

Rebecca reached across the table to take Cha Cha's hand. "We are going to get him, Darling."

I said, "And we need your help."

"You just tell me what I can do to help you get that mother fucker."

Kayne swept back his hair and responded with absolute precision. "It is important for us to talk to anyone who saw Ms. Murad leave Masque on the night she was killed."

"Where the fuck is he?" Cha Cha picked up her cell and hit a number on speed dial. "Le, come to my table with a bartender. Make it Milo."

Scott Le and Milo entered the Owner's private booth. "Milo, bring my guests another round. You know what I want." The handsome bartender practically bowed in acquiescence, turned, and left.

"How is it out there?" This remark was aimed directly at the club manager, a small, good-looking Asian around 30 years old. He was perceptibly nervous.

"Dead, Boss." Realizing his poor choice of words immediately, Scott said, "Sorry. It's just that word got around about Hadji, and folks are concerned about a serial killer on the loose. I've heard other clubs in the Manors are also having a slow night for a Friday."

Kayne spoke, "Mr. Le, you were the last person to see Ms. Murad alive. Please tell us what you witnessed."

"It's like I told Cha, um, Ms. Rosette. I left about three-forty AM on Sunday after closing. There was no one in the club except Hadji in the drag queen's dressing room. When I checked in with her, she said she would use the side door-- the one with the panic bar so I would not have to wait to lock up after her."

Scott Le took a deep breath and continued a bit more slowly.

"I've been having trouble with my motorcycle lately, so I was still in the back lot when Hadji left the building. As I pulled out of the lot, I remembered that she had dropped her bags. Then, there was this guy who came up behind her and helped her pick up her things."

"Mr. Le," Kayne said, "In addition to your being the last to see Hadji Murad alive, you are possibly the only person to have seen her killer. Please take your time and tell us about the man in the parking lot."

Scott Lee paled and started to tremble. "Jesus, I don't like the sound of that." Sitting closest to him, Rebecca took him by the elbow and helped him into the empty seat next to me. Cha Cha passed him her unfinished cocktail and made a "drink it" motion. Scott did.

Milo returned with our drinks. He looked at the shaking club manager with a surprised expression.

"Milo, water. Bring a pitcher and glasses."

When the curtain parted, I got a view of the club. Mohka Mirage was on stage doing a torch song, and the strippers were moving on and around the main bar. I thought I saw a familiar figure among the patrons seated at the bar opposite the owner's alcove. He was looking in our direction but too far away for me to ID him. Determining that this warranted a quick look, I wanted to excuse myself to investigate. Still, I decided to remain to hear the rest of Le's story.

Scott, trying to compose himself, continued, "Something about the guy was familiar. I told Ms. Rosette that he was one of the homeless guys living in the bushes behind the club, but the more I think of it, I don't think so. I think he was one of our patrons. He was a pretty big guy, and the homeless back there are usually pretty scrawny."

I asked, "Mr. Le, what else can you tell us about him, clothes, ethnicity? Anything you can remember is important."

"Pretty sure he was a white guy. Hard to say. I didn't see his face. He was wearing shades and dark clothes, blue or black. Look, I'll admit I did not hang around and get a better look. Should have, yeah. But I didn't. I guess I got caught up a bit with my own troubles."

Kayne stared intently at the young man, then looked up at me. From across the table, I could tell that he was thinking the same thoughts as me. Scott Le was far too hesitant. Just what was he hiding?

Milo returned and placed a water pitcher on the table with two glasses. As he parted the beaded curtain, Rebecca reached up to stop him. He turned and bent his head down as she whispered in his ear. She slipped him some folded bills. He looked up at me and left.

"Look, can I get back out there, Ms. Rosette?' Scott pleaded. "I left Tommy on the door, but we need him in the back." Looking around at Kayne, Rebecca, and me, Le added, "Never know who is going to come into this club."

"You think of anything, you let me know. You hear?" Cha Cha dismissed her manager.

As Scott left the alcove, I remembered I had wanted to check out the patrons. I stood and said, "I need to excuse myself for a minute."

"Know where it is, baby?" asked Cha Cha.

"Yes, thanks."

Kayne stood, excused himself, and left with me. "I'll talk to you in a bit, Nick." He followed Le to the entrance of the club.

I looked around, trying to find the man I saw from across the large room. The seat at the bar was empty; there was no sign of him. Sam was on one of the smaller platforms diagonal from the main stage. His jock was seductively askew and decorated with bills. The boy was apparently a favorite with what few patrons were present.

Rebecca's "Omar Shariff/Sheriff Ali" was stepping over the drinks of the few customers that were in the bar trailing his whip. He had removed his cape and headgear to gyrate seductively in his black g-string and desert boots. His slicked muscles reflected the ambient light like a sleek desert panther.

A few feet to the right, Sam jumped down and came up to me. I asked him about the mysterious customer.

"Yeah, I saw him. That jerk's a shit-assed tipper, let me tell ya. Comes in here often, too."

137

He moved closer to me and slipped a hand under my shirt.

"He doesn't like to be touched." Now, moving both hands along my abs and pecs, he continued exploring a bit lower. Then he added, "But you do, Officer. Don't you?" His mouth was inches from mine.

Sam's caresses were interrupted by Rebecca, who had extracted herself from the owner's table and held her cell phone in one hand. She was highly agitated.

"Do you believe this shit? Major fuckup at Miami International. My shipment from the Prado for the exhibit is being held up in Customs. That was my assistant curator. Fucking, twelve-thirty in the morning. I gotta get down there and straighten out this mess."

Cha Cha Rosette emerged from her alcove and came over to us. She spoke to me.

"If I find anything more from folks around here bout Hadji, I'll let you know, Baby. Leave your business card. Meantime, I need to go home. Not much sleep lately,"

I thanked her for speaking to us. Rebecca embraced her with an expression of sympathy for her loss.

"You think about what I said, Gorgeous." Cha Cha Rosette walked away.

Turning back to me, Rebecca said, "Can you make sure that Kayne gets back to City Hall for his car?"

She placed Sam's hands back on my chest and said to him, "Milo, take care of you, Darling?"

Sam nodded. "And I am going to take good care of my Officer Beefcake here." He looked at me with a lascivious grin.

I gulped and allowed him to lead me in the direction of the private dancer's room.

Turning to look at Rebecca over my shoulder, I saw her reaching up to the exotically hot Farad and placing a bill in his ample pouch as she exited the club. I was sure her phone number was on the tip.

Chapter Twenty-Two: Ket
NICK SECHI'S JOURNAL

"Look, Nick." Kayne pointed to the computer screen. "Our man is fearless, and he has planned out this abduction carefully. He wants Le to see him but is trying not to be recognized."

Through some pixelated static, the figure on the screen paused as he followed the drag queen, being careful to keep her unaware of his stalking. She raised her hand to wave off the departing Scott Le while her scarf, her bag, and valise spilled in a pool of parking lot light.

The killer halted a few paces behind her and waited until she saw him before moving closer.

"Nick, look, he is hunting! Cheeky bloke!" Kayne shot his hair back and pointed again at the computer monitor.

The shadows of the trees kept us from getting a clear view of the killer. The windy parking lot of Masque Bar last weekend resembled the rolling seas of the Atlantic at night. Patches of light and dark skated over the asphalt, creating a chiaroscuro pattern blending surface, trees, and one lone car. In an impressionistic overlay of black and white, two figures encounter each other in what would end up being a deadly dance.

My fingers tapped the keyboard. I tried to expand the image on the screen. Still, the resolution of the killer's picture into an identifiable face wasn't happening. Also, the static and the jerky motion made the figures appear and disappear at random in a haphazard pattern of colored squares. Kayne dropped a hand on my back as he stood looking over my shoulder in my home office.

"Mary can get one of her computer geniuses on this. Your video program tools are not that sophisticated. Perhaps a good tech can resolve all this pixilating mess so we can get a face." He tipped his watch. "Too late to call her now. In the morning, we can give her this and the camera. The FBI works on Saturdays, Mate."

He unconsciously moved his hand up and gently squeezed my trapezius to emphasize his point. The feed continued to play, looping through the time coordinates. I thought again of the look, smell, and touch of him in the City Hall parking lot.

We had left Masque about 30 minutes ago. Thanks to sexy Sam and his erotic choreography, I felt like a much better man. On the way back to my place, Kayne explained his follow-up discussion with the club manager, Scott Le.

In the passenger seat of my convertible, my Professor related a very detailed story. In the dark, his blue eyes betrayed his constrained excitement.

***

After leaving the owner's table, Kayne approached the entrance desk of the club. He and Scott stepped outside, walking to the rear parking lot. The young man lit up a cigarette with trembling hands.

"Mr. Le, since we began this informal interrogation, you look like a man who is shitting razor blades, Mate."

Scott said nothing and proceeded to walk Kayne to the rear of the club to the abduction scene. Kayne had stooped and examined the asphalt where the entertainer dropped her bags. Likewise, he studied the parking space and the surrounding area. Bending over to the debris that bordered the lot, Kayne reached into his jeans pocket for a cocktail napkin and carefully extracted a hypodermic needle from the brush. He stood up and looked at his companion.

"Let's go, Mr. Le. What are you not telling me?"

"I swear that's it, Mister. I don't know anything about drugs back here, but, like I've been saying, a lot of homeless folks live around here.

As if he had been queued up to make an appearance, a dark figure shuffled out of the undergrowth and caught Kayne's arm.

"Are you the Devil?"

Kayne took a step back as Scott Le looked on in horror.

The man was ragged and broken, badly in need of food, decent clothing, and basic hygiene. He remained attached to Kayne and struggled for words, mumbling and stammering. His head turned as he searched the dark places for the evil he was convinced lurked there.

"Easy, Mate. No, I am a friend. How are you doing?"

"You look like the Devil. Crafty. I've been waiting for you. It's like my Agnes told me. You seen her? I need to find her before he comes back." The man shifted and rubbed his face, lips, and nose running with slobber.

"It's OK, Mate. You live here?" Bending a bit, he could see a mattress in a hollowed-out space carved in the bushes next to a pin oak tree. Kayne approached the unfortunate. "Tell me your name, please."

In a voice tinged with mania, the man responded, "Prestor John, I am King in these parts. I tell them what to do, Agnes and me. I keep back the Devil with his dark angels." Soft rustling in the bushes indicated more homeless in the vicinity.

The man raised his voice and waved one arm, gesticulating randomly. "We used to get food, but that stopped. They want us gone, Mr. Devil, 'cause we see too much. Things we are not supposed to see."

The man's eyes were rheumy, red, and runny. He had trouble focusing. They rolled in their sockets, and he blinked as he scanned the two men and the parking lot. Scott raised his mobile to call 911.

Growing excited, Prestor John pulled out a cell phone from the pocket of his worn pants, the charger cord hanging from one end. He waved it, hollering, "Go on, Bub. I got one of those too. See?"

Kayne put out a hand to calm them both.

"Have you seen the Devil, John?"

"Right where you are standing, asshole. Last week sometime. Yes, I saw him."

"I believe you, John. What did he look like?"

"Big and with wings, and shit, hooves, tail – the Devil, he was here. Now is his time. He took her. Stealed that lady away. He feeds on souls that one does."

"Whom did he take, John? What did you see?" Kayne touched Prestor gently on the shoulder. The King reacted as if he had been tasered, howling and falling to the asphalt in jerky spasms.

Kayne stepped back and pulled out his phone, about to get help, but the man jumped up and pushed his face close to Kayne's.

"His touch is fire like yours. He comes from Hollywoodland. That is his kingdom. He took her there to be his queen. That pretty lady... my Agnes. Just like my Agnes."

He made a dash for the surrounding darkness but stopped and turned back as if remembering something. With a switch to lucidity, he punched at the cell phone. Holding the phone toward Kayne, he said, "See? See? Behold your doom!"

Kayne grabbed the phone from the bumbling man and quickly viewed the screen. With excitement, he tapped the device and then pulled out his phone to check the transfer.

The agitated homeless man grabbed for his instrument and raged, "Give it back!" He shook a fist at Kayne, "Seek him there in La La Land. There he rules." He was gone, into the bushes, into the night.

Kayne tapped in a number and called in the encounter to Mary Chaffee. He then dialed a hotline requesting a call back to set up some services for Masque Club's colony of street folks.

Kayne said to Scott, "Untreated schizophrenia. He needs medication desperately, among other basic things. Why there is a church only two blocks from here. Such a disgraceful state of affairs in such a wealthy country."

Ignoring Kayne's social concern commentary, Scott remarked somewhat nervously, "Jesus, everyone has a cell phone these days. How the fuck does he charge it?"

Kayne pointed to the outdoor outlets on the Masque building. "There, I surmise. People with schizophrenia sometimes have extended periods of lucidity. It could also belong to his Agnes, who seems to be absent."

He continued, "The police will need to impound that phone, surely. I hesitate to bring them back here. Our friend may bolt."

He tapped the top of his iPhone.

"But I have the feed."

As they returned to the club, Scott added, "I have been trying to get Cha Cha to fix those broken security cameras."

He pointed to the eaves of the club.

"Likewise, to get some more muscle in this club, but she says that times are hard and there is no line in her budget for extra security. So, it's me, Tommy, and broken cameras."

"That kid is a security officer here?" Kayne had referred to a young pup who took over the front door when they ventured out to the parking lot.

"Don't let his looks fool you, Sir. Tommy C is a black belt master — a total badass. Last week, he took down not one but two assholes, both twice his size. He was working the lap dance parlor. You know these guys-- get wasted, go back there with one of the strippers, and think it is a fuckin' bathhouse. Tommy enforces rule number one like a bastard— *The Customer Does Not Touch the Dancer*."

As he spoke, Scott's eyes shifted all over the immediate vicinity. Kayne pressed, "Scott, did you have a relationship with Miss Murad? Is that what you're not telling me?"

Le took a deep breath and let it out. He looked up at the night sky and then down at Kayne. He spoke very deliberately. "No, I helped her get through the night a few times, but it wasn't anything like that. She needed a shoulder to cry on sometimes. People can be so fucking cruel. I felt sorry for her."

He continued, "So we were like buds for a while. Then, we had a knockdown drag-out over something stupid about three weeks ago, and it was pretty public right before opening. Both said some dumb stuff."

"What did you fight about?"

"She found out I was seeing someone and got pretty crazy about it. Said I was a user like all the rest. She was going a bit apeshit at the bar where folks could hear. Hadji felt more for me than I did for her, Mr. Kayne. Total misunderstanding."

The young man continued to show prolonged agitation as he went on.

"Anyway, she said she would make trouble for me if I tried to junk her like all the rest of the people she knew. Tommy broke it up and got very nasty with her. Told her she was bringing everyone down here at Masque with her tired old show. It got pretty bad, and Ms. Rosette was very pissed. The Boss looks out for everyone despite how she acts. She always could put Ms. Dawn back together after she broke."

He failed to contain his emotions and blurted out, "Fuck, so from the way you're looking at me, I am sure you think I had something to do with this. A suspect, huh? Shit!"

Scott Le became utterly unglued as they walked back to the club entrance.

"Easy, Mate, I just want to find out what happened. As I said before, you were one of the last ones to see her alive. We are taking your word for it that there was someone else in the parking lot when you left Hadji. This was now corroborated by a very sick individual whom we most likely will never see again."

Scott got red-faced and grabbed his black hair with both of his hands as if to yank it out.

"Jesus, man... I am so fucked!" He went dumb.

After a minute, he was calm enough to speak. "Look, Mister, a strange man at the bar was paying a lot of attention to Hadji that night. Big guy like, I said before, on the creepy side. Asked me what time she finished her act."

"Did you tell him?"

"Yes, but I didn't think he was gonna off her."

Kayne cocked an eyebrow and said, "Could he have been the man you saw in the parking lot, this guy?" Kayne showed Scott some of the feed on his mobile.

"I don't know, man. It was dark, fixing to storm... I guess so. Jesus!"

Trying to contain his panic, Scott continued, "OK, look, I know you work with the FBI, mister. They can't know anything about me or that I was involved in this."

"Why, if you didn't... "

Scott would not let him finish.

"I'm DACA, man," Scott said with a shout. "My parents were illegals from Kazakhstan. They brought me over when I was two. You know what it's like to know that you could be sent to a country that doesn't like your family or your kind? They hate gays there."

Terror filled his eyes.

"They torture and kill gay boys like me. I can't go to jail here or there, man, you understand? These Republicans will deport me as sure as shit."

"Did Ms. Dawn know any of this?"

"Yeah, know what she said? She was like, 'Scott, I'll marry you, and then you'll be legal.' I mean, how crazy is that? For a while, I considered it, but then this other guy...."

The club manager stopped, not wanting to implicate another person in the matter.

When he went on, he explained, "So far, I have managed to fly under the radar here. Masque is a place I can hide. I avoid too much involvement with strangers. ICE is fucking everywhere. I keep my head down and steer clear most of the time.

"That's why you left quickly Sunday night.

"Yes."

"It took some help to get this gig, to be honest." He gestured to the club. "I've been on the run before. There is this guy in Miami who can help you disappear and come back as someone else. I gotta stay outta this whole mess or else...."

"Run away?"

Scott Le had looked up from the ground and into Kayne's eyes. Le's were the eyes of a lost young man. He said nothing. A few minutes later, he spoke.

"Nowhere to go, man. Nowhere"

***

"Fuck me hard! We have the actual abduction," I exclaimed. We both watched the man in the circle of light choose his position strategically as he bent over and helped with the pile of Hadji's spilled belongings. Once he had collected her gear, he said something to her and led her to the passenger's side of the car. He deposited her possessions in the back seat. She turned and faced him as if to say thanks.

Now, the image scattered across the screen in small, colored squares, lines, and blank spaces for a few seconds. When the feed resolved itself, the two figures had blended-- Hadji slumped against her killer.

"That was where he injected her with the Ketamine," Kayne said. "The pharmacology report from the autopsy will confirm, and we have the syringe. Remember, you spotted the injection point on the neck of the corpse at the Riverwalk?"

"What makes you think it was 'K,' Boss?" I said as I turned to Kayne.

He pointed to the screen and straightened up. "The immediacy of the effects and the ease of availability on the street. Also, the odor of the residue in the syringe."

His ice-blues were sparkling in the dim light of the computer screen. He continued. "This date rape drug takes a bit of time to act when powdered and slipped into a cocktail. He mainlined that unfortunate woman, and she passed out in a matter of seconds."

On the screen, Hadji's car was backing out of the lot, the killer in the driver's seat.

Referring to the feed I retrieved from Kayne's phone, I said, "Say again how you got this?"

"Crazy homeless man with a cell phone."

"You are so shitting me."

146

He raised his right hand. "On my life, Mate. I am working on taming the poor guy with some food and healthcare to secure his phone as evidence and find what seems to be his lady love, someone named Agnes. But look at that. The poor blighter has the shakes bad. Looks almost useless, eh Nick?"

He leaned in so that his face was over my right shoulder and gently placed a hand on my left shoulder. I caught the intoxication of his scent, clean, despite hours in a smoky bar. Kayne's natural fragrance was unencumbered by cologne or aftershave but laced with the spices and tanginess of Hudson's best cognac. I felt the feather's touch of his breathing and completely lost my train of thought.

Kayne stood and picked up his snifter, quaffing the shimmering contents.

I turned in my desk chair to pour more of the golden liquid into my glass and put a bit more in Kayne's. The fire of the liquor tasted so good as it went down. We were both in our bar clothes, having rushed back to my place, looking a bit like who done left it and ran.

"Kayne, is Scott Le a suspect? How about this Tommy What's His Name?"

"Grayson. I believe that, based on what is on this feed, the police will not hold Scott as a suspect in the woman's abduction. However, the police will consider him and Tommy as persons of interest deserving of continued investigation. Also worth finding is the man who inquired about Scott Le about Hadji at the bar."

A memory of the mysterious Masque patron I had spotted from behind the beaded curtain came back to me. I started to bring it up to Kayne. However, I lost my train of thought, distracted by my attraction to the man who stood so close.

I think I had hit every intense emotional peak in the human repertoire in the last 24 hours, including some primal lust with the very sexy Sam. (Talking: *Look ma, hands-free finale.*)

I felt my brain and body starting to shut down– hitting the wall hard. Feeling quite drained, I tried to focus on what Kayne was saying, but my eyelids were drooping considerably.

I managed with, "Any chance Scott and Grayson knew Jared?"

"I'm not convinced, Nick. Nothing we have puts the Petty Officer at Masque. We need to look at other places frequented by Jared Christiansen, specifically the gym and the leather bar. Someone saw something, and we need to run down any leads we find. It is futile to connect the victims beyond the fact that they were both gay and abducted in Wilton Manors. Like most psychopaths, our killer targets victims who fit the profile of his murderous interest. Their victims usually have no common associates."

His words had a strange echoing quality to them. Behind me, the loop played over again-- the hunter and his prey. I looked up at Kayne and started to ask him if he wanted to stay over and skip the late-night drive. I felt my legs go wobbly as I attempted to stand.

"Come on, 'Officer Pretty.' Let me help you up."

As I stepped into his arms, I noticed he was looking over my shoulder at the computer screen. Just before I passed out, I heard him shout.

"Bleedin' ratbag!"

Chapter Twenty-Three: Twist

Hell Boy saw something that made him shiver.

"See something, say something." Since the Palm Killer started his butchery in Paradise, those signs and billboards were everywhere. People were afraid to go out at night. Fear was everywhere, especially among Kayne's Shadows-- an army of darkness that often found themselves in dangerous situations despite many safeguards.

By 2:00 AM, traffic was thinning to the point of desertion. The boy's panhandling at the major intersections was bringing in little cash. His street waif looks usually evoked some pity from passing motorists, especially on weekends. Small in stature and able to affect a pitiable façade, he also, at times, faked a limp. Tonight, there was just no one around.

The arrival of the strangers earlier that evening at the Claypools was a signal that he needed to get back to the streets. He slipped out the back way, hopped a fence, and hopped into a crowded bus headed downtown. Rush hour was the best time to travel mass transit. He could get on and off without paying.

Hell Boy was back at being an updated version of "The Artful Dodger," cute, street smart, and slightly criminal. He still had the dirty, dog-eared copy of Dickens the Professor gave to him when he joined the Shadows, along with a cell phone, both now stashed in his backpack. Without letting his buds know he was a reading geek, he would often slip out the book and have a good go at tales of Victorian London's underbelly. It passed the time, especially on chilly winter nights.

John Cochran Dawkins, Esquire, unlike most 15-year-olds, who sought to look and act older, preferred a younger presentation of himself. Small and slight physically, he used the little boy look to his advantage – large, soft brown eyes convincing his public of innocence and boosting "contributions."

Help, a poor kid, mister.

He chuckled silently.

And if anyone messes wif ole Jackie D, thinking I'm a tyke, I smashes 'em like a full growed bruiser. Fucks'em up.

The small orphan stealthily climbed over piles of rocks and sand. The trucks and empty freight cars near the cement company adjacent to the tracks that cut through just north of downtown provided welcome shelter. Last winter, they parked an abandoned caboose in the rail yard for about a week. It was like he had checked into a luxury hotel, dodging in and out of the shadows late at night.

Now, he was afraid. He was scared shitless of what he saw and fearful of the big man who moved in the spaces between the heavy equipment next to the unfinished tracks. Huge shadows were cast by the diverging light beams that came from the plant's security floods perched on two tall storage silos. Light also bled across the yard from the surrounding street lights. The man's arms were loaded down. He was dumping something.

Jesus, he had seen this guy before, creeping around in the darkness like some crazy vigilante. The chav was a "watcher." One of those guys who lay off in the perimeters and shadows, waiting for the right moment to move in, to strike, to attack. He had outwitted lots of these assholes because of his ability to camouflage his presence, blend in, looking odd and inconsequential. But this one was different – giving off a Resident Evil, Jack the Ripper vibe, and it made the boy's blood run cold.

Hell Boy was scared.

He hadn't talked to Mikey in a couple of days. Not since he told her about the Warehouse 221 stuff. Considering the closeness of this Big Bad, he could not call her or the Boss now. He needed to remain still and not risk a struggle to get to his phone in his backpack and send a text. He concentrated on how to get out of the train yard without the berk seeing him. Carefully sliding under the tanker car that separated them, he lay flat on his belly on the crushed stone trackbed. The big man came closer.

Holy shit, the dude from Number 221, Crikey!

Jack started to sweat.

"Stay icy, numbnuts," he said to himself softly. "Do not blow this." He remained face down, waiting for the right moment to dash it.

Nearby, he heard the soft clanking of machinery followed by a louder whooshing roar and a sound like marbles rattling in a garbage can coming from the big man's direction and his bundle. Two rocks, the size of billiard balls, rolled under his tanker. One tapped him on the nose. A slowly passing freight train provided some cover sounds for whatever the scary man was doing just a few feet from where Hell Boy was hiding.

The train had slowed to a walk. Choosing what he thought was the right moment to scramble from beneath the car, the boy dashed for it. He counted: one, two, three, four steps. Timing his approach, he hoisted himself onto the couplings between the cars. Swinging across to the far side of the freight car, he jumped down and sprinted across two sets of tracks, shooting through a hole in the fence.

He was panting after he dove into a stand of brush just outside the perimeter fence. Hell Boy remained motionless for what seemed like an eternity. Finally, he pushed himself up above the screen of the weeds and looked for the big man. Shit! His backpack lay open between the second set of tracks. His copy of "Oliver Twist" tossed on the rock bed, pages fanning in the night wind.

He stood up, trying to decide whether he should split or rescue his stuff. Before he could turn around, he felt a hand grip his shoulder.

"Please allow me to assist you, Son."

Thomas Paul Severino

Chapter Twenty-Four: Aquaman
NICK SECHI'S JOURNAL

Damn, my head hurt. I was severely brain-dead. I delicately opened one eye as I lay on my face in my bed. As consciousness began to flow back through my grey matter, I slowly began to make the following observations:

One: My mouth tasted like I swallowed an ashtray.

Two: The brightness of the morning sun through the bedroom's patio doors seared my brain and indicated that it was most likely mid-morning. Saturday? Yeah, Saturday.

Three: I was naked and very "indisposed."

Painfully rolling over and sitting up, I examined the other side of the bed through squinting eyes.

So yeah, here's Four: I had not slept alone. *Holy shit!* I covered my eyes with both hands, trying to recall the events of the previous night.

Could my life be more complicated right now? Holy crap!

I groped to my right, snatched my Nightwing sunglasses from the night table, and headed to the bathroom. As I glanced in the mirror, I was shocked. I looked like someone had pulled me through a knothole. Clawing at my dark red hair, I finished a long piss while my morning tumescence subsided. Grabbing a robe, I headed out to find black coffee, my dog, and my bed companion in that order.

So, where the hell was my so-called watchdog through all this anyway? I thought our agreement included protecting me from ravishment. As I poured a mug of freshly brewed, I stumbled to the patio doors between the kitchen and the dining room. Chouko was barking in the yard. I also heard laughing and what I thought was Japanese. Looking out into the brightness of the patio as best I could, I saw my Akita and my randy professor mock wrestling in the glistening waters of the pool.

Chouko emerged and doused me with a soaking "doggie shake-shake." He bounded over, intending to jump up in a "two-wet-paws-on-my-shoulders" position, complete with long, slurping dog kisses. Before he could reach me, I pointed to the ground with my left hand and called out, "*Chouko, orosu!*" It hurt to talk loudly. Shit!

Chouko hit the ground, looking up at me with that curled-tail-wagging-wanting-more-play look. "Not this morning, Handsome. Daddy's hung."

"How can anyone see with all this light," I said to no one in particular.

Smiling, Kayne climbed the steps of the pool, sparkling water cascading off his muscled body. He picked up a towel and began to dry himself, shaking his black hair in imitation of his roughhousing companion. A double-headed imperial eagle spread across his left rear shoulder blade. The black, gold, red, and white glistened in the sun.

Excellent tat, I thought.

I ordered Chouko to roll over and stay. He loved enjoying the warm sun after a swim.

"The dead have arisen. Way too much carousing, my lad-- bad mix for a crime-fighting superhero." Kayne tapped my rather juvenile sunglasses and made his last point, touching my nose.

"Ow! Easy there, big fella." My head still hurt like hell.

He plopped into the deck chair next to me. I reached over and tugged the hem of his boardies, my boardies, actually. They fit him rather nicely.

"Dr. Sorenson, I have a few questions," I said mockingly. Still snagging the leg of his swim shorts, I asked, "And just what else did you help yourself to last night?"

He guffawed and did his signature hair sweep. "No, my young friend. Your innocence, of whatever degree one would find it after your Mr. Sam Stripper Boy had his way, has remained sacredly intact."

With one index finger, he crossed his heart and looked heavenward. He continued laughing through sips of coffee.

"I like my strong boys fully conscious."

Continuing to feign seriousness, he turned again to face me and added, "Next question, Officer Sechi, Sir?"

Seed Blood

"My guest room was not to your liking?" I slid my sunglasses down my nose, looked over them, and looked at him inquisitively.

"Well..."

Was he blushing?

"It's like this, Nick. Your dog snores. You do not. In any case, not as much. And I refer to my previous statement in my continuing effort to assure you of my very respectful behavior. Although I confess, it was a monumental, personal struggle requiring a Herculean effort to stem my raging passion."

He was over-the-top histrionic and beaming his best shit-eating grin again.

A confirming snore came out of the sleeping dog at our feet.

Before I could continue, Kayne held up an index finger. "Please allow me to anticipate your next question."

I closed my mouth and let him continue.

"You want to know who got you in the 'nuddy,' as we say in Oz."

I steepled my fingers in front of my face, impatiently tapping my index fingers together, looked over at him, and said, "Yes, and I am waiting for your answer, Dr. Sorenson."

"Truthfully, I invited over a bunch of my very energetic mates, and we... ah... well... You know, I think I may have lied a bit ago about there being no hanky-panky."

My turn to belly laugh.

If only, I thought, but naw, I would've wanted to be awake for that.

Jeez, he was mouthwateringly hot and cute at the same time. I was such a man whore thinking this way. Hud was barely 24 hours out the door.

Dropping the banter, Kayne looked me in the eyes and said, "Nick, I saw on the mobile's feed...."

Before he could finish, Chouko leaped up and ran around to the side gate just as we heard the bell. Kayne pressed the remote to unlock it. A familiar voice called around the side of the house, "Are you decent, Darlings?"

Rebecca sailed into the backyard, her Saturday brunch costume, a vintage, pale yellow, one-piece Esther Williams bathing suit complimented by a large pair of Jackie O sunglasses and rhinestone strappy sandals. Her sheer, floor-length aqua bathing coat was entirely off her shoulders and trailing behind. At her wrists, silver bling shimmered, and, in her hand, an impossibly large straw hat.

She hit a mock, hands-on-hips, judgmental pose as she came into view.

"Well, Professor, I am appalled. Overnighters with your students. Didn't we talk about this, Dr. Sorenson?"

She wagged a finger at Kayne as he approached her in a head-down artificial repentance pose. They did a Euro, double-cheek kiss.

He held her around the waist and said, "Everyone's of age here, my girl."

She rolled her eyes and caressed his chin. "Harrumph!"

I stood to add a smooch. However, Rebecca, extending one arm, held me off. She raised her Dolce and Gabbana's and cocked one eyebrow at Kayne after appraising my looks. She said, "Whatever did you do to this man? He looks like hammered shit. Sorry, Darling. But... I suspect, totally rejuvenated, in any case." She winked.

Before either of us could answer, a second combination of the gate's bell and the commotion of the dog brought a second familiar beauty around, his beefy arms bearing packages.

"Call off dog, Niko!" The sexy baritone of Gints Bergovic in his gym togs showed no fear of the Akita, just friendly annoyance.

"Chouko, *yameru*!"

Rebecca joked, "I forgot. Right after I texted you regarding your whereabouts, I met this sexy gym god at Einstein's." She added playfully, "Whatever his name is, and we decided to bring breakfast. Play your cards right, Buster," she winked at Kayne, "And I think he just might be on the menu. Ohhh, such eye candy, Darling!"

She caressed one of Gints' biceps.

Gints leaned my way for a smooch, all smiles and muscles, while Rebecca unpacked bagels, schmeers, and a box-o-coffee. Gints then rounded on Kayne. Nose to nose, he inquired, "And you, Big Doctor, why you don't call, Gints after very sexual Greek dancing and make out?"

Kayne took a step back and spread his hands widely, smiling at his gorgeous friend. Seems 'Bad Boy' was doing a lot of explaining this morning.

Gints turned his back, stretching his big arms to remove his string tank. "We gonna see about this right now."

He let the shirt fall, and turning back to Kayne, he added, "Ahhh, so you through with Gints again. So sad you play with emotions and use this body. You must be taught lesson." He faked a slumped-shoulders, broken-hearted sniff, then took on a mischievous expression and ran full speed into Kayne, knocking them both into the pool.

Rebecca danced away to avoid the splashed pool water. "Play nice, Darlings. Don't wet my Maylana. It's an original – beautiful but dry clean only."

Gints and Kayne wrestled mock strenuously in the heaving blue water, diving under and over each other in a test of strength that sent the water sloshing from side to side. Rebecca and I let the boys play and attacked the bagels. Having second thoughts on a queasy stomach, I settled for more "brown drugs." I refilled my cup.

Slap!

Gints slammed Kayne's boardies on the deck of the pool. He gave a lascivious wink as Naked Boy Kayne jumped up on the muscled stud's broad back and dragged them both under. Chouko, released from his stance, barked at the two men grappling in the pool. The water rocked and overflowed with the power of a small tsunami.

Slap!

Kayne surfaced and slammed Gint's gym shorts and jock on the deck next to his "bathers" in a scorekeeping motion. His arms shot up in an alpha victory pose. Gints surfaced like a Leviathan and took Kayne from behind in a neck hold, pulling him back against his shimmering chest and roaring.

Like a spectator at a salacious Greco-Roman wrestling match, I adjusted myself in my robe. Noticing my movements, Rebecca lowered herself into Kayne's chair and pointed to the shiny, naked, and wet gladiators. She said, "How do we morph this soft porn into a classy brunch gathering?"

I laughed. "Good luck."

Now, both resurfacing, Gints and Kayne stood eying each other, chests heaving. They each took deep breaths, exchanging the macho stares of two combat warriors. Kayne said something in what I thought to be Latvian that made Gints smile and nod, finally embracing his opponent in a long and passionate kiss. I could not hear the rest of their exchange.

With the muscle man pacified for the moment, Kayne pulled out his secret weapon. Turning away, Kayne shouted, *"Chouko, kōgeki!"* My "Beautiful Butterfly" flew through the morning air and took Kayne's place with the battling Gints. Dog and muscle boy both fell into the water in a playful embrace.

Kayne motioned in a pleadingly embarrassed way, and I tossed him the boardies. Covering up his "enthusiasm," he climbed the steps of the pool and flopped into a vacant chair.

"That boy exhausts me."

"Apparently, in more ways than one." Rebecca handed him her coffee.

"Nick, Kayne, I need to update you on the opening of this new exhibit at the museum. On the one hand, it will dazzle all of South Florida. On the other, I am going to have a complete breakdown due to my frustrations with this community.

"As of five this morning, US Customs, Miami, released the sequestered paintings from Spain. I managed to drop some names that led to a few strategic phone calls and presto, an immediate reversal of the holding order. Also, I have been getting significant push-back from the local clergy, most notably, the Catholic hierarchy. It's like they just realize what this exhibit is about."

"You mentioned your rather frustrating meeting with Archbishop Costello," Kayne said.

"Yes, and his local representative in Broward, Monsignor Ciccone. They are concerned that the exhibit will cast the Church in an unfavorable light."

"And, did you flash your advisory board's curatorial credentials for the project?"

"Hello? Yes. Numerous times, Darling. Three project team representatives are local clergy, and another three represent al Musei Vacticani. Director Barbara Paolucci personally worked with us on *Seed Blood*.

She sighed in exasperation. "I mean, what is the problem? This is a historical exhibit. Facts are facts. This exhibit evokes the fervor and the passion of the Apostolic Age of the Martyrs from both outside and inside the Roman Church. Politics, religion, and death – you know, the good stuff."

I passed over the irony of the exhibit's subject, given the current serial killings, and instead commented mockingly, "How surprising! You mean religious leaders are going out of their way to cover up a dark past?"

"Not quite a cover-up, no. Mostly, the hierarchy wants to spin history to cleanse any guilt involved. Church leaders do not see a need to emphasize the violence that comes with religion right now."

In front of us, a hunky and very naked Aquaman battled the "Hound from Hell" across the screen. Opps, make that across my pool.

"How are you dealing with this, my dear?" Kayne picked up his phone, glanced at the screen, and texted a short message.

"Well, Preston and his Board are all for moving forward. He is fortifying my arguments with calls to key figures. His foundation is the presenting sponsor. I relish the fact of standing up to these assholes, to be honest. I am one woman they cannot silence. Art should be free of politics. It is evocative. Leave off with the spin doctoring and other bullshit."

At the mention of Thomas Mitchell Preston, I cringed inwardly but said nothing.

"Good for you, Rebecca. Let me know how I can help."

"I was just getting to that. It is imperative that the methodologies of our serial killer do not get leaked. 'Palm Killer' is fine. If the press gets hold of the martyr theme, it will create devastating publicity that will sink the Church's backing and that of many of the other sponsors of *Seed Blood*.

"But most likely boost attendance," Kayne said.

"Agreed, but if it's going to break, I'd rather have the excitement after the grand opening. I don't need boycotts, and I do need the clergy there. The Archbishop has purchased four tables. Educational collaborations with the Museum and the Archdiocese will result in more revenue. You know that there's some asshole with a Twitter account out there that's going to say I am behind the killings in an effort to boost ticket sales."

I asked the question I knew we all were thinking, "Do you all think that the killer and the exhibit are connected in some way?"

"I thought of that, Nick," Rebecca said. "Mary Chaffee had her agents interview my staff. So far, she has not shared her findings with me. Has she indicated anything to you, Kayne?"

"No, but if you recall, your colleagues do not match the one essential characteristic of a psychopathic killer."

"Right, my administrative staff is entirely female. These women had many questions as to why the FBI was interrogating them. It has been difficult keeping them focused."

I asked, "What about the support staff, the construction and assembly crew, security, the docents, your service providers?"

"I gave all that contact information to the Feds. Mary's agents are going through them all. The Feds are even interviewing my Board. I suspect Mary will alert you to any concerns, things like prior arrests, any records of violence, that sort of thing. They are researching personal social media for anyone close to the Museum's exhibit. It's a lengthy process that, frankly, Darlings, has created a bit of paranoia around the opening."

Kayne added, "From what Mary has shared with me, the FBI has come up with no serious leads in connection to those associated with the Museum, but their investigation is far from complete. It is important to remember the most notorious psychopaths in history were experts at blending in. In short, they aren't easy to spot."

Gints emerged from the pool following Chouko's hasty exit. It was hard to say who won the bout.

Without any modesty reservations, Gints plopped himself in the chair next to me. I handed the big guy a towel. "Thank you, Niko." He indicated the water-shaking dog, "That dog is champion. He keep you well protected, yes?"

"I thought so, up until last night." I looked at Kayne, who threw a towel at my head.

Rebecca interrupted and said, "You know, that reminds me, I should have brought some sausages this morning. I suddenly have an appetite for...."

Kayne placed a cautionary hand on her arm, "With propriety, my dear, please. You are practically a representative of Holy Mother Church at this point. Did you take my advice and order a nun's habit for the opening?"

She stuck her tongue out at him.

Ignoring them, Gints said to me, "You, Niko, you call Kostas, yes? He hunger for you. Why men do not call intimate, very loving friends is puzzle to Gints." He said this last sentence looking accusingly at Kayne.

I thought, *What a small town this is. Does everyone know that Hud left me?*

Gints stood, drying his ample crotch and rock-hard bodybuilder's butt. He grinned at Rebecca, unashamedly aware of what he was doing. He sat down next to me.

Before Kayne could say something, the gate/dog system went off again.

Kayne took up the gate remote again. "That will be Mary. I took the liberty to text her, asking her to pick up the latest evidence." He went to shut down Chouko and meet our newest arrival. I reached over and arranged Gints' towel over his manhood and upper thighs.

"Latest evidence?" Rebecca turned to me questioningly.

"Yep," I said, knocking my Nightwing glasses from the top of my head back to the bridge of my nose. "Your crime fighters have been very busy, Ms. Quinto. It wasn't all drinks and lap dancing last night."

Special Agent Mary Chaffee rounded the house to the patio.

Kayne dashed into the house to get the camera and the hypodermic.

Rebecca and Mary pressed cheeks in a mutual greeting. I introduced Gints, who stood to adjust the front of his towel with one hand and extend the other.

"Special Agent Chaffee, this is our friend Gints Bergovic. Gints, Agent Chaffee is with the FBI."

The expression on our muscled Latvian was one of consternation. "Gints totally legal, Miss Officer. I have papers. What you call the card of green."

Mary's expression spoke softly, almost to herself, "Where does Kayne find these hotties?"

"Chilllax, Gints," Rebecca said, "No one is hauling your ass away unless it's me." She nudged the Special Agent, who dropped a look in the direction of Mr. Bergovic's naked glutes."

Coming out of her semi-trance, Mary said, "Nice to meet you, Gints. Not to worry. I am working with your three friends on the recent murders in Ft. Lauderdale and Wilton Manors."

Kayne came out of the house with the two crucial pieces of evidence. I was about to ask if the Bureau's part of the investigation turned up anything since the briefing. Still, Mary's facial expression seemed to anticipate my question.

"I want to let you know some significant developments. First, I received your message about the man in the Masque parking lot. Your cautionary strategies were correct and followed. We managed to question him with the support of Social Services and received his phone as evidence. At this point, he is under observation for health reasons, as his evidence on the abduction of Hadji Murad is hard to decipher.

"We found a retired social worker, Agnes Jackson, who has adopted the Masque homeless community. She gave them a cell phone, which

162

ended up in the hands of Prestor John the night the killer took Hadji Murad. She wanted the group to have some way to contact the police if someone accosted them. There was a very grisly case of aggravated assault on a homeless family near the downtown bus station about six months ago. Ms. Jackson said she had no idea the video was on the phone. The other homeless folks in that colony have no recollection of the abduction of Hadji Murad. Perhaps more will come."

Rebecca said, "I sit on the city commission to address the needs of our homeless community. We need our politicians to produce the funds to put a viable plan in place. They seem intent to look away."

Kayne looked intently at Mary and said, "There is more, isn't there? You could have called Nick with that intel. What is it, Special Agent Chaffee? What has happened?"

Mary looked at each of us in turn before speaking.

"It appears there's been another killing."

Chapter Twenty-Five: Stephen

NICK SECHI'S JOURNAL

The train yard just east of Sunrise Boulevard was cordoned off, and traffic stopped in both directions. Police vehicles and ambulances filled the property of the cement company. An assembly of law enforcement personnel combed the tracks and side lots that cut through the plant and the surrounding urban scrubland.

Sheriff Crawford, Chief Mays, and the team from last week's discovery of the Navy Officer at the Port of Everglades stood just behind the first responders working on the body of a man lying amid a pile of rocks next to the newly constructed tracks for Florida's newest luxury train, the privately-owned Sunline. Representatives of the transportation company and their construction company partners stood off to the side, speaking with detectives. Because of the presence of so many law enforcement members and the rescue team, again, our examination of a pristine crime site was out of the question.

As Kayne and I approached, Crawford was explaining that construction workers noticed a human arm projecting from a pile of ballast, the rocks that made up the roadbed and stabilized the railroad ties. Construction delays had resulted in weekend crews on-site this Saturday morning. The discovery was quickly made known to the police.

Upon inspection, hemp wrapped a green frond to the hand of the buried person-- the signature of the "Palm Killer." Paramedics were desperately trying to revive what was most likely an hours-old shattered corpse. A partially emptied dump truck loaded with rock stood open next to the body. Its truck bed slanted, the rear door hanging open.

Kayne looked at the body before us and spoke one word, "Stephen."

I started to ask for an explanation, but the activity around the victim immediately focused our attention on the rescue effort. One of the paramedics applied the paddles for what was to be the fourth and most likely the final time. Another used mechanical ventilation on the nose and mouth.

"Clear!"

With a full-body, convulsive arch, the young man's body jumped up off the ground before falling back. The medic applied the stethoscope and listened for about 5 seconds. He announced, "We have a pulse! We are back into sinus rhythm." The surrounding investigators stepped back to allow other paramedics to continue the rescue.

Dian Crawford spoke to Kayne, Rebecca, and me, "The victim is Danilo Santos, according to a business card in his pocket. Our intelligence indicates he was a porn star, exotic dancer, and male escort. We are trying to get information on his actual ID, as 'Santos' is a stage name. But there is some conflicting information there."

Before I could ask for clarification, there was a shout from a police officer who had been walking the perimeter fence. He waved us over and pointed to a clump of tall weeds. Crossing the tracks and passing through an opening in the barrier, we saw the body of a small boy lying on his back. His dead eyes were staring into the morning sky. His throat had been slit with what appeared to be a brutal force. The killer had nearly decapitated the unfortunate child.

Next to the boy's body was a worn backpack and a ragged opened copy of *Oliver Twist*, its pages fluttering in the breeze.

Chapter Twenty-Six: Quads
NICK SECHI'S JOURNAL

The repeated sound of the impacts echoed above the background noise and standard gym Muzak. "Damn, dude! Pulverize that sucker. Come on, Doc. Show me the moves." Chad Hilton cheered the shirtless, dark-haired kickboxer warming up on the speed bag. He had trained with Kayne, and together, they had amazed onlookers with some of the best examples of combat sport, especially in their sparring sessions.

The clientele at Quads Gym in Oakland Park was diverse, incredibly fit, and intent on making fitness gains. Many guys and gals were getting their Saturday night pump on, lifting free weights, training on the cardio equipment, or doing aerobics on the main gym floor. It was late afternoon on the day that the bodies of Danilo Santos and the street waif, John Cochran Dawkins, aka Hell Boy, were discovered on the train tracks.

Kayne hadn't said much since the discovery of the mutilated body of Hell Boy, the youngest of his network of Shadows. At the site, he knelt beside the dead boy for a long time. I suggested that we head out for a workout after the police completed their investigation and removed the bodies. He was numbed to the core by the discovery of the ravaged urchin.

Once we had arrived at Quads, it was clear that he needed to be alone. As we undressed in the locker room, Kayne said nothing, but I could feel the grief mixed with rage. I warmed up and then went into my acrobatic training routine but stayed relatively close to him. The possibility that he was coming apart concerned me, and I was glad that feisty Chad was checking him. As he warmed up and donned the gloves, I came off my handstand pushups to assist him in his workout since Chad had moved off to train another client.

Kayne slammed the heavy bag with ferocious intensity. I stood behind it, keeping it steady and allowing him to exert maximum force. His round body kicks from both left and right were high and expert. I stepped back from the bag each time to avoid getting side-clipped. From time to time, I pushed the bag into a swing. Kayne danced around the moving target, delivering coordinated, powerful jabs, right crosses, and rear leg push kicks. His movements were continuous and expert, elbows in, gloves up, and scraping his eyebrows. He delivered sharp and powerful elbows and knees in close range in the form of the Muay Thai.

His attacks on the body bag exhibited an extraordinary, almost maniacal force and speed. Around us, gym rats were leaving their workout stations to stand in a circle and watch his mastery of mixed martial arts. Covered in sweat, the top of his hair pulled tight in a small man bun, Kayne trained bestial-- perfect timing, distance, proper cadence, and accuracy, all movements sharp and crisp. He leaped and pivoted to land powerful kicks high on the bag. These strikes, punctuated by yells that came from deep in his guts, drew murmurs of admiration from the spectators. However, nothing changed the focused, brutal expression on his glove-framed face as he tried to batter his frustrations into oblivion. He ignored the bystanders and me.

After 40 minutes, panting from the ordeal, he reached into his bag to exchange his boxing gloves for the fighting, open-fingered kind and, without looking at me, tossed me a spare pair. Removing my tank top, I kicked off my running shoes. put on the gloves, but opted not to add the required head protection. The odds should be even. I slipped in a mouthpiece and slammed my palms together, circling the tautly muscled fighter.

Now Kayne's anger had become a cold, ticking rage. His eyes narrowed, and his gaze was frightening as he dropped into position, tracked me with footwork and arms raised, fierce and focused. We circled each other, and the dance began with Kayne rushing and exploding with a big knee aimed at my chest. He connected, but I managed to partially block the powerful blow and lessen the impact by creating a wall with a bent right arm and leg, connecting knee to elbow. The result brought a jarring realization. I knew we were not sparring. This was a bout, and he was beginning to see I was a worthy opponent.

Spinning off his left side, I pounded two sharp jabs to his lower rib cage just above his hip. We exchanged a few high-impact hits, landing some and ducking under others to deliver a counter-attack. He dropped with a leg sweep, but I returned with an elbow to his head as he came back up. Blocking, he took most of the force but slammed my upper right side with a rib-jarring series of hooks. As he connected with my recent wounds, I thought, *This fucker means business.* I faked right and came in with a left that hit at the level of his right eye, drawing blood.

Payback's a bitch, Brother.

Kayne pivoted, and I took a right uppercut to my left side but countered with a right followed by a spin and a rear right leg pushback, throwing him off balance. Not for long. He rotated back, and we collided in a Muay Tai clinch, "the Plum." Our faces were inches away as Kayne locked his arms around the sides of my head and clasped his hands behind my neck. I struggled to keep his lower body off balance with kicks. Still, he stepped away while maintaining the vice-like grip of the clinch.

In return, I took a few expertly aimed knees while glancing into eyes I hardly recognized. Through spit, blood, and sweat, Kayne taunted, "That all you got, Pretty Boy?" I cussed and struggled to focus. Both of us were breathing hard in an intense match of skill and strength.

Rapidly, I pushed up on his triceps and shortened the distance between us. Taking him in a body lock, my hands gripped together behind his back. I used my upper body to push forward against his chest. He went down, toppling onto his shoulders and back.

As he fell, I ducked down, coming out of the clinch. When he hit the mat, I could tell he was furious, realizing he had gotten sloppy. Emotions dominated his thinking – a deadly mistake in combat. I remained on the top, dominant position, striking my opponent while changing sides. My attempts to keep him from settling with short strikes after the takedown proved futile.

A superbly placed kick pushed me back almost on my butt. Kayne used this power switch to push up off the floor in a spectacular "kip-up," drawing muted cheers from the observers. As his feet hit the floor, he stood upright, spun, and crashed a right kick into my chest with a lightning offense. Again, I felt the blow close to the spot where the bullets had smashed into my chest. I reeled with pain, attempting to move away and regain my balance.

Finally, countering with an expertly aimed elbow between my shoulder blades, he brought me down, grappling me into a triangle chokehold. I struggled to use the standard techniques for breaking the grip of an attacker. Still, his body wrapped tighter around me like an anaconda crushing its prey. His breathing was hot, rapid, and intense. Hitting him on the hip, I signaled submission to his superior strength and expert skills. No response. I slapped the mat and gasped his name, struggling for air and fighting a blackout.

Chad and another trainer pulled us apart, helping me up from the ground. On my knees, coughing and sputtering, I held up my hands in a feeble protest that I was all right. Kayne was flushed and seemed unsuccessfully trying to gain control of his rage, fending off gripping hands. Like a trapped animal, his eyes scanned the horrified spectators and the situation, trying to make sense of what had happened. He looked around, embarrassed and confused, as if coming out of demonic possession. Chad, holding him back, was speaking softly to calm him. Kayne's eyes settled on me, and with a look of shocking surprise, his face dropped remorsefully, but words would not come.

Once able to breathe again, I insanely wanted more and started for him, fists raised.

"You guys need to take your grudge match somewhere else. We want no injuries here," said Nathan, the trainer who was checking me. He pushed me back, calling my name and continuing to make sure that I had my wits about me, breathing regularly. Over Nathan's shoulder, I answered Kayne's gaze with a defiant look of intense vehemence. I pushed back the crowd and hit the locker room, seething with anger. *This shit ain't done!*

"Fuck!"

***

Kayne entered the locker room. Blood seeped from a cut over his right eye. His body was coated with sweat, and his mouth drool. He pulled at his gloves.

"Nick, I... I apologize for..."

I was fucking pissed! Slapping my gloves on the bench next to my open locker, I slowly walked over to him. Our eyes were locked. I roughly put my hands on his chest and forcefully pushed him back into the lockers, hoping the impact would emphasize what I was about to say and bring him to his senses.

"You total asshole," I spat at him. "That boy's death was not your fault. Not your fault! And it sure as hell was not mine."

170

Seed Blood

Our faces were inches apart. Nevertheless, I was yelling. Kayne's arms hung limply at his sides in physical and emotional defeat. Others in the changing room were stunned by the interchange and either stared or quickly left.

He dropped his eyes from mine and tried to look at the floor.

"Look at me!" I pushed him.

He did. His ice blues filled with a brokenness that went to his core.

I spat out the words one by one, "It's! Not! Your! Fault!" I punctuated each word with a moderately powerful open hand to his rock-hard, sweat-slicked chest.

I pointed in the direction of the club entrance. "There's a monster out there, and he's dog-shit crazy. You are not responsible for his actions. You did not fuck up, Kayne. You did a lot to keep Hell Boy safe. He tragically happened to be in the wrong place at the wrong time." I squinted back tears of rage and frustration, wanting to crush him into my arms as we both fought to overcome the maelstrom of fear and evil that surrounded us.

I took a breath and pushed him away. "Give yourself and the rest of us a fucking break. Get off your God damn ego trip! Let yourself and me off the hook."

A large teardrop jumped the bottom lid of his right eye and sailed down his cheek to be followed by more from both eyes. He looked up at me with tears mingling with the sweat, blood, and spit on his face. I gulped back a lump in my sore throat, keeping myself from joining him in blubbering like a fucking baby. I hate when strong men cry; I just lose my shit. This felt like drowning – terribly helpless and fatal.

Kayne searched my face and said in a low, croaking voice, "I could have protected him. Jackie was one of mine. He was a willful little boyo, but I was this close to getting him off the street for good."

Kayne's anger started to rise again. He heaved a deep, sputtering breath and spat out, "You... you had to send in the Feds. Do you realize the possibility of them reining him in scared that boy back onto the streets?"

He slammed the locker to his right with a ferocity that spewed out his rage explosively and finally. He could take no more. Speaking words that resembled the coldness of a steel scalpel, he looked at me and said quietly, "You? Protect and serve? Not bloody likely. You're two for two, Officer Hotshot." His blue eyes were seared with anger, and his face was a frightful mask of icy accusation combined with mockery.

I rushed to grab him by the throat but stopped inches away. Instead, my hands went to either side of his head on the lockers. As my fury subsided, I involuntarily lowered my head against his chest, panting and utterly devastated. Within my clumsy embrace, Kayne pushed me off and turned his face away.

I stepped further back, feeling the floor beginning to slip out from under me. A feeling of complete confusion, anger, and guilt overcame me. Collapsing on a bench, I held my sore head in my hands.

Speaking from what felt like an abyss of sorrow, I said, "I did the right thing for that kid's sake. Played it by the book. I went with my training. Hell Boy should have been reigned in long ago for his own safety. The problem is the fucked-up system's safety net for kids that forced you to create the Shadows. He had a knack for escaping from protection. Jackie was at the wrong place at the wrong time. Why can't you see that?"

I was shouting again. Kayne was unmoved and unresponsive.

Then, I began to realize that something else was gnawing at me from the inside.

The ferocity of this public brawl made it evident to me that neither of us had been able to keep this case on a purely professional level. I had blurred the lines between work and relationship – so fucked up! Whatever I was feeling for this man was shattering with the nightmarish force of a firestorm.

I grabbed my gear and said in a level voice to the floor between us, "Look, I need to be away from you right now. I need some space, Professor. You intelligently deal with this, and maybe we will talk again. For now, stay the fuck away from me."

Pushing by him, I exited the locker room into the club. Without thinking, I landed a punch on the wall next to the door, cracking the wallboard.

Chapter Twenty-Seven: Rey

Nick Sechi's Journal

As I headed to the parking lot, intending to go somewhere, anywhere, and then deciding on going home to brood, a woman who was also leaving the gym stopped me.

"Man, was that some kind of lover's quarrel or what? Jesus, you boys must have some issues. That got pretty savage."

I felt my temper rising again. I was so over-dealing with crazies. I turned and faced a very fit woman in gym togs. She cut her blond hair into a military buzz, and Latin script coursed down her right shoulder and arm. *Aut viam inveniam aut faciam.* Translation: I will either find a way or make one.

"Another guy, right? Men can be such pigs sometimes."

My mouth opened to ask why she thought this was her business, but before I could say anything, she pointed at me, saying, "Hey, you're that cover boy, the 'Hot Cop.' Sechi, right? Now working on the Palm Killer?" I remained mute.

Without waiting for a reply, she continued, "I'm Raymonde Isaacson. I am an entrepreneur here in South Florida. Me and my wife, Rose MacDill, own and run three restaurants on the Drive." She held out a hand.

Ms. Isaacson's grip was firm. She continued, "Would it be possible for me to speak to you privately? I realize that this must be a bad time, but it could be important. We could grab a bite if you feel like some food."

I looked off across the darkening parking lot for a few seconds and then back to my companion. Do I really want to do this? I was distraught, dirty, bruised, and bloodied but not a bit hungry – in no condition to walk into a restaurant in sweaty "jock chic," even in Wilton Manors.

"Um, sure." I caved. "Coffee Talk, on Twenty-Sixth?"

"Perfect. Meet you there."

***

As I pulled into the café's parking lot, my phone chirped. Mary Chaffee. *The hits keep happening, Nick boy,* I thought.

"Hey, Mary. What's up?" I faked calm.

Ms. Isaacson pulled into the next parking spot, saw that I was on the phone, and pointed, signaling that she would meet me inside.

"Nick, I'm up to my ass, but I wanted to get back to you as quickly as I could regarding the evidence I picked up from you earlier."

"Go."

"The hypo-- no prints but, as Kayne surmised, traces of Ketamine. Like that found in the body of the deceased Hadji Murad. The camera-- also no prints. The tech folks could trace the feed, however."

"The location?"

"Wilton Manors Public Library, six blocks from your place."

"Fuck," I said.

"He likes getting close to you."

Gooseflesh.

"The video feed of the Masque parking lot was a mess, but we were able to clear it up a bit. Nothing traceable on a face ID. It's almost as if he knew he was being filmed. A few times, he kept looking directly into the camera. We did get a read on the ball cap."

Just before I passed out in Kayne's arms last night, I remembered that he cussed big time while looking at the screen behind me. He never told what he saw.

"Mary, what did you get?"

"The ball cap on the video feed carries the logo for the Los Angeles Dodgers."

***

"I saw this morning on the news that they found a body of a porn star, the third victim of the Palm Killer," Raymonde said as she gestured to the seat next to her. I dropped into the chair and took a sip of the coffee she had picked up for me – black. Indicating the rather non-example of a designer coffee, I said, "How did you know?"

"My dad and three brothers were cops. No whipped cream, flavorings, or sprinkles for them. Besides, with that beating you took," she gently touched what was becoming a real shiner. She continued, "I figured you needed some pure caffeine to jolt your system. How 'bout some ice for that shiner?"

I winced. My right eye and cheekbone were tender. "I'm good." I showed her the three ibuprofen in my hand from my stash in the glove compartment, and I threw them back with another swallow of the hot brew.

Responding to her opening statement, I said, "They took the 'vic' to Broward General, and he seems to be hanging on by a slender thread right now."

"I know, Rose and I were there before I hit the gym, but they would not let us see Dave. Rose is still there. I go to the gym when I need to get my frustrations out. I'll relieve her when we are through. I was going to go over to WMPD when I recognized you."

Raymonde stopped talking and stared into space for a moment, tears welling. Once she had her emotions under control, she looked back and continued, "Rose and I met Davey about four years ago. That's his real name, David Miller." She handed me a picture of a scrawny teenager with a reversed ball cap, torn jeans, and a skateboard over his shoulder. He was a cute kid with dark eyes and curly hair.

"He was just closing in on 16 and on the street. Father was a real abuser back in Mobile, Alabama. Many gay kids get thrown out by their families when they come out. They head for South Florida because of its large LGBTQ community, figuring that they will be accepted and get to be with folks like them. But I am not telling you anything you don't know."

I nodded, "Yeah, about 60 percent of homeless kids in the State of Florida are LGBTQ. Unfortunately, they get here, and the social services are insufficient. The result is they get trapped in the local sex industry and drug trade. Some guy offers big money, and they are willing to do almost anything to survive.

"I met a young woman when I first came on the force who was pushed out at twelve. She slept behind the dryers at a local laundromat over near Five Points when she was growing up. Tried to commit suicide twice. Doing fine now, thanks to some community help. She is currently a student at Florida State, honors program."

"Amazing. For every one of those stories, there are 100 like that little kid who got his throat slit. So very, very sad." Ms. Isaacson choked up a bit before going on.

"Officer Sechi…"

"Please call me Nick."

She smiled, pointed to herself, and said, "Rey."

"Nick, something evil is happening in this town. I recognized that Navy guy they found at the Port. Used to see him at Quads on occasion. Great smile on that kid. Can't believe he was murdered. And that poor woman from Masque. Folks are getting scared. My restaurants are empty, especially the late-night crowd. Wondering who's next."

"Rey, when you saw Officer Christiansen at the gym, ever notice anything suspicious?"

Rey Isaacson thought for a moment.

"You talk to Mike Crowley? They were buds."

"Yes, he was pretty devastated."

"No, sorry, I can't be helpful. The Navy guy was very popular. Had a lot of fans when he trained, but can't really say I saw anything strange.

"Big guy in a Dodgers cap?"

Rey shook her head. "Afraid I have no recollection. I tend to get tunnel vision when training. Rose says I go into a zone when training."

I smiled.

"Nick, that little boy… sure didn't look fifteen…."

I thought of poor Hell Boy and the anguished, guilt-ridden Kayne Sorenson. I found it difficult to say the dead child's name.

178

"Jackie was a runaway from the world of human trafficking. Also identified as gay."

"More and more kids know at an early age."

Returning to her account of David Miller, aka Damon Santos, Rey continued, "Nick, Rose, and I hired Davey to work in the kitchen at one of our restaurants. He was about to close out of the foster care system, so we pulled a few strings. We arranged for a place for him to stay, a suite above Restaurant Piaf. Once he trusted us, he turned out to be an excellent employee. Having someone on site at night was crucial for security-- his, I mean. Plus, he felt a bit important in his role as junior security. Rose and I live in the townhouses next door to the place, so he was constantly being supervised. He was a good kid.

"We got him in school, too. St. Simon's Academy. At graduation, he was super proud that his two moms were in the audience. Broward College accepted him. He had just begun a degree in sociology when things started to go south.

"Just as his life was getting good, he started lying about his age and started dancing at a local boy bar. He invented a stage name for himself and started spending a lot of time in the gym. He caught the eye of a talent scout looking for hot young bodies for gay porn. The rest happened pretty fast."

"You have a name on this porn guy?"

"Jay Nolen or something like that. He got Davey into Hawk Studios. He was one of their top executives. Davey became one of their exclusives, appearing with their biggest porn stars even though, during the first years, he was underage. Kids doing porn lie about their age all the time. What a fucking world."

She sipped her brew and continued. "After about three years, Davey's contracts began to slow. For some reason, and I don't know why, he never did get into the drug scene. That's so much a part of the porn industry. One of the guys he was close to overdosed and died. Davey really took it hard.

"He used to say there was a lot of politics involved in staying at the top of the porn star chart. Casting couch stuff. He started on PrEP when the demand for barebacking got intense. By then, he had moved to Los Angeles."

Rey pulled up a studio shot of Damon Santos on her cell phone. It was easy to see why he would have a huge fan base. He was crazy hot and very well-endowed.

"After a while, his popularity dropped off, and he came back to South Florida. It was about that time that he started escorting. Explained that he needed more cash because his meds were costly. Like many in the industry, he desperately wanted to transition to modeling and legitimate movies. About a month ago, he got a call back from Hawk. They were marketing his proposed next film as 'The Return of Damon Santos.' No longer a bottom boy but a more mature, versatile star. They would have started filming in Ft. Lauderdale beginning in January.

"Dave started hanging with a bizarre guy about that time. Big dude and very intense. Started out as one of Dave's clients who kept hiring him for one-on-ones. This guy was in his mid-thirties, I'd say. Real lousy vibe about him. Always referred to Danny as 'Mr. Santos.' Like I say, creep city."

"You met this man? Got a name, Rey? Sounds like a person of interest."

Rey shook her head, "Dave used to refer to him as 'The Deer Slayer.' No one uses their real name in porn or in escorting, for that matter, especially the Johns. Not sure what the context of this guy's nickname was, but Rose and I thought, with this attempt on Dave's life, the "Slayer" part may point to something important."

"Do you think you could pick him out of a lineup or from photographs?" I unconsciously rubbed my left lower ribs. Was the ibuprofen ever going to kick in?

"Fuck, yes," Rey said quickly. "Absolutely unforgettable."

"Where can I find this guy, do you know?"

"No, but when he met him, Davey was cage dancing at the leather bar in town."

"Prowl?"

"Yes. A good place to start." She stood to go.

"I gotta get back, Nick. We need Davey to get through this. If I can be of any help, here's my number." Raymonde handed me her business card.

At that moment, the sounds of a news broadcast coming from the overhead monitors filled the coffee shop. I looked to see a cashier with a remote turning up the volume.

"... wrapping up his press conference, Wilton Manor's mayoral candidate, Reverend Cale Norton, where he called upon law enforcement to do a better job of finding the Palm Killer. An open mic caught the Reverend's comments about the killer."

The video froze the picture of the high-profile leader of a local fundamentalist church. To the right of the image, words spelled out as his voice came over the feed, "Yeah. If you ask me, he's killing all the right people."

Chapter Twenty-Eight: In Memoriam

Nick Sechi's Journal

The eulogist fought through copious tears as he finished, "Jared never asked anything of anyone except acceptance. He wanted to live his life as an authentic human being, making no apologies for who he was and with a friendly welcome for all. He loved his family and served his country in the United States military. He was strong and quietly dedicated, with a desire to live with authenticity and honor."

Michael Crawley wiped his face, took a deep breath, and continued, "He was truly a loving man, giving life to every situation and person he encountered. His days were ended much too soon, and I knew and loved him all too briefly."

Overcome with grief, he was unable to continue. The pastor of the Sunshine Cathedral of the Ft. Lauderdale Metropolitan Community Church, the group hosting the memorial service, assisted Michael from the pulpit to his seat in the sanctuary.

Navy Captain Anthony Rota spoke of Christensen's exemplary service and dedication to the United States Armed Services before returning to his place in the front row of the assembly with a group of Navy men and women. The program continued, complete with the obsequies of a military funeral. Flowers banked the closed coffin between the American Flag and the Navy flag. A massive spray of resurrection lilies adorned its top.

Pastor Stevens, a dazzling white surplus over his black cassock, invited others from the group to offer reflections on the life of Jared Christensen. A few members of the congregation walked up to the sanctuary and, through many tears, shared loving memories of the young man.

I noticed a black-veiled Rebecca sitting in the middle of the assembly. The broad-shouldered man seated next to her had an all too familiar shock of jet-black hair, which he unconsciously pushed off his forehead from time to time. Next to Kayne sat Gints, who kept pulling at the collar of his starched shirt. The muscle boy was more comfortable in far looser and less clothing. Bob Mays, Dian Crawford, and Mary Chaffee sat behind the Navy contingent with a few members of their respective cohorts, local law enforcement, and the FBI.

I stood in the back, feeling very anti-social but scanning the group. I had a premonition that our killer may be present somehow. It would have fit his profile as a twisted voyeur. A small group from Professor Sorenson's class sat far in the back. I wondered if this service served as appropriate field research.

Kayne also scanned the assembly. He tried to catch my gaze, but I deliberately looked away. At one point, he leaned in to speak to Rebecca, who turned to observe a woman in the far back corner opposite where I was standing. Seated on the aisle, Rebecca quickly slipped out of her seat and headed to the back of the Cathedral.

As she passed me, she silently leaned in for a smooch. Pulling away, she pointed to my now very black eye and chided, "What the fuck, Darling? You two, I swear." Shaking her head, she continued to cross over to the seat next to the weeping woman in the back row.

As the service continued, Pastor Stevens invited the churchgoers to come forward and take a carnation from a vase in the sanctuary and place it on the coffin. The members of the Navy stood and assembled at the front as an honor guard. Michael Crawley took the hands of each mourner as they came up to pay their last respects. As Kayne approached the bier, he picked up the ribbon of the bow that held the spray of lilies on the top of the coffin. He examined the script on the white fabric carefully.

At the same time, Rebecca, supporting the woman from the back row, came up to me and introduced Myra Christiansen, mother of the deceased.

"I am truly sorry for your loss, Ms. Christiansen."

"Thank you, Officer. I have so much to be sorry for." Not only was she in the depths of grief, but regret for her rejection of her child also filled Myra Christiansen with sorrow.

"My son, my beautiful son...." She looked at the coffin at the other end of the Church and cried desperate sobs into her handkerchief."

Seed Blood

Not wishing to intrude, Mary Chaffee gave me the "call me" sign as she passed next to us on her way out of the church. Rebecca assisted Jared's mother up into the sanctuary to the body of her only son.

I noticed Kayne and Gints heading my way down the aisle on the far side of the Cathedral. I turned quickly to the center aisle. I walked up to pay my respects. Approaching the sanctuary, I watched Michael Crawley take the hands of the tormented and sobbing Myra Christiansen.

Behind them, among the lilies on the coffin, a gold ribbon was inscribed, *Deo Gratias*.

Thomas Paul Severino

186

Chapter Twenty-Nine: Karoline

Hudson Ch'en's Saturday night date was not going well. It had been four days since he moved out of Wilton Manors and back to his condo on the 16th floor of a 20-storied high rise in the Las Olas section of Ft. Lauderdale. Getting back with his ex was not going to happen. How do you morph a sex bud into "Relationship Guy," especially if it didn't work the first time? Without the excitement of cheating, something had gone out of the mix.

Roy Angsley had shown signs of increased interest now that Hud also numbered Nick among his exes. However, it seemed Roy was over-fascinated about the sex tape that had gone viral. His intimations had included a hint at a three-way sometime. Hud thought, Seriously? Hot for Nick? Some shit never changes.

Roy was a player. He had been when they were together. Their status right now was purely sexual, which seemed to be agreeable. Their history was such that Hudson was sure that's where it would remain. "Fool me once...." He was also aware that he was very numb to the whole crisis right now.

Karoline was a trendy four-star restaurant on the Intracostal in Oakland Park. The beautiful people flocked to this high-end venue, especially on weekends. Hudson moved his seared scallops across his plate and responded to Roy's last question about his job.

"I got word this morning. The Foundation will not be taking disciplinary action, considering that someone made that tape without Nick's or my knowledge. "

"You must be relieved."

"Yes, but that did not prevent them from issuing a written warning-- all about bringing embarrassment to the organization. Preston took a meeting with the Archbishop, who was royally pissed about the scandal."

"Why should the Archbishop be involved in this?"

"Preston is a huge Catholic. The Foundation has partnered with the Archdiocese on many projects. They are buds. His Excellency is on the Board."

"How do you feel about all this?" Roy cut off a piece of his filet, put it in his mouth, and looked up at Hud.

"To be honest," Hudson raised his eyes to meet Roy's, "I really do not give a fuck. Dusting off my resume if you want to know the truth. I'll be glad when I can get past all this and get on with my life."

"As hot as he is, Nick must have been hell to live with, Hud." Roy was trying to show genuine concern.

"Hot is a very relative term. Looks can be deceiving." Roy just stared, not understanding.

Hud did not want to have this conversation – "I'm On the Rebound from My Last Boyfriend. Help Me Get Him Out of My System." He shifted uncomfortably in his seat and looked wistfully at the yachts passing in the channel. He tried to change the subject with, "So, how are things going with you, Roy? "

"So, good, yeah," came the response. Roy was a freelance writer and reporter for the "South Florida Gay and Lesbian News," a prominent media source for the LGBTQ+ community. He was also working on a second novel.

He offered, "I have been trying to get an exclusive from the FBI on the progress in the Palm Killer case, but they are a totally closed shop when it comes to the press. I may just have to bed their hottest profiler to get what I need."

That's about right, Hud thought. Throughout their two-year, open relationship, Roy, good-looking and hypersexual, led a parade of hot men through their bedroom. Hud, at first, was all in, as it were, but it got very stale very fast. Without smiling, he said, "Some post-sex pillow talk, hidden recorder on the nightstand?"

"You know it, baby." Roy smiled and raised his Maker's Mark on the rocks in a mock toast. "Speak into the sex toys, Agent Studly."

Hud forced a smile and said, "You know, Roy, those 'wrist talkers' are mostly straight." He pantomimed an FBI agent talking into an up-the-sleeve microphone. "Very difficult to bed, even for you?'

Roy gave Hud his slyest look and provided his usual solution for seducing a straight guy.

"Two shots of tequila."

***

The man at the bar was behaving strangely, thought the bartender. Although packed with patrons, there were a few empty seats from time to time as tables became available. This guy apparently wanted to sit in a particular place at the far end of the bar, directly across from the tables near the windows.

He spoke to no one and alternated his attention from observing the couple seated in his chosen place and punching his cell phone. The bartender noted that the two young men occupying a window table seemed to be the weird guy's object of obsession. A stalking, jealous lover, she figured. When one of the men left the table to use the restroom, the creepy guy followed him like a surveillance camera. The troller punched in data to his mobile with rapid finger movements as he followed.

***

When Roy returned to the table, he did not sit. Holding his cell, he said to Hudson in slightly hushed tones, "Hey, Boy, I just got a text from a source on the serial murder case. I need to meet him ASAP down in Dania Beach. He says he has some important intel for me about that preacher, Norton. Let's go. I'll drop you at your place."

"So, if it's OK with you, Roy. I think I'm going to stay here for a while. Mellow out a bit. I can Uber home."

"Cool." Roy shrugged and made a move for his wallet.

Hud extended his right hand over the table and moved it in a slightly circular motion.

"No, I got this."

"Thanks, Hud. If it's not too late, I will call you later. We need to get so into some nasty tonight." He moved closer for a kiss. "Talking hot, sweaty, headboard slamming, man sex, like we invented it— make you remember how a real man makes you beg for more."

Again, Hudson forced a smile that froze and faded as Roy turned and exited the club.

Catching the eye of his server, he pointed to the bar as he moved to occupy the nearest empty seat. The waiter brought the dinner check, and the bartender took his drink order. She returned with a brandy snifter shimmering with a golden green swirl of Cointreau.

Hudson Ch'en fought back the feelings of depression as he lightly swirled the brandy. Just what did he want in the big picture? Twenty-five, two relationships that crashed and burned in the last four years, what's next?

Hud intensely wanted Nick right now. The breakup had been quick but very painful. He also realized that missing Nick because of his cop overtime was a big part of being with him throughout the last few months. How fucked was that?

No, leaving him was best for both of them. He needed a man who made him his priority. With Nick in his own Marvel Universe, that would never happen. Also, there was an inverse correlation between Nick's libido and his obsession with his police work. As the latter swelled with intensity and he actualized his role as a crime-fighter, the former grew limp with disinterest.

He regretted having to attend Thursday's gala at the Museum. The exclusive VIP premier viewing of the new exhibit, *Seed Blood*, presented by the Preston Foundation, would draw many notables from South Florida's wealthy-- art philanthropists, religious hierarchy, business leaders, and politicians from Broward, Miami-Dade, and West Palm. The press would turn out in droves. He closed his eyes and saw the images of the sex clip. The event would further complicate his life, pushing him even more into the public eye.

He sipped his drink, thinking back to his boss' reprimand.

Seed Blood

"Mr. Ch'en, the Board has decided to take no major disciplinary action over this incident," said Thomas Mitchell Preston earlier this morning.

"We find that your involvement was a case of stolen identity. It was not your intention to bring salacious public interest to the Foundation. I would like to remind you that the Board voted to be the presenting sponsor for the Museum's new production. You are aware that I voted against it. The Preston Foundation is committed to being a private, behind-the-scenes philanthropic organization. Publicity of any kind is our nemesis, especially the public attention generated by the lurid activity on that tape."

He gulped, upending the brandy snifter. The burning liquor was like an anesthetic. What the fuck was he thinking? Nick would be at the opening. He had asked Roy to be his "plus one." What a recipe for disaster.

He reviewed the Roy situation once more. The deal with Roy was going nowhere, and he knew it. Better to face this at the beginning than get sucked into a repeat. The erotic passion was explosive, but if they continued to see each other, it would be a no-strings only. Roy was way too shallow to be his 'happily ever after.' Hud was resolved not to get tied down in another romance. Not for a long while, anyway.

Wanting to escape the madness of obsessing over the loss of Nick and the fear that murder had brushed terrifyingly close, he ordered another drink. The bartender brought Hudson a strange concoction.

She explained, "This is Queimada. It comes from Ukraine, compliments of the man sitting over in the corner. Made according to his clear instructions. It would seem you have an admirer, Handsome." She gestured over her shoulder.

The seat behind her was empty.

The drink was on fire.

Chapter Thirty: Prowl

NICK SECHI'S JOURNAL

"Yeah, sure. He comes in here a lot. A real creep. Into *muy* extreme sessions. You know what I mean?"

On his first break of the evening, the muscle boy looked up at me with an adorably cute, inquisitive expression. It was 12:30 AM, and he had started dancing in the cage at 10:00 PM.

Henry Moreno was Columbian, 23, and 5'9". He was definitely a "roid boy" but not on enough juice to get massive. He maintained a jacked and ripped physique, just swole enough to keep his different jobs as a trainer, barback, and very popular dick dancer who offered a few additional services.

His gig in the cage would bring him some big cash tonight. Prowl's monthly Fetish Dance packed in the leather men "balls to the walls." And they loved a hot, sultry, muscled-up cage tease willing to indulge their sexual fantasies. Also, they paid top dollar for one of his used jocks or leather thongs.

A landmark of the South Florida leather scene, Prowl raised a tent in the front parking lot and set up two full bars and displays of leather gear for sale for this standing-room-only event. At the height of the evening, leathermen would pack both the club and the rafters. The crowd would spill out onto the street and adjacent parking lots. Throughout the night until closing at 3:00 AM, cruising patrons paired up or left in groups for an evening of very edgy passion.

The club's music was house grind with a deep orgasmic baseline. The lights on the dance floor created a circuit party atmosphere of pin spots, laser beams, and jets of fog. A macabre cast of leathermen, boys, and occasionally women, appropriately costumed in fetish gear and dungeon wear, cruised and gyrated in the decadent, dystopian gloom.

Men in varying degrees of leather, some masked or hooded, some in chaps and harnesses. Most patrons were shirtless and in jocks and boots. They rubbed against each other, moving through the club, dancing, getting drinks, and pausing to make out in one of the many dark corners.

Armbands, keys on hips, colored insignia, tattoos, and piercings provided signals on sexual proclivities of the leather men and their "boys'—meaning anyone consenting to play a submissive role. On screens throughout the bar and on the back patio, porn clips looped above the patrons' heads and the smoke of the crowded establishment. Security passed among the determined revelers in an attempt to keep all contacts lawful.

Henry continued, "*Ay sí, Papi*, I know because a buddy of mine got into some real trouble with that *pendejo*. Many scars and bruises." I traced a healed wound on the front of his shoulder and raised one eyebrow. "A buddy, *chico*? You fibbin' to your Papi? Have you been doin' *la vida loca* with the brutal guys again?"

I had found a relatively empty corner of the back bar and bought him a beer. He put his hand on my naked chest as we spoke and pouted at my admonishing. He looked up at me through long lashes, making sure I knew that he found me attractive.

"Oh, no, *Nickito*, you know I am savin' *amore caliente* for you, only." Henry fake-sulked. He lied, and I smirked. "Plus, he was here that night with that hot white boy, the sailor. The one who got killed. Security had to bust them up three times. *Mucho* frisky, you know? Back by the pool table... he hold that boy by the throat. Scared your Henry when I saw."

He lowered his eyes and looked up at me with another so innocent but ready with the wild, passionate look he had perfected. Henry was seductive as hell tonight, but then again, he always was a fiery, energetic Latin boy. The kid loved a bigger man to take charge in a heated, ravaging mode—a man to keep him from getting scared and overly satisfied.

I just love undercover.

He pushed off from a lingering kiss and pointed to my chest. "You stay away from him. You are too *guapo* to mess with him with all those muscles and that hot *pelo rojo*. Henry remembers you are red down there, *también, si*? No, I forget. So, show your Henry."

He made for the top button of my codpiece. "Easy there, Chico." I pushed his hand away as the side of my face caught a beam of light from the dance floor, sending sparks and colors across our skins.

194

I leaned closer. "What can you tell me about Damon Santos? He danced here. You must know him. Any connection between him and the rough dude?"

Henry shifted uncomfortably. Looking around, he said, "I know nothing about that, Baby. I gotta be careful, *tu sabes*? Poor hombre, he really got messed up."

He glanced cautiously around the club and then back to me. Almost in a whisper and with a terrified expression, Henry said, "That guy you lookin' for, Papi, is a lot of trouble. Very angry and brutal with the gay boys. But do you want to know something? That devil, he cannot, you know...." He pressed my hand against the stiffness encased by the thin cotton of his jock. "Not like my *Nickito Caballo*. Is very strange."

He left my hand where he had placed it and gave me a wicked look.

"*Ay*, who did that to your eye, Papi?"

I moved my hand up to my cheek and said, "It's a long story, *mi sexy pedazo de culo*."

"Mmm... crazy hot masculine, Nickito." Henry mugged a bewitching expression as he pulled in closer and let one hand drop again to my groin. The near-naked muscle boy's voice was husky as sin as he said, "Listen, my last set is finished at three-thirty. How about we go to your place after and you can *cógeme* to hell and back? You remember, best you ever had. Sex with Henry will set you on fire, my Stallion."

The farewell kiss I gave him was firm but final and with no promise of a late-night hookup. I pulled back and said, "You see this guy we talked about, Henry, you tell me."

"*Sí, Jefe*. But you must promise to keep Henry out of this. I do not want trouble, and this *hijo de puta* is deadly, Nickito."

"So, just text me." I knew he had my number.

Around us, the bodies of the leathermen condensed in a swirl of alcohol, sweat, smoke, and testosterone. I blocked like an offensive lineman as we pushed through the crowd. We wove our way into the club and to his cage at the edge of the dance floor. He would remove his black jock in this set and use a hand towel to cover his privates as he danced for the leathermen and their boys. I stuffed three twenties into his waistband and slapped his hot ass as I moved off into the crowd.

***

Did you ever get the feeling that someone was watching you to the extent that the hair on the back of your neck stood up? This was a pretty ludicrous idea, given that one is in a packed leather bar at 2:30 AM, where heavy cruising is an art form. My leather drag included chaps – featuring my bare buns, a snap-on codpiece, black Wesco boots, a Muir cap, and a leather vest. The whole thing was so Al Pacino in "Cruising," circa 1980.

After his last set, I watched Henry climb out of the cage and head back to the storeroom to change. On the way, he paused to talk to a few patrons. He stopped to make a transaction at the door and walked bare-assed to a liquor closet to put on his street clothes.

I backed up to a bench on the far edge of the bar and stood in the dim lights. Overhead, porn images filled the screens with rough leather sex and fetish fantasies. To either side of me, couples made out with an intensity that was startling and liberating at the same time. As closing approached, patrons began the preliminaries of what would take them to other venues in a night of passion and lust. A very hot bartender in a black do-rag and mirrored shades on the farther side of the bar kept sending me complimentary "Mick Lites." The space between us was so crowded that the only thanks I could offer was a tip of the beer bottle, a touch to my cap visor, or a smile that I hoped he caught. He was super busy anyway and tempting as hell.

Looking over the bartender's head, I saw a man in full leather who was partially covered by the shadows in a corner directly opposite me. On his head, an executioner's hood obscured all but his nose and mouth. Strange that I could feel his frightening stare from across the room. His presence sent a sheet of sweat dripping down my torso.

He was a big man, and I was looking for a regular patron about his size. A much younger man approached him, and they talked a bit. As I watched, the dark stranger pushed the boy to his knees below my sightline and pulled the youth's head to his crotch. The man in the hood looked up at me across the bar space as he pushed himself against what could only have been the open-mouthed face of the boy.

Suddenly, a glint of steel, caught by a stray shard of light stabbing through the dark from the lighting array above the dance floor, flashed above the head of the boy. The crowd at that end of the bar, including the staff, were oblivious to the two caught in the fatal sex play. Drawing nearer, the big man was grinning at me like some monstrous fiend, his tongue hanging from the corner of his mouth. I lost sight of the boy and the knife as a group of three hefty men struggled to make way for me to pass through the crowd. I yelled into the throbbing din and pushed desperately through the liquored-up bar patrons between the predator and me. When I reached his corner, the would-be executioner was gone. The young leather boy was coughing and spitting but unhurt.

***

I left Prowl about 10 minutes later and headed down the walk of the first side street to my Mustang, hoping to catch the escaped demon. It was dark, and the shops on the block had been empty for hours. It was unusually warm, and I was sweating from the press of so many bodies at the club. I removed my vest.

As I passed a utility alcove in the darkest section of the walk, wedged between two storefronts, a body slammed me into the blind end of the tight enclosure. Before I could go on the offense, I felt the blade of the knife on my naked back just below my shoulder blades. With his other hand, the intruder pushed my face into the crumbling cement wall, rocking my head against the rough surface with the palm of his hand. He delighted in squashing my already bruised eye against the rock wall.

"You do not want to mess with me, Pretty Boy, or do you? Huh? Do you? Perhaps we are fated for a fatal encounter, and that is what you crave."

The killer kicked my legs wider in a broader stance, keeping me off balance and unable to break his hold in the cramped alcove. He pushed his lower body against my ass and thighs as he spoke with the huskiness that comes with insanity. "I possess unlimited power, boy. You cannot hope to overcome me."

I shifted, attempting to gain some leverage. However, the beast slammed closer with full-body contact. "Keep your hands high on the wall and listen to me carefully, Hot Shot," he growled in my ear. "Or I will open

197

you up and spill your hot blood." He leaned back a bit and skimmed the flat of the knife over my back.

I followed directions as he continued, "Your foolish attempts to thwart me last time have only succeeded in making me stronger. Although you feel my strength. I will soon unleash my full power." I felt his spit and the touch of his snarling teeth against my ear and neck as he hissed his threats into my soul. "I will enter you, boy. You cannot escape me, ever. I will possess you in your dreams. Totally mine. I am he who makes your balls shrivel with fear."

As he spoke, he returned to pressing his body against my back and legs. This time, his hold increased as if he would entirely contain and stop my breathing in a deadly full-body smothering. His mouth moved from my ear and across my cheek to an inch from my lips. He intoned, "Vengeance arises. Make no mistake; I will crush you if you continue to interfere. Your only choice is surrender."

The heat of his breath in my ear and on my neck was scorching. I squirmed slightly to gain an advantage, but he pushed again against me with the heavy weight of his upper body. My assailant worked his legs up so that he was mounting my splayed torso. I bucked backward, but he quickly pressed into me, his forearm against the back of my neck. Next, he slid off but stayed against me. I felt the blade and the wetness of his slobbering mouth as he continued to speak.

"You cannot stop me. Continue to annoy me, and next time, I will eat your fuckin' heart!" His nightmarish voice slowly ramped up with rage and hatred so that he scream-whispered the last part of his vow in the bestial shriek of an insane assassin. To emphasize his point, he slammed my face into the wall again. I felt the darkness coming and fought unconsciousness.

Our bodies were stuck together with sweat and spit. I remember we were both breathing heavily. The slaughterer continued his rage, his lips dripping foul threats and vile utterances of coercion inches from my left ear. "Shall I leave you with a souvenir, Officer, or save it for your boyfriend? He is sinful... yes... also begotten of corruption. No, some purifying fire for him, I think."

There was a commotion coming from patrons finding their cars and heading out. My attacker now began to move quickly. I felt the knife cut and the wetness of the seep and drip. I screamed into the darkness. It was over in a second. He stomped on the backs of my knees, and I went down. He left.

I slid down the rough cement, barely conscious. I was drowning in horror. In the opening of my cement prison, figures moved in the darkness and dim light.

The next sound I heard was three beeps from a cell phone in the doorway of the alcove. The silhouette of a tall figure filled the opening. "We have an officer down at...." The speaker gave the address. The pieces of my cognizance began to come together. Security, I figured... a 911 call. I struggled to stand.

I felt strong arms pull me from the cramped space and seat me against a store window, placing my discarded vest between me and the wall. I looked up to see the friendly bartender still in the mirrored state trooper shades and do-rag.

"Easy, Nick."

Kayne Sorenson caressed my wounded head like an errant lover, stood me up, and carefully put me into a fireman's carry across his naked shoulders, helping me to an approaching ambulance.

Thomas Paul Severino

Chapter Thirty-One: Confiteor

The man unlocked the links that held the gate closed. Stepping through the opening, he pulled together the chain and relocked it. He turned and entered the decrepit building through a service entrance door on the first floor, climbing to the top of the staircase to the fifth floor. He opened an abandoned suite that faced the river and the village beyond. The rear of old commercial one-storied buildings lined up directly across the water. From his sanctuary, he could see, along Dixie Highway, the industrial buildings of the Wilton Manors Municipality Compound, the stately buildings of the Pride Center, and the Portiuncula Complex with its glowing bell tower. The glittering ribbon of Wilton Drive snaked its way to the south from the busy Five Points intersection.

There was no electricity, but he liked the dark. Cell phone illumination was enough. Some candles and the city's light pollution below added to the obscurity. On the horizon, one building dominated downtown Ft. Lauderdale. The rehearsal of the lighting display for the upcoming Museum's gala opening sent gleaming spears of light into the night sky.

His space was spare and cluttered with a few books, bar publications, magazines, and empty takeout containers. There was a broken club chair left behind by the movers. He sat for a moment under a spray-painted rendering of the Archangel Michael at war with Lucifer on a wall that had once been someone's office. The opposite side had another rendering, that of the crucified Christ. The Savior's corpse ran with blood over the face and downward from the deadly crown of thorns. Rivulets of more blood seeped down the legs from flesh worn raw at the knees caused by the three stumbles under the weight of the cross. The gory slashes of the scourging covered the body of Jesus. Beneath this horror was written a single word, *Memento*, Remember.

His makeshift hideout was a refuge from the evils of the world. He knew he was transforming, becoming an angel of justice, a light bearer enthroned in the darkness above the city of sinners. The child had been collateral damage. Sometimes, you have to take a step to the side of evil to serve the light. He had no feelings for any of them. They would all see the coming terrible retribution. The holy fire will reign down... soon and very soon.

He removed his boots and leather gear and folded the pieces into a neat pile next to his street clothes. Kneeling naked on the bare cement floor, he took up the handle of the leather flagellum, the ends weighted with small shots of metal. He raised his eyes to his murdered Savior. He began the prayer, *"Confiteor Dei, Omnipotenti.* I confess to Almighty God...."

The first savage strokes over his left shoulder brought the blood. He did not feel the ripping cuts on his back and shoulders. The Penitent continued into the night until the blood pooled on the floor.

Outside, it started to rain. The psychopath left the office and descended the stairs without dressing to stand in the cleansing downpour amid the roar of thunder and the sky fire of winter lightning.

Drenched, he returned to his sanctuary and stood naked in front of the dark windows. In the reflection, the enormous wings of the Archangel spread out on the wall directly behind him. Naked and erect, he stared at the combined reflection. He was becoming an avenging warrior of the heavenly host. Forked bolts of light lit up the stormy sky, accompanying his furious movements and flashing the image on and off.

The mercenary of terror and righteousness cued up a video on his phone and placed the mobile where he could see it during the ritual. A trance descended like a shadow into his brain, and he heard the words over the gasping audio of the two men.

He would bring the light, the cleansing fire, soon... for He is like a refiner's fire... and He will purify the sons of Levi...

He brought the blood-stained knife to his mouth. His tongue and lips scoured the blade, taking the red communion. His other hand slid lower, and he closed his eyes, seeing only one person in his mind.

Pretty boy.

When he finished, he dressed. He watched the faraway lights of the Museum dim and fade in the storm. As he left the decaying lair, an open page of glossy advertising drew his eyes-- the Fritcher Museum's new exhibit.

Chapter Thirty-Two: Blade

Angela Brown couldn't sleep. She had tossed and turned since she went to bed at 11:30 PM. Images of madness filled her waking dreams. Dr. Sorenson's last assignment was a review of the research on contemporary American serial killers through history by modus operandi, signatures, and staging of some monstrous predations. She found it challenging to stop random thoughts of cannibalism, torture, rape, murder, and mass graves described in the profiles assigned to the class for review. This subject was humanity at its most savage. The winter rainstorm raging outside only heightened the mad, soulless atmosphere of destruction that kept her awake. She wondered where the light would come to hold such darkness at bay.

At 4:00 AM, she heard her roommate return. He went straight to his room, and the sounds of his TV came through the wall. Not long after, she heard him turn off the monitor. A bit later, she could hear him snoring.

As spooked as she was, she decided to change to reading a favorite novel from a small pile on the night table. Sitting up in bed, she snapped on the bed stand light. After a few minutes, the lamp flickered, and the power in the apartment went out. Lightning storms were always cutting the electricity in this neighborhood – old transformers. Angela decided to use the flashlight feature on her iPhone. Checking, she saw that she only had a seven-percent charge.

"Damn!" She thought.

Then, she remembered that her roommate had a storage battery charger. She tiptoed into his room and pulled his backpack over to the window of the bedroom. Two of the walls of the room were stacked with computer equipment, the likes of which always startled her. She knew he was a corporate web designer and a consultant on cybersecurity systems, spending hours at his keyboards and monitors each day. It appeared that many of the components had switched to battery backup because of the power outage. Small red and green lights blinked in the darkness.

Opening the heavy satchel, she stopped and searched for the charger. She knew the guy carried one around for emergencies. Her eye caught a pair of thick black leather boots near the night table.

Suddenly, her blood ran cold.

Strapped to the outside of the left boot was an ominous-looking weapon's sheath. A hunting knife was embedded in the nightstand next to the sleeping man. The handle and upper part of the blade were stained with blood.

Chapter Thirty-Three: Swab
NICK SECHI'S JOURNAL

I sat in the ambulance, answering Sheriff Crawford's questions as the paramedics prepared to dress my cuts and bruises. My face looked like chopped sirloin. A tall, slim woman sat to my right, applying antiseptic to my swollen and discolored right eye, cheek, and jaw.

"Took a nasty left hook there, huh, Champ?"

"Old wound, to tell the truth. The newly embedded grit is making it hurt like hell."

As she picked out the sharp specks, I winced at the application of the red-brown medicine and whined Chouko-like.

"Mercurochrome, tough guy. You'll live, and that kisser will heal good as new. You'll still be a handsome bruiser."

Prowl and the surrounding area were cordoned off for an extensive search. Most of the patrons were gone. The civilian excitement on the street was primarily due to the lateness of the hour. Patrol officers were going house-to-house in search of the fugitive. As Dian Crawford listened, I explained my encounter with the killer, omitting mention of Kayne's bartender incognito routine. Once he delivered me to safety, he too, melted into the night.

Despite having close contact with the slaughterer in the tight space of the darkened alleyway, I couldn't add much to the description details that would strengthen our attempts to identify him. Suddenly, I remembered.

Late into the encounter, a car, pulling out of a parking space close to the opening of the confining alley, cast a glaring light into the dark hole. The killer was in the process of making sure my left hand was pinned against the wall. For a second, I saw the design on the inside of his left arm.

"Wait! He had a tattoo. It was simple -- two lines, each forming an opposing crescent, joined at one end and crossed at the other. Hold on."

I put my hand up to stop the nurse working on my eye.

"May I?" I swiped a pen from her pocket. Turning to Dian, I drew the design on the inside of my left forearm.

"Looks like a fish," the doctor said and went back to treating my eye.

I looked at the Sheriff, hoping to get a response. "We'll get the description to the FBI folks and the detectives," she said. She instructed an agent to snap a picture of my "inked" arm.

Dian mentioned that yesterday her detectives had interviewed the Wilton Manors library staff with not much of an outcome regarding the spy camera used on my home. Many college students had been using the computers lately, and usage was very high on the night of the videotaping. Sheriff Crawford's tech team theorized that the killer programmed one of the PCs to record the camera feed from my house to a flash drive that had been left on the computer and was retrieved the next day.

"We are considering log-in sheets but are having little success. Most likely used a fake name."

"How about the coffin flowers with the same Latin phrase as in the first message, *Deo Gratias*."

"Phone order. Appears to have been with a stolen credit card."

"Dian, you or Mary get anything on that preacher, Cale Norton?"

"Very strange, Nick. I thought Mary told you. The Reverend was extremely belligerent about being considered a person of interest in this case. Believes his opponents are out to get him and that the press reported his words out of context."

"Seriously? Such a sleazeball."

"You got that right. Anyway, Norton has an alibi for each of the killing dates. But, it's his wife's word. She says they had gathered for private family prayer during those times. Kayne seems to think he does not fill the profile of a psychopathic killer. So, we believe we are pretty much stuck with just your Grade A homophobe."

"Jesus."

I felt gentle fingers on my back. The male member of the medic team was about to cleanse and treat the knife marks between my shoulder blades. I looked over my shoulder. "Nice back, man. Training is paying off," the cute responder said quietly and with a wink.

"Hold on a second, Mike," Dian said to him. "Officer Harris, look at this. She pointed to the knife cuts. Detective Tim Harris examined my last and rear delts and moved his close gaze up to the back of my neck.

"Looks like you got a nice cross going here, Officer. Bloody but not too deep. Won't scar much."

Harris paused, turning to the attending paramedic. He said, "Get me some of that... right there... see it? ... and up here." The attending paramedic reached for some sterile swabs and a couple of saline tubes.

Opening the swabs, he took samples from the wound and at the side and nape of my neck. He dropped the swabs in the tubes of saline.

"Officer Sechi," Detective Harris said, "Despite the scarification, it seems the killer likes you very much."

"I'm not sure I know what you mean?"

Looking at his boss, Tim Harris explained, "Some effluvium that is not perspiration... I think we got some saliva, and that could mean DNA."

Turning back to me, the agent said, "That monster tasted you."

***

Greg, the paramedic, covertly handed me his card in case I needed more "attention" to my wounds. As I stood up to exit the mobile medical unit, swabbed, antisepticized, and bandaged, attempting to leave on my own reconnaissance, my phone chirped. It was a text from Captain Robert Mays, one word, *Awake*.

I bolted from the ambulance, sprinted down the parking lot through the driving rain, and climbed into the driver's seat of my Mustang. I put my emergency light on my dashboard as cops lifted the crime scene tapes to let me leave. I took the shortest route to Broward General, speeding through traffic lights, my dash strobe flashing blue and white light shards into the newly rain-slicked, vacant streets.

Arriving at the hospital, I parked in the emergency room restricted area and, flashing my badge at the entrance, bounded down the corridor, taking the elevators to the ICU level. As the doors closed, I caught a look of myself in their mirrored surface. *Holy shit! My ass hanging out of my chaps and the leather vest will go over big with my boss. Fuck it. Welcome to Undercover in the Manors.* With that, the doors opened on the 4th level, ICU.

To say that nurses, doctors, and police officers stared in amazement would have been an understatement. I never saw so many open-mouthed gawkers. *S'matter dudes? It's not like a bare ass is out of place in a hospital.*

Chief Mays swiftly strode over, intercepting my approach to the doors of the glass-enclosed unit that housed the conscious Officer Eshani Shahnawaz and an assortment of life-support equipment. The upper portion of the bed was elevated so that Shan was in a partially sitting-up position. Staff had removed the breathing tube, and she was sipping the contents of a cup through a bent straw. Around her were members of the police department.

"Nick, you can't go in there."

"But, Sir, she's awake. How…"

Mays persisted in his attempt to stop me. "Her doctors said that at about 3:40 AM, she just came out of the coma. They are amazed at this stage of her recovery. She continues to be under observation to determine the extent of the damage from the bullet."

"Let me talk to her, Chief."

"No way, Nick. Shan is the prime witness in the Internal Affairs case against you. No *ex parte*." He had his hand on my chest, holding me back.

Mays continued, turning me back to the elevator, "Let's you and I talk about what happened tonight but not here. I heard you got into a bit of a scrape. I know Dian will compile your testimony and send it over to my office. I must say that I will not be pleased if I find out you were in pursuit mode of a dangerous criminal totally on your own, Officer."

As I turned to leave, I caught Shan looking at me in my bare-assed leather man's outfit.

She smiled.

Chapter Thirty-Four: Bind, Torture, Kill

NICK SECHI'S JOURNAL

"In our last class, we discussed possible brain abnormalities in the biological profiles of psychopathic criminals – specifically the connective tissue as compared to that which appears in normal brains. The research asks whether psychopathic behavior may be caused by a structural or functional abnormality within this brain area."

On the screen, Dr. Sorenson compared MRI images of brain scans of psychopathic and non-psychopathic criminals. He explained.

"Using electromagnetic imaging, we can see the abnormality here." His laser pen circled portions of the color images in each scan. "Please notice the normal brain shows more connective structures in the white matter than the brain of the psychopath. Notice and compare this structure."

He changed slides.

"This is the amygdala. Please explain its purpose."

Hands shot up.

Kayne selected Sélaisse Coquilleau, a young nursing student. "There is an amygdala on each side of the brain, there and there." She pointed to the images on the screen. Kayne followed with highlights. "They are thought to be a part of the limbic system, which is responsible for emotions, survival instincts, and memory." Her soft Haitian intonation gave her description an inviting sonic texture.

"Well done. Observe the scan of the psychopath's brain. It shows reduced functional connectivity between the cortex and the amygdala. Consequently, decreased brain connectivity is a characteristic neurobiological feature of psychopathy.

"Also, there is evidence of an association between this lack of brain connectivity and the male chromosome. The conclusion, therefore, is that the abnormality is grounded in the psychopath's DNA and not an acquired personality trait."

Professor Sorenson brought the lights up in the classroom. Looking a bit haggard, he stared down at his notes. An angry red cut over his left eye stood out in the beam of the podium light, as well as a fading black and blue patch on his right cheekbone and a swollen, split lip. He looked as if someone mugged him.

Looking up at the class, he requested, "Postulate for me using the research, please. How does this biological factor manifest itself in the behavior of the psychopath? Let us see who did some homework."

Jill Epson, in the third row, was quick to respond.

"The abnormal biology of the amygdala and the connective tissue of the cerebral cortex results in the personality characteristics we discussed. These are a predisposition to violence, a low tolerance for stressful events, and psychological trauma. Likewise, psychopaths do not typically feel nervous or embarrassed when caught committing a cruel act.

"Correct. The psychopath may literally lack the normal brain pieces to care what others think. Well done. What else?"

"Emotionally, they often are impulsive and high-risk takers. They do not feel empathy when other people suffer," another student ventured. "Unlike most people, the serial killer feels attracted to murder and death."

Kayne homed in on the last comment, "Yes, Mr. Barrows, the suffering they inflict characteristically causes feelings of euphoria, sometimes sexual fulfillment, and a sense of powerfulness. From childhood, the killer has a predisposition towards sexualized and aggressive fantasies."

The class was enervated and eager for more learning. Kayne pointed to a woman toward the back of the classroom. As he walked to the rear of the room, he said, "Dr. McGrath, please summarize for us the characteristics of the family environment as it relates to the psychopathic mind."

The white-haired, beautifully attired woman, seated three seats from me, stood to give her answer. "Traumatic childhood and adolescence experiences of serial killers are indeed significant. In an extremely disruptive family, the serial killer loses the sense of his reality. This reinforces his low self-esteem. But Professor, here again, the research is inconclusive and contradictory regarding childhood social trauma. I refer particularly to the stability of the home and the formation of the psychopathic personality."

"Please elaborate."

Barbara McGrath looked down at her notebook before responding with, "Although serial murderers like Charles Manson were abused and neglected children, the list of those with a normal childhood is extensive. Jeffrey Dahmer, Ted Bundy, and Dennis Rader grew up in healthy households with seemingly loving families."

"And does this research ring true with your experience as a family counselor, Dr. McGrath?"

"Yes, Professor. Many families I have counseled are at a loss to find the cause of their child's violently anti-social behavior. It is easy to see why so many in the past, and still today, believe in demonic possession.

"Fascinating. The reasons for serial homicidal behavior can be complicated. Resident evil, family environment, or chromosomal abnormality. Nature or nurture. Or even perhaps nature, nurture, or the devil? But let us stay with the science, please."

I had eased into the classroom through the back door shortly after class began in the dimmed light of the projector. My feelings remained unsettled in an alarming way over the events of the weekend, and Kayne Sorenson seemed to stand at the center of my emotional quandary. I grappled with his presence in my life. Getting struck by lightning in the romantic sense was turning out to be quite a bitch.

Additionally, for the last two nights, recurring nightmares resulted in more bouts of screaming. I tossed about the bed linens, with images of knives, blood, and dark concrete alleys swirling in my head. *What is it you fear, Officer?*

Sleep escaped me.

I was acutely aware that my feelings about the course and my professor had become very ambivalent. I sat back and observed as Kayne hit his stride. His combination of intelligence with personal charisma was both a highly accomplished educational style and a masterpiece of grand seduction.

"Let's look at the next series of topics for this evening. I have taken the liberty of sending you yet another compilation of the research on what we refer to as the killer's signature. Those of you with your electronics are free to pull these up. Others may take notes from the display."

He pulled up an outline while class members tapped away at their laptops and tablets or put pen to paper. "The signature of a serial murderer serves the psychological needs of the psychopath. To express this, he often poses his victims. This staging comes from emotions and symbols within the offender's psyche, reflecting a deep fantasy about his victims and his world vision. He is respecting a specific ritual order which is necessary to represent his personal worldview— a monstrous invention."

He strode around the room, aware that I was sitting in the back and not in my usual "teacher's pet" place in the front. Standing next to me with his back to the rear wall of the classroom, he continued, "Students, please review the summary provided by the Morelli study group of the previous class. Ms. Morelli and her group provided us with some valuable conclusions regarding the imaginary life of the psychotic killer. Liesl Morelli and her group members sat up at the mention of their summary.

"They reported that a psychopath's fantasy life develops slowly, increasing as time goes on. These notions are born of trauma and low self-esteem, assimilated even before he killed his very first victim. The killer creates his distorted view of life from relationships and behavioral patterns developed at a very young age. Childhood guilt, anger, and frustration build a schema of delusion that motivates the psychopath throughout his lifetime. Thus, a pattern emerges based on the choices he makes in his disaffected mind."

Without looking at me, he said, "Officer Sechi, condense for us the assigned research regarding the crime scene of a murder by a psychopath, please.' My inside voice said, *Sure, put me on the spot, Kayne. When the fuck do I have time to do classwork when I am running bare-assed all over town chasing some real, and not a theoretical, serial killer asshole?* I was sleep-deprived and running on pure caffeine and a bit more alcohol than usual.

The slashes on my back felt like they were open again and weeping into my shirt, so I sat forward in my chair. Using my outside voice to respond to Kayne's question, I stammered, somewhat incoherently choking on words with a slight rasping sound. The class turned in their seats to stare at what was rapidly becoming a fallen and slightly unbalanced superhero in this town.

"Well, Officer? Crime scene? Research?" And then, with of bit of an arch in his tone, he added, "We are waiting. But we can give you a moment to collect your thoughts if needed." Kayne kept his distance from me, now waiting for my reply at the front of the class.

He had been there to retrieve the ravaged aftermath of my late-night leather encounter. Why was he demanding such a Spartanly swift and stoic return to normalcy? I wanted to crawl into a hole and brood after my confrontation with pure evil. A thought crept into my restless mind about wanting to lick my wounds. Still, the disgusting image of the lips, tongue, and mouth of the maniac on my body shocked me out of my self-pity.

With conviction, I took a deep breath. I said, "Sir, it has been my experience with systematizing offenders that there are three separate crime scenes. First, where the killer approaches and abducts the victim. Second, where the victim is slain and finally, where the perpetrator disposes of the victim's body and, in many instances, stages the remains." I looked down at my open notebook. "The research into the methodologies of serial killers confirms my summary with certainty, most notably, Bhatt, Roy, and Westborough, et al."

Crushed it, boys and girls!

Kayne looked away with an unreadable expression on his face, offering no affirmation of what I had said. Having engaged me in the discussion, he was not willing to let me slink back into my dark reveries. He challenged, "I would like more elaboration, please. Criminal investigators sometimes find deliberate alterations of the crime scene or the victim's body position at the scene of the murder. Can you tell us why, Officer Sechi?"

"Right, the perpetrator alters any or all the crime scenes for two reasons: One, to confuse. Two, changes to the crime scene can be a part of the crazy play of the murderer for compulsive reasons. Posing can also be used by the perp to send a message to the police or public."

With an unreadable expression, Kayne said, "What message, Officer?"

Seriously? Are we really going to do this, Kayne?

I drew up with what little courage I had left and tried to steady my voice. I took a deep breath and continued.

"He wants us to know that he is a primal force, unrelenting, unstoppable, and aware of our darkest fears. He uses that power to crush anyone and anything that stands in his way. A bloodsucker emotionally and literally, this guy is...."

My fists were clenched, and I was full-out sweating. Aware that all eyes were on me in that stunned onlooker way, I stopped and tried to come to my senses. The awkward silence was unbearable.

Stay strong, Nick. Hold on.

A very nervous Angela Brown raised her hand. "Officer, how do these theories match with the current murders in Broward County known as the Palm Killer Murders?"

Still looking at me, Kayne nodded as if to say, *You can do this.* I stood and took the question.

"Unfortunately, I cannot be specific regarding the details of an ongoing investigation. I will say, however, that the case to which you are referring has many of the classic elements that Dr. Sorenson has mentioned in this class." I hoped that my switch into official tones had covered my meltdown.

Kayne quietly added, "Organized killers are very difficult to apprehend because they go to excessive lengths to cover their tracks. In addition, they often are familiar with police investigation methods. Put this is often paradoxical.

"Please allow me to clarify. So twisted is a serial killer's behavior that they attempt to foil the police while craving capture. They slip up. They leave clues. Unconsciously, the intensity of their crimes is too painful to endure."

As I came back from the brink of hysteria, I paused to make eye contact. In Kayne's gaze, I sensed the accusation regarding the lost boy was still there.

Kayne continued, "We must acknowledge the details of the relationship of the killer to law enforcement. In his mind, the police represent a flawed, puny attempt to thwart his avenging rampage, and he revels in toying with them before a fatal strike. I refer you to the notorious communications between Jack the Ripper and Scotland Yard, London, 1888 to 1891. He teased them in an infamous game of cat and mouse.

"The serial killer is adroit at preying on the mind of those who seek the beast. His weapons are fear, speed, and brute force. He will stop at nothing to obliterate the opposition. He attempts to punish all who stand in his way once he has attained the status of a super-being."

Kayne seemed to be winding down. With a note of weariness in his voice, he continued, "Law enforcement divisions international, federal, and local are elite units of the best men and women the profession has to offer. It is essential that these professionals keep their motives pure. By that, I mean staying focused on the data and experts' findings with a minimum of emotional response to the horror.

"The psychological dread of the crime fighter will create a diversion, an inability to act, or an overreaction resulting in the reckless endangerment of the public. One needs to control one's anxieties to fight crime effectively. Specifically, the law enforcer must be in total control — must be fearless and dispassionate in the pursuit. Fear, hatred, and passion fuel the beast."

I looked beyond him through the window into the night. *What is it you fear, Officer?*

Again, there was silence in the room.

Snapping back, I wondered to whom he was addressing his last remarks, the class, or was it a bit of unconscious soul searching, confession, and repentance? *Poor Hell Boy*.

Kayne pointed to the ceiling with one finger like an Old Testament prophet. "Where do we go when crime makes no sense? How do we catch a criminal when motive becomes elusive, the pattern becomes indiscernible, and emotions cloud our judgments?"

"Remember, the psychopathic killer is addicted to bloody mayhem, mentally, physically, and sometimes sexually. It is a fearful craving, this acute hunger for murder of the most depraved fashion. We talked a bit tonight about the fact that he is a divided soul. His addiction will be checked by his unconscious desire to be caught. He wants to end his own rampage.

"Only by building a psychological profile of the murderer from the evidence, based on an understanding of the research, can we enter the mind of the horror. And then..." he paused theatrically. The index finger of his left hand remained pointed upward as he rotated his gaze to take in the glances of the entire class.

His words hung in the air. He was Mesmer The Great, and we were his subjects-- a grand hypnosis unfolding.

"And then?" I asked.

He lowered his finger and pointed at me.

"One has no other choice. You draw close to evil and end it."

***

"I need to speak to you privately, please. It is very important."

Angela Brown had caught my arm as the class exited the room. While she moved over next to Kayne and got his attention, she addressed her request to both of us.

In his academic office, a few steps from the classroom, Kayne motioned for us to sit as he stood leaning against the corner of his cluttered desk. I remained standing.

"Early Sunday morning, I found this in my roommate's room."

Angela withdrew a hunting knife wrapped in a kitchen towel and carefully placed it on Kayne's desk. Dried blood caked the handle of the blade. I recognized it as the knife I saw inside Prowl and in the alley.

Kayne picked up the weapon, covering his hand with a handkerchief. It was sharp and deadly. "Ms. Brown, are your prints anywhere on this?"

"No, Dr. Sorenson."

"Does Jonathan know you have this?"

"Jonathan?" I was completely thrown off balance.

Angela shrugged her shoulders and answered excitedly, "By now, he does. I left before he awakened. I have not been back there since."

I looked from one to the other. "Jonathan?" I repeated.

Without answering, Kayne replaced the knife and reached into his satchel to remove a file. Extracting a single page, he placed it next to the murder weapon. It was a printout of a student's University ID picture. Beneath a blue and white Dodgers baseball cap, a face stared blankly -- Jonathan Yurick.

He lifted his eyes to meet mine. "Welcome to La La Land. It appears we have our killer, Officer."

Thomas Paul Severino

Chapter Thirty-Five: The Curious Dog in the Night

NICK SECHI'S JOURNAL

"You call Gints, and Gints is here."

The muscled-up beauty strode into Kayne's office, big arms spread wide, palms up as if accustomed to a fanfare whenever he entered a room. He plopped into a seat after giving Kayne a smooch, smiling at Angela Brown, and giving me a lascivious eye flash and fist bump.

I picked up my mobile, and Kayne introduced his muscle to his student. "Ms. Brown, my, ahem, colleague is the soul of discretion and, as you can see, very able-bodied."

I ended a call to Chief Mays' office requesting a patrol unit and SWAT team to Angela's Wilton Manors address, advising that the suspect was armed and dangerous. We continued our conversation with the young woman.

"Officer Sechi, I've known Jonathan for about four years. I had no idea he might be a dangerous person. He has always been very private and quiet."

She looked from person to person. "We met when we were undergrads and poor as all get out. We decided to share an apartment a couple of years ago to economize. He had been coming out of a bad time. I got the feeling it was the loss of a parent, but he would never say. He was also in the process of changing his job. When I chose to go on and get my graduate degree in criminology, Jonathon came along for the ride."

"Friends?" Kayne asked.

"None, nobody, in fact. Although, from time to time, I had the feeling he was seeing someone. He never brought anyone home."

"Jonathan works at home doing tech jobs free-lance, systems security, corporate web design, and marketing analysis. That sort of stuff. Lately, I had the feeling from some overheard conversations that his computer work was not exactly above board."

"Why do you say that?" I asked.

"So, he was getting some calls that he would take to the other room. I think they were about cyber surveillance for one of his clients. He kept telling someone on the other end not to worry, and no one would find out. Not my business, I remember thinking at the time, but then I began to wonder. I even looked for him on social media pages, but he had none. Told me he hated Facebook. Thought it put too much personal stuff out there."

"Ever talk about family?"

"Never. I got the feeling my roommate was an orphan."

"Can you tell us about his comings and goings from the apartment, Angela?" I expressly referred to the dates connected with the attacks on Christiansen, Murad, Santos, and Hell Boy.

"I'm afraid I did not pay that much attention to dates and times, Officer, to be honest. He went out at night a lot, often not returning until just before dawn, lately even more and more. I figured it had to do with installing cybersecurity for his client companies. His work occurred when offices were vacant. Once, I asked him. He said I was right and that he also liked taking long walks at night. He said it helped him to think. And that was cool with me. My teaching job is very stressful, so privacy and solitude at home are very attractive to me. In that way, he was an ideal roommate."

Kayne asked, "Forgive me. Were you and he ever romantically involved?"

"No, never. I have to say that I am completely in the dark regarding even Jonathon's sexual preference. He is a completely closed book on love and dating, at least with me. We never went into that aspect of our life together. If I brought a guy to the apartment, he would leave. I attempted to ask him to join my friends and me on occasion, but he had no interest."

"Jonathan was not in class this evening. Any idea where he may be?

"No, Doctor Sorenson. Considering he must have realized that I swiped the knife, I'd say he's either hiding or waiting somewhere for me. As I said, I have not been back to my apartment. I am staying with a friend he does not know. In coming to class tonight, I waited until just before the start to go into the classroom. I wanted to see if he was here."

I asked, "Angela, when you found the knife, why did you not take it to the police? Why wait a whole day?"

Angela looked at me and blinked back tears. She answered, "I'm not sure. I have been so conflicted about this. Like I was frozen or something. Perhaps I could not come to grips with the fact that I had been living with a killer who knew a lot about my family and me."

She looked down and continued, "Jonathan has a nasty temper. I guess I thought he might find a way to come for me. He once bragged that he was so technologically savvy that he could outmaneuver even the most sophisticated surveillance. I just don't know. Finding that was such a shock. I have felt so frozen since the night before last. I'm sorry. I decided yesterday to turn it over to you after class tonight."

"Did you and he ever discuss the Palm Killer murders or the subjects covered in this course?"

"No. I asked John to study with me once, and he just blew it off. I figured he really had no interest in the highly publicized murders or this class. He seemed very superficial about this course and the people in it. No real buy-in, sort of like he was going through the motions.

"I'm afraid he did not share much enthusiasm for you or your methods, Professor Sorenson. He also did not like that you were in class, Officer Sechi. He mentioned you a few times and not very respectfully. Referred to you as 'teacher's pet.' I remember thinking that he sounded like a jealous kid. "

Kayne looked away and then back at Gints and finally back to Angela.

"Angela, I'm afraid your life right now is in grave danger. You have inadvertently shattered his fragile identity, and your obstruction of his fantasy will cause him to lash out with dangerous fury. Officer Sechi will see that you have police protection, but I want you to allow Gints to stay close to you. Is that possible?"

Angela Brown seemed to shrink before our eyes. She trembled visibly. "Um, I am not sure. My friend with whom I am staying...."

"No, that will not do, I fear," Kayne interrupted. He picked up his cell and, stepping away for a moment, made a call from his list of favorites.

221

I took the time to ask, "Any idea where Jonathan would go if he decided to go underground? I'm pretty sure that when the police arrive, they will find he is not at your place."

"No, Officer. I have no idea."

Kayne returned to the group. "Ms. Brown, Gints will take you to stay with a friend of mine. We must make sure Jonathan will never be able to track you there. We are dealing with a hunter, my dear, and we need to take appropriate precautions."

Kayne looked at me and said, "Rebecca."

"But, Dr. Sorenson, my family, my job."

"I advise that you continue to call in sick until we resolve this."

Angela nodded. "I do have a bit of sick leave."

He nodded to Gints, who stood and, with sincere gentility, took both of Angela's hands in his.

"Let's go, pretty lady. All is well when you are with Gints. No harm will come."

"You two." He said before turning to exit. "You get his fucker, yes? But is more important you take care of each other." He left but not before eyeing us both with a quizzical look on his face that implied, *What's up with you two, anyway?*

"One more thing, please," Kayne said to Angela.

"A landscaping company trims up the shrubbery around your apartment complex each month, I would surmise. They do not haul away the branches. Rather, they leave them for bulk trash pick-up. Can you confirm, Ms. Brown?"

Angela turned with an astonished expression that communicated, *Why ever should that matter?*

She answered, "Why, yes."

***

Once we were alone, Kayne shifted uncomfortably and then began to pace. Doing the signature sweep of his forehead, he avoided my eyes and addressed some new facts of the case.

"The flora around the Brown/Yurich place will be found to contain *Phoenix theophrasti,* date palms. Upon analysis, the blood on this knife will be found to be yours. It is interesting how it is confined to the upper part of the blade and absent from the lower part and the tip, considering your scarification. He has partially wiped it or...."

He did not finish the sentence. The hair at the back of my neck stood up, and I felt flushed – either anger or nausea at the thought of my blood licker. I turned away and unconsciously massaged the back of my neck, feeling the wetness of newly oozing blood lower down on my back.

Very quietly, Kayne added, "Furthermore, the police will confirm this knife as the murder weapon used on the poor dead child near the railroad tracks."

"If you would, please take charge of the evidence." This last sentence was said in a hushed tone as he gazed into the night through the window of his office. He seemed very remote or even confused.

"Of course."

He looked at my reflection and, noticing my stiffness, said, "How's your back?"

"Fine." I lied.

Hud always said I had trouble talking about emotional issues. There is a typical emotional paradox, at times, within my Italian American family. Significantly, we often shout, "I love you" and "I hate you" in the same tone of voice. Yet, no matter how passionate we were, when it came to some sensitive issues of the heart, our mantra was often "I don't want to talk about it." Sometimes, we are the masters of repression.

Apparently, the same dynamic applied to Kayne.

In the past three weeks, we had crossed some personal boundaries, especially considering the occurrences at Quads and Prowl. It was apparent that each of us was struggling to re-establish a purely professional relationship in the insanely high-charged atmosphere of the

Palm Killer Case. With the chaotic collapse of my relationship with Hudson Ch'en, I could not be sure of the authenticity of my feelings for someone as attractive as Kayne Sorenson. Emotionally, I wanted to run.

So, as men do all the time, we avoid unfinished and unspoken personal issues. We focused on the job, anticipating the killer's next strike. I imagined what Rebecca's reaction to our evasive behavior would be. *Fuck, Darlings, say what you have to say and get back in bed. Then you can tromp on this guy's ass with impunity.*

Kayne felt strongly that the killer would ramp up his activities with acute savagery now that we were getting closer. We talked a bit about the possibility of multiple murders. I could see the headline "Palm Killer's Grandest Act of Murder. Police baffled."

He touched the window glass in a self-conscious move.

"By this time tomorrow, the dragnet for Jonathan Yurick will extend across the state and begin to go nationwide. The tri-force investigative team, headed by Mary Chaffee, will continue tracking every lead with precision while sharing crucial intel with us. The press has reinforced panic in the community. Consequently, every attempt continues to be made by the team, however unsuccessfully, to keep elements of the case from leaking."

He continued, "Nick, you do realize that he has focused his rage and sexual obsession on you. We have to use that to stop him. Not only is he hunting you, Nick, but you also continue to be his mouthpiece. This is how he keeps his illusion of power and terror alive. We need to exploit that fact with extreme caution as we draw the net tighter. We know who he is, and he knows we are coming for him."

"You are talking about using me as a lure." I walked to the window a bit of a distance from him and looked out into the city's nightscape. I shifted in my t-shirt, the back sticking and pulling.

He looked over at me and answered, "Unfortunately, yes. But carefully and protectively." I slowly turned to face him as he continued, "You have had intimately close contact with him."

He paused as if to let this sink in.

"And, typical of the psychopath, he is toying with you. I believe he has marked you for a significant role in a spectacular denouement of power and destruction. He is transforming into what he considers an all-powerful being, and the act of possessing you, he envisions as the apotheosis of his complete investiture with demonic power."

Kayne turned nighty degrees and faced me. I continued to look into the dark night.

"I am of two minds regarding our expanded partnership with the police and the FBI and their ability to catch him at this time. The potential for them to bungle the operation could result in more lives. On the other hand, we need to make sure you have adequate protection. You are his prey. He will continue to stalk you and destroy you."

My fists clenched, and I felt myself redden with rage. I turned my back to Kayne. Defiantly, I thought of the night monster who haunted my dreams. *Bring it, fucker*!

After an excruciating silence, the anger began to subside. Without looking at him, I said, "Kayne, um, I... about the boy ..." I stopped without the words to continue.

Kayne stepped closer, and looking at my reflection in the glass, he said almost in a whisper, "May I help you with your wounds, Officer? You seem to be bleeding. I have a first aid kit in my file cabinet." He touched my shoulder and turned me to face him.

The beauty I found in his soulful stare floored me. I felt an almost overpowering need to pull him into an embrace, climb into his back pocket, and stay there forever. What was I after? Security? Protection? Passionate sex? Love? Lately, I had pretty much destroyed all of that in my life.

In my mind, I heard Hud's accusation. *Do you superhero types ever stop to consider how those who love you feel? Because it feels like... no, it is like death, and it draws closer by the minute.*

Then, an eerie overlay sounded in my head. *What is it you fear, Officer?*

Kayne reached gently to take me in his arms as I stood riveted to the floor, fighting to control my emotions. This resulted in a sudden reflex

225

reaction – a premonition of blood and destruction. My pulse raced. I broke into a sweat and pulled away from him.

"Sorry. I just need...."

"Nick, may I just say how... please, can we...?."

He stared perplexed as I avoided his blue-steel bedroom eyes and interrupted with, "Thank you, Professor. I think I'll just head home."

I backed up and walked to the door.

"Good night."

***

Chouko was raising holy hell, racing through the house.

I rolled over and climbed out of bed, removing my Glock 17 from its shoulder holster hanging from the corner of the headboard. I noticed the digital display. It was 3:37 AM. Someone was in the yard.

Walking through the dark house, I peered through the patio doors into the far corners of the yard while pulling on a tee shirt and gym shorts. Something was happening where the landscaping brought together the back wall and the side privacy fence. The motion detection lights were on, but deep shadows gathered in some spaces just beyond the beams near the cabana house.

I could see the toes of his boots where the shadows ended. He was there in the corner, standing still. As I became fully awake, I felt my blood turn to ice in the all too familiar images of darkness and danger in the night.

Remember your training. Check the corners. Make a silent approach.

Going back for my cell phone, I called for backup.

Chouko barked and threw himself at the glass, growling and baying in a frenzy. I slowly slid back the patio door. Before I could signal the dog down, he raced past me and headed for the intruder at the far end of the yard. So much for a silent approach. An acrid smell filled the yard. There was a spark of a cigarette lighter in the dark.

Seed Blood

I stepped out onto the patio, ducking behind a pile of stacked deck chairs. I called out to the intruder. "Drop your weapon and move to where I can see you."

Chouko took his position in the open yard between the stranger and me. Fearing for him, I dashed forward and hit my stance behind a palm tree. A blinding instant later, the pool exploded in a roaring conflagration. The surface of the water erupted in flames six feet and higher. I hit the lawn with a roll to the slide away from the pool and against the house's foundation.

Looking up, I saw Chouko in mid-leap. His body twisted impossibly as the bullet hit him. My dog crumpled to the ground, his maniacal baking ending in a whimper.

The yard, the house, and the perimeter wall blazed with the reflection of the roaring flames, a surreal inferno that was the burning swimming pool. Dashing forward to the cover of the cabana house, I heard the sirens from the Wilton Manors police cruisers arriving in the neighborhood.

Coming around to confront the intruder in the corner of the yard, I stopped, gun raised.

He had vanished.

Chapter Thirty-Six: Anselmo

NICK SECHI'S JOURNAL

"The surgeon removed a bullet from his neck where it lodged near his collarbone after passing through his skull. The team of veterinarians made extensive repairs to the surrounding tissue. I am not sure what effect it will have on his brain. To be honest, that is unknown territory. The bullet missed important blood vessels on its way out of his skull. Right now, it is too early to tell. He is strong and has every chance of making it through. But, Nick, we just don't know."

I had been staring at the floor, too numb to think about anything but my "Beautiful Butterfly." I looked up at the chief veterinarian as he continued.

"Now, all we can do is wait, Nick. I have your number should we have a significant change. My office will keep you updated as things progress."

"Thanks, Mark," I said to my family vet. I wanted to stay and wait to find out, but Kayne and I were scheduled to follow up a lead not too far from the animal hospital.

"What about you, Nick? You look really worked over."

I had gathered up the body of my Butterfly and raced past the arriving police and fire departments. I felt Chouko's labored breathing against my chest. The animal hospital was a few blocks away. The paramedics launched into action to get him and me to the vet.

While Chouko was in surgery, I briefed the police, who followed us to the hospital.

"I'm ok, Mark, thanks. All in a night's work."

"I'll let you know how it goes, but it may be a while."

Still in shock, I repeated my thanks.

As I left, I asked my colleagues to drop me home.

***

"Professor Sorenson, the man in this picture, entered our Juvenate when he was 14. Yes, I know exactly who he is."

"I'm sorry, Brother Fintan. Juvenate? Please explain," I asked.

"Certainly. At St. Anselmo's, we ran a high school for prospective members of our order. Upon graduation, these boys could be accepted into our Novitiate and begin their year-long preparation for first vows as members of our order. New brothers profess poverty, chastity, and obedience each year for three years. If the novice passes scrutiny, they can profess perpetual vows. Some in our community go on to ordination."

"We had a ridiculous custom back in those days to identify our own. This is my class mark." He rolled up the sleeve of his brown habit to show a tattoo on the inside of his forearm. It was a crude Celtic Cross. "Most of my classmates were Irish Americans. Each Novitiate class chose a different and unique design."

Kayne asked, "Brother, tell us what you know about this design, please." Kayne took out a small notebook and drew two facing curved arches, one on top of the other. They touched at one end and crossed at the other. "Do you know the significance?"

"I believe I do," answered the little monk. He explained as he took up a yardstick from his desk, standing with it as if it were his walking stick.

"In the early centuries of the Common Era, it was illegal to be a Christian in many parts of the Roman Empire. Christian travelers would identify themselves to strangers when entering a new region by drawing an arc in the sand."

Imitating an approaching pilgrim, he illustrated using the yardstick sweeping across the tiles in a half-circle at our feet.

Realizing mid-story that Kayne was familiar with the lore, Brother Fintan handed him the yardstick, and Kayne took up the narrative. "If the welcoming Roman was a fellow believer," he came around to the other side of the scribed arc. "The host would put the tip of his walking stick here and trace its opposing image overlapping the ends of the two arcs. The result was the outline of a fish-- in Greek, *Ikhthus*. Written in the and in the Cyrillic alphabet, it is a mnemonic for the Christ."

230

"Yes, indeed. Correct. A secret sign like a password." Brother Fintan smiled with eyes twinkling. "Well done, Dr. Sorenson. The school lads in our Juvenate were mere children and loved games of that sort. I was no exception." He rolled down the sleeve of his habit, covering his tattoo.

"I was the director of that program," he continued, "until we decided to close it down. You see, there were some, um, improprieties regarding the staff and the students." Brother Fintan looked away for a few minutes.

After a pause, he said, "That was indeed a terrible time for many in the Church, especially the youth."

He took a breath. "This boy's home life was quite unhappy and very volatile. He came from a wealthy family and, from an early age, began to show some very aggressive and rebellious behavior in previous schools. His counselors believed it was pent-up aggression toward his father. By enrolling the lad in our high school, the family thought we could correct his unruly behavior.

"Upon completion of his sophomore year, the boy requested admission into the Juvenate, but Jonathan's father resisted his entry into the order at first. I saw the request as a rebellion of the boy against the father. Regardless, many of the brethren felt that the boy had an intense desire to serve God – a passion, in fact. There was, apparently, a scene in private, and the next thing we knew, the father signed the acceptance papers into the first program."

"Although very devout, Jonathan was a questionable student throughout the two-year Juvenate program. His grades were average and slightly below standards. Without many friends, he usually kept to himself. He had his prayers and his computers. Very interested in the lives of the saints, he spent many hours in the Abbey library. He was a technology expert and brought our operations into the modern age, both here and at the Abbey. Whereas his religious fervor was exemplary, he seemed unable to connect with his classmates or teachers. A bit of an air of superiority, I'd say. And then there was the business of the animals."

"The animals? Do you mean at the Monastery?"

"Yes. You see, toward the middle of Jonathan's junior year at the high school, we began to find some of the livestock mutilated over a year or so. The police never found out who was doing this. At the time, many thought that vagrants on the property might have been responsible. This was when Jonathan was having trouble convincing his family to consent to his admission to our Novitiate, the next step towards the profession."

Taping the picture of the man, Brother continued, "This young man, following his first profession of vows at the end of his Novitiate, took the religious name of 'Jonathan.' It is our practice to reject our 'name in the world' and choose a new 'name in religion.' When we profess vows, we are taught we become a new person, empowered in the Spirit. We believe that we leave the old person behind. My birth name was Kevin, you see. Now I am Brother Fintan, named after an Irish saint."

"Throughout his Novitiate, Brother Jonathan became a very close friend of the Assistant Novice Master, Father David. Too close, to be honest. I became aware that they referred to themselves, and others took it up as well, as the David and Johnathan of the Hebrew Scriptures, inseparable, heroic male lovers.

"Now, in religious life, we have a maxim, 'Seldom one, never two, often three.' This rule was meant to discourage particular friendships and the risk of improper behavior. Nevertheless, Brother Jonathan and Father David persisted in their closeness. Their relationship came to be common knowledge. I advised my confrere of caution. Johnathan found in David the father he had sought throughout his tender years. Father David found... but I am getting ahead of myself."

The little monk stood up and walked to the window to stare at the parking lot, where a significant number of homeless people were lining up for the medical and social services provided by the Center. He was pensive and silent.

"Please continue, Brother Fintan," Kayne said in a soft, reassuring voice.

Still gazing through the window, the little friar continued, "Please allow me to backtrack a little, gentlemen. We had accepted a substantial gift from the family at the time of their son's admission to the high school program. Jonathan's family built and endowed this center for our urban ministry to the poor. They insisted on no public recognition for their generous donation."

Kayne and I exchanged a look as Brother Fintan continued.

232

"Upon his eighteenth birthday, when his father could not prevent it, Jonathan petitioned to be received into the Novitiate. I was the lone vote against his acceptance, but Father David had some influence on the order's leadership by then. Specifically, Father David was a very gregarious fellow with many supporters in the order's leadership. He also worked with Jonathan's family to continue funding this Center. He convinced the boy's father that the order and the Center were Jonathan's future. There was talk of expansion of services, and this, unfortunately, led to certain matters being overlooked."

Kayne asked, "Was a gregarious fellow? You speak of Father David in the past tense."

"Yes, Father David became director here in the years preceding the end of his life. Young Brother Jonathan served as Director of Operations here with him. The youngest to hold that position. Fr. David died, unfortunately, five years ago. A long struggle with HIV/AIDS tragically compromised his health."

The monk was silent, staring off through the window at the Portiuncula's chapel with its high bell tower. He pointed to the foot of the six-story tower crowned with a cross. "We found him out there. He jumped when he could not stand it any longer. I honestly do not know how he made it up those stairs without help. His entire body had just about shut down."

Kayne murmured as if in a trance, "James, the Brother of the Lord."

"There was some controversy with the Archdiocese when the news of his death became public. Suicide has always been troublesome in the Church. Poor Brother Jonathan took this very hard and left the order and the Church, I believe, soon after his friend's death."

Brother Fintan rustled through some volumes in his library, producing a file that he handed to Kayne.

"Here is the personal file of Brother Jonathan from his acceptance through to his graduation and entrance into the Novitiate. I am not quite sure why I have it. When I took over as Director of the Center, I brought it from the Abbey. Young Brother Jonathan was so very bitter after the death of Father David. I remember how much rage and hate he had inside. He seemed to strike out on all sides."

As he took the papers and turned through them carefully, Kayne asked, "Brother, what was Father David's name in life?"

"James Yurick."

Kayne looked at me as the shock of the last statement hit both of us. The student in Kayne's class, Jonathan Yurick, had left the religious order and had taken the last name of his beloved friend. They were joined in life and death.

After reading the papers, Kayne handed me Brother Jonathan's application to join religious life in the Monastery of St. Anselmo. He lifted the index finger of his left hand and brought it down on a line near the top of the first page.

Kayne had pointed to the entry filled in under the heading "Name in the World."

Holy shit!

Chapter Thirty-Seven: Police Work

Bob Mays was working late on a Friday night. He longed to start the weekend with his family but needed to tie up some important loose ends. He sat in his office and reviewed the current paperwork on the third victim of the Palm Killer. The Chief set the file aside and picked the investigation reports of the shooting of the 17-year-old drug dealer from mid-December. Mays scanned the official forms.

Internal Affairs read Officer Nicola Sechi's testimony into the record. They deposed him two days after the shooting of the 17-year-old, which resulted in the death of the youth. His lawyer accompanied him, and Nick provided details of the incident. Officer Sechi had met with the officers from Internal Affairs in the bandages from the chest wounds resulting from the young man's attack. His Kevlar vest stopped the bullets, but the three shots had resulted in deep, painful bruises, as indicated by the medical reports. The impact knocked him onto his back in the darkened crack house.

When asked by IA to explain his decisions in this enforcement action, the Officer provided several justifiable reasons to show that shooting the boy to prevent the assassination of his partner was according to standardized protocols, i.e., within the guidelines for encountering an armed and dangerous suspect holding a hostage. He provided evidence from his shoulder camera regarding the severity of the situation, namely the dead bodies of the mother and sister, the murderer's heightened state of agitation, and a relatively clear video of the capture and restraint of Officer Shahnawaz.

In addition to the charge of shooting and killing a minor, IA accused Nick of dereliction of duty by taking a fatal risk at the climax of the stand-off with the young drug addict. Further, the investigation confirmed that the boy and not Nick had shot the police officer.

Because the only other witness to the shooting remained comatose, the compliance review hearing, designated by law to be conducted within ten working days after the request, was delayed by an agreement of both the officer and the Department of Internal Affairs. An alternate date would be set following the recovery of Officer Eshani Shahnawaz of the Wilton Manors PD or her demise.

Shan met with the Compliance Review Committee in her hospital room at Broward General to answer their questions 24 hours after returning to consciousness. Nick's testimony was a matter of record. The Board would issue its ruling in the coming weeks.

Closing the file, Mays next reviewed the plan to provide enhanced security at the Art Museum's new exhibit scheduled for the following evening. He had briefed assigned officers just a few hours earlier. Dr. Sorenson was sure that the Gala would be an opportunity to catch the Palm Killer. So far, the murderer's whereabouts still eluded law enforcement.

Cathy Wayne, head of cybersecurity, stuck her head in the door. "Got a moment, Chief?"

"Sure." Mays waved her in. "Whaddya got?"

The petite Pakistani American woman took a seat opposite May's desk. She explained, "We have a very sophisticated asshole out there, boss."

Mays tried hard to switch his exhausted brain into a very focused mode. Cathy was a technology expert but tended to forget the rest of her colleagues, including him, were not. He had to very carefully try to decipher what she was about to say because he knew it would be like a foreign language for his non-technological mind.

He said, "This is about the security breach from the Palm Killer, correct? So, how'd he get in our system? And tell it to me like I am in the second grade."

Cathy nodded and continued, "Evidence is showing this is a zero-day attack, Boss." Mays raised his eyebrows, signaling to her that she had already lost him.

"OK, so the attacker engineered a malicious software that opened a vulnerability window, allowing him to manipulate Officer Sechi's computer and our network before we were made aware of the threat."

"How did he get through the firewall, Cathy?"

"Firewalls do reasonably well as mitigation against network breaches, but they are not infallible. These days, my team spends most of their time processing, testing, reviewing audits, and preparing documentation to take advantage of the latest security patches."

She added, "As I said, this guy is good. We looked at the latest attack weapons like exposed servers, forged IP addresses, and rogue wireless access points. We came up with a methodology that is as simple as it is effective. He had physical access."

"Cathy, you mean he got on one of our computers. That's not likely with visitor security, passwords, and the like. Are you telling me the killer is an employee of the Wilton Manors Police Department?"

"Possible, and that would suggest a disgruntled employee. But I am going to say 'no' to that. Most likely, he used a method we call Sneakernet. Specifically, he introduced the Stuxnet worm or something like it with an infected USB flash drive via an unaware employee. That is how he was able to get control and send the two messages."

"I thought we had protocols for portable drives."

"Boss," Cathy looked at him with a wry expression. "Rules are only as good as the people who follow them. Not everyone follows instructions."

Mays thought of Nick Sechi and grunted.

Cathy said, "So, circling back. The killer plans this well ahead, right? He gives someone on the Force an infected flash drive. So, that could have been some time ago because of the zero-day scenario. When my department sweeps for incursions, it is too late. The worm is already in the system. We think we have neutralized it, but it lies dormant, waiting for a programmed code to set it in operation – most likely a date and time. Bingo, the asshole has accomplished breach and has control."

"Anything traceable, Cathy? We need to find this guy."

"Not yet. As I said, this guy is genius-level. We continue to work on it."

Mays said, "Thanks, keep me in the loop."

Cathy stood up to leave. "Boss, you need to head out. You look like hammered shit."

Mays chuckled at the candor of his Security Officer. "Yeah, lotsa hours and a big deal at the Museum tomorrow night."

Cathy Wayne stopped at the door and addressed her superior, "One more thing. I know from the briefing that you are working on a sting at that Gala. Boss, make sure your team does not use their cell phones and stick to their communicators. Likewise, the FBI."

Why?"

"Ever hear of iSpy?

"The 60s TV show?"

"Boss, I was not born until '92. So, that means nothing to me. iSpy is one of the best cell phone hacking tools, illegal but highly effective. Your perp has the level of sophistication to be using this program to track targets and manipulate their phones. That puts him close. Real close. And capable of some serious confusion."

"What you're telling me is that the extra security I am putting on the lure for the killer can't let the bait know he's being watched. He or his security can't use their cell phones without blowing their cover."

"Yes, with one adjustment. Let the setup guy use his phone – that's the trap, Boss. Your guy will draw the freak into the trap."

The Captain thought, *Provided the lure isn't nutso himself – freakin' Hot Shot.*

Mays turned to look through his office windows on the mid-January night, an eerie glow lighting up Wilton Manors and Ft. Lauderdale.

Chapter Thirty-Eight: Seed Blood
NICK SECHI'S JOURNAL

On a scale not seen in South Florida, the unique lighting design for the long-anticipated opening showered Ft. Lauderdale in elegance. Rebecca's team had hired a French company to produce a *Son et Lumière* spectacle comparable to the dramatization of historic places like the Great Pyramids, the Palace of Versailles, and the Parthenon. The international design company used the palate of Downtown Ft. Lauderdale to sensationalize the event of the season. Grants, sponsorships, and individual contributions for the exhibit enabled the Museum to create a stunning affair.

At city crosswalks, pedestrians stepped across a light-generated logo for the exhibit that splayed across the sidewalk and seemed to appear out of nowhere. Within a five-block radius of the Fritcher Museum of Art, surrounding buildings dripped in scarlet. At the same time, symbols of the Roman Empire in the early centuries of Christianity cascaded across any flat surface in the urban landscape above street level. Spotlights sent revolving beams into the night sky, reflecting off the glass high-rises as well as the waters of the New River and its bridges surrounding Museum Plaza. Blood red and gold splashed the Broward Center for the Performing Arts at the west end of the downtown Riverwalk.

Seed Blood had arrived!

Spiraling ruby, gold, and white lights bathed the white monolithic surfaces of the Museum itself. Here moving religious figures and symbols paraded above the VIPs assembling in the central courtyard. Giant feather banners framed the entrance with the logo and images of the new exhibit. A gobo projector lit up the pylon directly to the left of the gateway with gigantic letters of the exhibit's title, *Seed Blood*, in their signature colors.

In the circular drive off SE 2nd Street, valet parking attendants were dressed as *tirones*, basic trainees in the Roman Army. The attendants jumped into luminous Cadillacs, Bentleys, Jaguars, and Teslas as they emptied occupants between the sleek limousines and gleaming town cars. I recognized a few as undercover cops. From time to time, scattered across the plaza, I saw a "suit" speak into his wrist.

Guests stepped onto the red carpet dressed in their most exquisite – jewels, winter furs, and latest designer fashions. City, county, state, and national leaders turned out together with the heads of the corporations and not-for-profits, as well as Fine Arts leaders from as far away as the Hermitage in St. Petersburg and the National Museum in New Delhi. In the background, the baroque strains of the *Dies Irae* from Mozart's Requiem filled the courtyard.

Day of wrath and doom impending, heaven and earth in ashes ending.

Clergy, decked in cassocks, capes, veils, and pectoral crosses, sported the traditional colors of their religion, red, black, or purple. The Orthodox Metropolitan arrived from Miami in long, flowing black robes with a small retinue of priests and nuns. His Excellency the Patriarch leaned upon a gold and jeweled crosier topped with a pair of dragons curled to face each other. The ornate symbol of his spiritual authority evoked the bronze serpent made by Moses in the Book of Numbers.

Orthodox, Reformed, and Conservative Jewish leaders from South Florida were in attendance. Some were conspicuously dressed in the Tallit, the prayer shawl of sacred tradition. Some young community members sported the *yarmulke*. They moved through the outdoor gathering space designed like an ancient forum filled with various faiths and cultures representatives.

Near the fountain in the Museum Plaza, an Imam made his way forward with members of his flock. The "Shepard of the Faithful" trailed the folds of the prestigious, black *bisht* cloak while nodding in his immaculate white turban as he made his way to the entrance of the Museum with his striking entourage. The men in his company were stunning, with dark eyes and close-clipped facial hair – an array of Eastern princes. Some in flowing white *thawbs,* others in hand-crafted Italian suits, they tossed the ends of their red and white *keffiyehs* over one shoulder as they ran interference for the regal spiritual potentate.

A trio of Armenian bishops in black conversed with a small group of Nigerian Catholics from St. Agustian's church. The contrast between the clerics and the parishioners was striking. In double-breasted cassocks and pointed black hoods, the prelates were adorned with elaborately chained sacred medallions. The women and men in colorful Youroba native dress with head wraps resembling colorfully winged creations preached on distinguished heads were filled with the energy of their African roots.

Smiles and energetic greetings were everywhere.

Rebecca had raised the bar of extravagance for the city. "Darling, we are competing with Miami, Orlando, and even West Palm to create mystery, beauty, and overindulgence. As the Italians say, 'Anything worth doing is worth taking to the extreme.' *Capisce*?"

The Museum issued local universities and colleges a block of tickets to the opening and asked that students receive half of them. The faithful from churches, synagogues, and mosques turned out. Young and old moved through the courtyard to the exhibit's entrance under the gaze of an exuberant press corps and an enhanced security force.

Leaning on a stylish walking stick, Kayne arrived with Gints, who looked incredibly uncomfortable in his "fine feathers." They had been dressed by a high-end men's glamour couturier, "The Ultimate," on Wilton Drive. The upscale establishment specializes in dazzling dinner jackets, dramatic shirts, and exotically designed shoes. Tonight, they sported black tuxedo jackets shot through with gold, black, and red sequins. The shoes were exceptionally "Gaga," with swirls of black and red glitters finished off with gold metal toes.

As they moved toward the entrance, Kayne's limp seemed to suggest recent injury, as did the bruises on his face, but neither detracted from his debonair look. He shot his forelock and turned with his hunky escort to be photographed by a bevy of photogs. Local and international celebrities greeted him as he crossed the red carpet. Bending to kiss the ring of Patriarch Theodore, he exchanged introductions with a very noble Gints. He seemed to me to embrace the aura of beauty and mystery, mixed with a dash of horror like a high priest or a shaman intent on reading the auguries and interpreting the signs.

I initially wanted to come solo. No, scratch that. I honestly wanted to skip this posh gig and sit beside my Chouko at the animal hospital as he struggled to recover. I knew, however, that Rebecca would never forgive me if I blew it off. Late in the afternoon, Gints called me to say that Kostas Galifianakis, the cutie from Bistro Parakalo, had a tux and awaited my call.

"He is not proud, Niko. Will take asking by you at last minute. Do it. That how much he want you."

Kostas was indeed gracious and looked gorgeous in black formal wear. He had presented me with a blood-red rose boutonniere to match his. His dark features and handsome scruff caught the admiring eye of both men and women. When I drew his attention to the stares, he kissed me and said, "We make a very sexy couple, *Agápi Mou.*"

I showed my badge, ID, and gun in the shoulder holster beneath my dinner jacket at the security checkpoint. I nodded to the officers, scanning the faces of all who entered the exhibit. As I turned back to Kostas, I looked over his shoulder. I saw the limousine of the exhibit's presenting sponsor pull into the courtyard circle.

Thomas Mitchell Preston, escorting a stunningly beautiful woman, at least 20 years his junior, in a red Alexander McQueen and carefully selected white diamonds. The couple drew the flashes of the press cameras and actual applause from those lining the red carpet.

Preston and his date were followed out of the limo by two very handsome men. Roy Angsley looked exhilarated as he moved forward hand in hand with a striking Hudson Ch'en. Poor Hud, his first time in public since the internet universe saw how the foundation's CEO liked his man sexing. My ex looked somewhat pale and drawn as if he just wanted the evening to be over. Hud ignored calls from surrounding reporters as he followed his boss to security.

In a sudden desire for distance, I took my handsome Greek beauty by the arm and hurried through the entrance of the Museum to find that the main foyer was just as grandiose as the courtyard. Rebecca told me she wanted the space to echo Nero's *Domus Aurea,* the House of Gold, as a welcoming area for the exhibit. Throughout the atrium, servers in dazzling white Roman tunics, golden laurel crowns, and sandals proffered champagne and hors d'oeuvres to arriving guests. The primitively austere music of Ancient Rome washed over the lights and banners that drew us to the entrance arch, announcing:

Seed Blood
Torture, Death, and Redemptive Suffering
In the Early Church

Seed Blood

33 CE to 313 CE

The entry to the exhibit was a replica of the Emperor Door of the resplendent Hagia Sophia in ancient Constantinople. Above the door were the words, "The blood of martyrs is the seed of the Church – Tertullian, c. 200 CE."

Passing through this entry, we came to a space that exhibited two pictures, one to either side of a second doorway. Again, the gateway was a replica of the grand basilica, Hagia Sophia. This time, above the Splendid Door, the inscription read, "God and Christ help us."

At this point, the chant switched to Greek Orthodox sacred music. Two magnificent icons drew the viewer's attention. A gold-haloed archdeacon looked at the observer, holding a book of the Gospels and a palm branch. The second icon had three figures. The same archdeacon knelt with his hands clasped in divine entreaty. Behind him, three men stood with boulders, ready to kill the saint by stoning. The citation identified the subject, "St. Stephen, the Protomartyr." My thoughts went to Kayne's one-word remark on the discovery of the torn body of Damon Santos.

"Stephen."

***

The prelate in a red skull cap and a purple and red cassock pretentiously gripped his pectoral cross. He sounded very officious as he spoke to his friends.

"Scholars base the theology of martyrdom on an irony found in the writings of St. Paul, 'To live outside of Christ is to die and to die in Christ is to live.' For centuries, the faithful have been devoted to the memory of our martyrs and have sought their intercession in times of need. Anyone who dies for the faith is instantly raised to the status of Saint, their eternal reward a foregone conclusion in the eyes of Holy Mother Church."

Rebecca Quinto rolled her eyes at the pontificating Archbishop, took a huge gulp of her cocktail, and stepped around him and his admirers to extend her hand to Kostas and me.

"The two most beautiful men at my little soiree. Welcome, my Darlings." Kisses.

Rebecca, dressed in a floor-length, accordion-pleated, chiffon, drop-dead-gorgeous dress with matching Christian Louboutin pointy-toe pumps, did a little twirl to strut her glamour. The slit skirt allowed a peek at one fabulous leg. At her hip, the dress' opening ended at an enormous amethyst. She said, "I love that my dress was made especially for the opening by a design student at the Ft. Lauderdale Art Institute. The color is heliotrope magenta, Darling. Don't you think it is just too divine?"

Attempting to lighten my mood, I pointed to the shoes. "So, Katy Perry."

"Nordstrom's Boca – an obscene fortune, Darling ."

Nodding to the group she was blowing off, I said, "Rebecca, don't you have to escort His Eminence through the exhibit? We do not want to steal you from a Prince of the Church." Glancing over her shoulder at His Excellency, she commented, "No, Darling. My board chair can take care of the Archbishop for the rest of the evening. A little goes a long way with that girl – the priest, I mean."

She finger-waved to guests as we maneuvered through the crowd. Kostas on one arm and me on the other. "Be honest, Nick. What did you think of the entrance, the courtyard, and all? I'm not happy with it. Needs something more, a higher attraction factor. More sizzle, if you know what I mean."

Snagging an assistant, she handed him our empty flutes and her glass. "My usual, Tony Darling. And get these beauties some real gay man's drinks. I know you will know what that is, Sweetie."

She winked.

Turning to Kostas and me, she asked. "How dirty do you get?" We both smiled. "Your martini's, I mean, Darling." She mugged innocence as the server headed to the bar.

Kostas turned to appraise the departing attendant's butt in his short tunic. I elbowed him. Referring to the departing server, Rebecca said, "That boy loves doing squats, Darling. Lives at the gym. Could have posed for that." She waved at a very homoerotic portrait of St. Sebastian, by Caravaggio bound and pierced with arrows.

Seed Blood

"Nick, I can get some cover-up for that eye of yours. But, on second thought, you look so divinely savage – bruised and sexy in your formal wear. And so appropriate to our theme, the sacredness of suffering." Rebecca gestured to the art filling the galleries we traversed. She seemed to reign over the spectacle. A modern version of Nero's wife, Poppaea, our fashionable Executive Director, presided over the martyrdom of the early Christians in the Colosseum of the Fritcher Museum, hosting a very patrician audience.

The glamorous guests toured through a lavish but macabre expedition, beginning with the crucifixion of the Savior and taking in three centuries of persecution and gory death. *Seed Blood* featured masterpieces from all over the world, depicting the saints in their final ecstasy, claiming the crown of victory through tortuous martyrdom.

St. Lucy was crowned in glory. One hand held the palm of martyrdom while the other cradled a plate with her extracted eyes, staring at the viewer. Simon Peter, the apostle, was represented begging to be crucified upside down because he was not worthy to die in the same manner as his Lord. The beheading of Saint Paul, the filleting of Saint Bartholomew, the many tortures of Saint Thecla, these, and more were depicted in paint, marble, and story throughout the exhibit. Racked and tortured, the saintly victims raised their eyes heavenward, from whence came their glorification and salvation.

The fourth gallery was a stylized rendering of a Roman church hung with representations of the Apostles of Jesus, all of whom died a martyr's death. A painting of the Apostle James thrown from the tower of the Jerusalem Temple stunned me. My thoughts returned to Brother Fintan's account of the unfortunate Fr. David and his reported suicide.

On one wall was a copy of the mosaics of the Basilica San Marco in Venice. Beneath the reproduction of the tiled arches, His Excellency Patriarch Theodore was telling the story of the theft of the mummified body of St. Mark from Alexandria in Egypt and the entombment of this stolen prize in the Mother Church of the "Most Serene Republic of Venice," St. Mark's Basilica.

Referring to the looting of the relics by the Crusaders in 1204 from the Church of the Holy Apostles in Constantinople, the Orthodox Archbishop insisted, "It would not be the last time relics of the holy saints of the

Eastern Churches would be carried off by members of the Church of Rome."

The next gallery was dark and relatively unadorned. Soft, dark shadows suggested the shelf-like tombs of a Roman Catacomb. In the middle of the room, a series of intense spotlights illuminated the only work of art in the space, St. Cecilia's coffin effigy. This was the coveted centerpiece of the exhibit. The marble sculpture of the martyred patron of music, breathtaking in the solemn darkness, represented a significant coup for Rebecca and her team.

On loan from the Church of St. Cecilia in Rome, the gleaming white marble representation of the virgin depicted her lifeless form in the garb of a sleeping Roman maiden. She lay on her side, her head swathed in linen, with her face to the ground, the scar of her attempted beheading showing on her neck. On the dark, black, and reddish walls, the ivory script was timed to fade in and out, telling of the girl's courage during the Persecution of Diocletian in the Third Century CE. The chanting of monks filled the tomb-like chamber.

A Dominican priest on the faculty of a local Catholic university was explaining to his friends the symbolism in the depiction of the martyr's hands. "Even in death, Cecilia proclaims the faith. The extended finger of her left hand signifies the belief in the one true God. The two fingers of her right hand proclaim the dual nature of Christ."

I thought. *Nevertheless, she persisted*.

The next two gallery rooms displayed reliquaries containing the venerable and the beatified bones of those who refused to recant their beliefs even in the face of seemingly insurmountable pain and suffering. For centuries, these holy artifacts promised blessings of holiness and forgiveness of sin for many who revered them. The craftsmanship that contained the remains of those who gave their lives for the faith were extraordinary examples of pietistic art. Elaborately stylized maps and graphics testified to the growth of Christendom fueled by the fervor of the martyrs and inspired evangelists. Here and there, throughout the exhibit, were the instruments of torture and death with which victims received the crown of martyrdom.

The exhibit ended with The Nicea Icon showing the Edict of Milan of 313 issued by Emperor Constantine prohibiting the persecution of Christians everywhere in the Empire and ending the Apostolic Age of the Martyrs. Above the artwork was a massive cross of light. The inscription beneath it read, "*In Hoc Signo Vinces*-- With this sign, you will conquer."

***

Circling back through the galleries, we caught up to Gints and Kayne in conversation with members of the police departments attending the opening. Special Agent Mary Chaffee, looking resplendent in black and silver, was joined by her "plus one," a stunning woman in white and silver. They joined the Mayor and his friends for conversation and an update on the Palm Killer Case.

"We are closing in but so far cannot locate the suspect. We found an abandoned hideout in Wilton Manors, but he still eludes us. Sheriff Crawford and Chief Mays are making every effort to bring him to justice. We have doubled surveillance here at the request of Dr. Sorenson."

Interesting. That request should have come through me.

I stepped away from Kostas and Rebecca to address a couple from the Wilton Manors Board of Commissioners. They inquired about the serial murder case. As I looked up, finishing my somewhat sketchy report to them, I found myself facing Hudson and Roy, who were turning around at the same time.

"Hey, Hud."

"Officer Sechi."

"Wilton Manors' hot cop. How are you, Nick, my man?"

"' Sup, Roy?" *So nice of you to have been sleeping with my boyfriend, you fucking bastard.*

Angsley was his ebullient self, running chatter that attempted to be friendly and casual. I shifted from one foot to the other, visibly uncomfortable. Hud and I avoided looking at each other. The three of us understood that two of us wanted to be anywhere on the planet but here, together, right now.

Excusing myself, I rejoined Kostas, Gints, Kayne, and Rebecca as she ushered us into the museum's banquet hall. Kostas handed me a "Virgin Mary" instead of a "Dirty Goose." Apparently, he read my thoughts earlier that I needed clear faculties all around at this event.

"I thought you would like a drink more suited to the religious theme."

"Thanks, bud." I clinked with his martini glass.

"We can get to the dirty stuff later." He said with a salacious grin, adding, "Nick, you look so sad tonight." He gestured with his glass over my shoulder. "Is it Hud?"

Knowing that my ex was watching, I kissed Kostas in a very exaggerated way-- a juvenile grab for a "fuck you" moment.

"Easy, Nick," he said, not wanting to be my public rebound boyfriend. I stepped back and apologized for what was a stupid and objectifying gesture.

"It's cool, but like I said, Sexy, later. Perhaps that waiter boy can be convinced to come along for a ride." Kostas nodded to the youth in the white tunic who had apparently taken his fancy.

"Davin, I have looked everywhere for you, my Darling." Rebecca turned to kiss the good-looking man who had just approached us. "You are at my table, my satyr, with the presenting sponsors and the Archbishop. So, be on your best behavior. Mmm?"

Davin grinned and slid his hand down Rebecca's back, claiming his woman. "But you are irresistible, my Dear. You look scrumptious this evening."

She turned to the three men of her stunning entourage. "Darlings, you all are at the table next to mine. Stuffy speeches for days coming at you, so if you want to get up and wander back into the galleries, I will understand. Just stick to the pictures, boys. Avoid dark corners. No, ah ..." She wagged an index finger with a blood-red nail.

Leaning in, Gints nodded and said solemnly, "*Jāšanās*."

"Right," echoed our hostess. "None of that."

As she left us on the arm of sexy Davin, she turned once more to say, "Do not forget the after-party on the roof. A very select guest list, of course. The fireworks are by Grucci. That's Phillip and Debbie at table three from the award-winning pyrotechnic family. Divine New Yorkers."

We took our places at table two. In a very awkward arrangement, Kayne ended up sitting next to me. My ex and his new boyfriend were seated directly behind me at the Presenting Sponsor's table. Choosing the right moment after speeches and midway through dinner, I excused myself. The tense conversations with Kayne and the proximity to Hudson and Roy were getting to me, and I needed some distance.

Bending down to speak into Kostas' ear, I explained, "I need to walk the perimeter, bud. The job and all... Be right back."

I acknowledged Chief Mays and Sheriff Crawford and their table companions as I headed out of the banquet hall and back through the gallery.

Near the St. Cecelia exhibit, I caught the attention of the young staffer who had served us our first cocktails. "Would you bring my date another Dirty Goose, please? He is at table number two. Do you remember him?"

"I sure do. I mean, yes, Sir."

"Thank you." I knew exactly what I was doing.

As I strolled through the Museum, I took the time to sort out my feelings surrounded by the trove of art and antiquities. So many emotional dead-ends relationship-wise, Hudson, Kayne, and even Kostas. Yeah, that was going nowhere, and I was offloading it pretty quickly, sending him the hottie waiter. K Boy was an incredible guy, but...

I checked my voice messages for an update on Chouko— nothing. As I stood near a painting of the crucifixion of St. Andrew, I sensed evil in the dark corners of the galleries. I started to spiral downward, feeling the sudden imaginings of terror, torture, and sacrificial blood in tight spaces, among pressing bodies, and shot through scenes of impending doom. Eyes turned to heaven... clubs and knives raised... arrows and nails embedded in human flesh... I wrestled for clarity and strength of mind while fighting the coiling tentacles of terror.

What is it you fear, Officer?

As if knocking me back to clearer thinking, my phone chirped with a surprising text.

Nick, we need to talk. I think I made a huge mistake. Meet me in the roof garden—Hudson.

Chapter Thirty-Nine: Lawrence
NICK SECHI'S JOURNAL

A soft breeze stirred the myrtle trees spaced across the broad expanse of the Museum's roof garden. It was an elegant space designed for special events. The Museum's patio in the sky was landscaped and staged with outdoor furniture and potted trees behind sections of wrought iron fencing to create intimate seating areas. Multi-leveled platforms created environmental interest that promised comfort and intimacy. Seven groupings surrounded by fire pits were set up to warm winter gatherings.

Staff placed bars and high tops at the large outdoor living room perimeter for a charming post-event celebration. The entire atmosphere promised to bring together the glitterati and the cognoscenti, reveling until the first glimmer of dawn. Soft lighting caressed the city night, coming from below and reflected above. Technicians would switch on landscape spots just before the arrival of the most elite of the VIPs. The forecast promised a crisp, clear evening, ideal for pyrotechnics by the award-winning Grucci family of Bellport, New York.

As the doors of the north elevator opened and I stepped out, Jonathan Yurick came up from behind me, nailing me with a hypodermic to my neck. I spun around, reached for my gun, and immediately fell to the roof deck.

The last sound I heard before descending into complete darkness was a deep voice rasping,

"Good evening, Officer. Please allow me to assist you."

***

I awoke, attempting to shake off the grogginess of the drug. It took me a moment to realize I was suspended four feet above the decking by my wrists. Yuric had hung me from a utility crane used to transport heavy objects from ground level to the roof of the Museum. Jonathan had removed my jacket, tie, and shoulder holster. These were placed neatly on one of the couches to my left.

As my vision cleared, I thought I recognized the bodies of two police officers between the entrance to the stairs and the service elevator. They were bound together and gagged. I could see the killer working intently just beyond one of the low-burning fire pits on the opposite side. The monster was bending over the prone body of an unconscious man in a disheveled tux, his face turned away from me. As the demonic figure pulled away the shirt of his victim, I caught sight of the phoenix tattoo flickering in the dim light of the fire.

Hudson Ch'en.

Jonathan removed Hud's shoes and proceeded to lash him to a section of the wrought iron fence that had been disconnected and placed on the deck. The low, blue flames of the fire pit cast wavering shadows and spears of illumination across the bodies of the maniacal hunter and his semi-conscious prey. Beside the makeshift gridiron were the branches of a date palm.

I called across the expanse, "Jonathan, listen to me. We need to end this. Killing this man will not bring Father David back."

Yurick lifted the gridiron and its attached prisoner to a leaning position on the edge of the fiery pit. The mention of his friend cut his concentration for just a moment. He turned to me, trying to speak but only succeeding in a trance-like uttering of short phrases. He held a hunting knife in his right hand as he came at me, ranting in the night.

"*Passus est...* he suffered. He was not the first. There were so many in the early days of the plague. I helped him receive the palm and crown. He could barely make it up the stairs of the bell tower. He was so broken and weak. I carried him. He resisted, but he also embraced his death at the end, reaching to heaven as he fell. He eagerly desired it, as will this one."

The killer gestured to Hud, who was coming into full consciousness on the grill. The highly twisted logic of the severely insane filled the murderer's confession as he rambled on.

"Jonathan, Father David would not want you to do this. He was a good man. You remember, right? The good that he did for the poor and sick. The care and the love he gave. Not this. He sits in judgment on you, Jonathan. He wanted his friends to live."

Pleading, I tried to draw the murderer away from the purposed destruction of his next victim.

Not being deterred, Yurick grabbed my throat as I struggled. He placed the knife's blade against my neck in the cleft of my open shirt collar. The intimate proximity to pure evil was overpowering as I hung above the roof.

"Do you know how St. Bartholomew was martyred, Officer Sechi? He was fileted alive by his executioners. How's your back, Pretty Boy?" His eyes seemed to glare a nightmarish blood red in the night. His body seethed with a savage fury. As if to imitate skin removal, he ripped the knife blade down up my shirt front, sending the studs and buttons ricocheting across the decking of the roof.

Releasing my throat, he caressed my chest and abdomen with the open palm of his left hand. His fingertips stroked the bruises on my torso from the bullets and from Kayne's rage. He intoned in that familiar rasping voice, "Once his torturers removed his skin, Bartholomew was thrown from a great height."

As he brought his mouth and wet lips closer to my torso, he murmured, "... the lusts of the flesh... make us children of wrath...."

My arms ached, supporting my full weight. With all the strength I had left, I flexed my hips and swung up with my legs but missed ensnaring the neck of the killer. I did get in a knee to his chest, which threw him backward.

He came back and hissed, "Now, now, Officer. Didn't I tell you not to interfere?"

He shook his head and pressed his temples as if remembering to resume what was to be his initial execution of the evening on the fire pit. He returned to his first captive.

"The Father will see." He looked around. "He will be here soon. They will all be arriving shortly to be caught up in the Great Retribution. Roasted flesh and blood to assuage his anger."

Using tremendous strength, he positioned the gridiron and its prisoner over the pit. He stepped to the side, leaning down to turn up the flames. His ravings and the jostling of the roasting grill roused the captive. Hud screamed as his clothes started to smoke.

Out of the darkness, a figure leaped to land before me. He pulled a sword from his walking stick and began slashing like D'artagnan above my

253

head. Trailing frayed rope, I dropped to my feet on the decking. In the same instant, Jonathan raised the flames and tossed the key to the gas jet across the roof. He ran at the intruding Kayne, hunting knife drawn. The insane Yurick switched hands and grabbed a metal stanchion to fend off Kayne's approaching blade.

Hudson began to burn.

Freed from the crane, I vaulted over the distance that separated me from the fire pit, pulling at the writhing body of Hudson Ch'en. Using a discarded fence pole as a lever, I managed to lift the grill off the edges of the pit and away from the flesh-hungry, rising flames.

Framed by the raging fire, Kayne and Jonathan fought to the death a short distance away. The enraged killer hurled pieces of furniture, tables, and chairs. He toppled outdoor heaters as Kayne danced away every time. The Professor's proficient training in martial arts allowed him to execute a series of expertly placed elbows, knees and kicks to the killer's body, causing him to drop the metal pole. Nevertheless, Yurick continued his deadly onslaught with fists and knife.

Stepping back, Kayne addressed the monster by his "Name in the World."

"Thomas, have done! It's all over. You can stop now."

Screaming hysterically, Yurik covered his ears.

"Do not call me that name!"

The killer lunged at Kayne. "It is his name. The doubter... the faithless... the one who will not forgive. He who demands death."

As they locked together, a show of strength and rage amid a now chaotic setting, I frantically worked at the stout lashings that bound Hud to the scorching metal. I slapped at his smoldering clothing.

Jonathan drew back and attacked, slashing furiously with the hunting knife. He caught Kayne on the left shoulder, drawing blood. Kayne jumped, pirouetted with legs to the sky. Righting himself on the way down, he ran his sword through his attacker's ribs from right to left as he landed on his feet. Jonathan Yurick keeled over in a deathlike slump.

Kayne inspected his opponent, sheathed his sword, and jumped across overturned furniture. He stooped to place my Glock next to me as I sat cradling a shaking and gasping Hudson Ch'en. Kayne's left arm hung uselessly at his side, bleeding profusely. He was panting as he knelt in front of us.

"How is he doing, Nick?"

I ripped what remained of my tuxedo shirt. "Jesus, Kayne, we need to use this to stanch that arm. You both need an ambulance."

Freeing an arm from holding the agonizing Hud, I awkwardly shifted to remove his cell phone from the pocket of his tuxedo pants. Hudson clawed in panic at me, holding me in a grasp of desperation.

Explosive terror suddenly erupted. As I looked up, Kayne was lifted up and back from behind, his good hand pinned to his neck by a steel cable garrote as his left arm remained unmovable. A critically wounded Jonathan Yurick was strangling him from behind as Kayne knelt in front of us. Keeping Kayne on his knees by kneeling on the back of his legs, Yurick restricted the Professor's defense. The strength of the choke further prevented all resistance.

I raised my gun, finding myself in yet another stand-off, the head of the killer and his victim aligned too close for an unimpaired shot. My recurring nightmare of helplessly watching a loved one destroyed directly in front of me had returned.

Jonathan and Kayne struggled inches before my face while the weight of Hud's body and his agonizing wrestling to hold on to me overcame my every effort to help the choking professor.

"Hud, let go! Hud!" I was screaming.

As the death struggle continued, Kayne's eyes began to close. A predator's savage wrath filled Jonathan's flushed face. He strained with all his might on the garrotte. Then, like a wild beast preparing to eat his expiring victim, he leaned in to lick the blood-spattered neck of his dying prey.

Move, mother fucker!

255

I was unsure if I thought or yelled it, but I started to see a narrow opening for a clear shot.

Before I could pull the trigger, something from the back bashed the killer's head forcefully to the left, causing him to release his victim. As Kayne fell forward towards me, Jonathan, bleeding profusely from his head and torso, staggered to his feet. He backed up to the low perimeter roof wall. A red satin pump hung from the right side of his head, its heel deeply embedded in his right temple.

Hiking up her skirt, Rebecca rushed the killer, who staggered with arms flailing. She grabbed the impaling shoe and yanked it free. The force moved her to the right as the gored, bloody monster twisted off to the left. At the same time, I got off the shot with expert accuracy, which sent him over the parapet to the courtyard below.

Jonathan Yurick plummeted six stories to the earth, landing on the spikes of a wrought iron fence near the entryway to the Museum. On his way down, he clawed at the exhibit's massive banner, smearing the white walls of the Museum with his blood. The flag floated to the ground, covering the fallen monster like a blood-soaked shroud.

Rebecca peered over the roof, panting. "No way you were going to get one of my Louboutin's, you crazy fuck!"

I joined her at the roof's edge after calling for backup. As the elevator opened, police and security officers swarmed to aid the two fallen men and the bound police officers. Rebecca and I looked down at the bloody courtyard hung with a torn title banner raked by the corpse and gore of the serial killer.

Stepping daintily back into her shoes, she pointed at the now-teeming courtyard below and looked at me.

"Now, that's award-winning marketing, Darling."

Chapter Forty: Redemption
NICK SECHI'S JOURNAL

"The Preston Foundation is honored to support this project. This is a place where transgender people, young and old, will be safe and will thrive."

A slightly pale Hudson Ch'en stood at the podium beneath a portrait of Hadji Murad. An easel next to him held a large check for ten million dollars signed by the Chair of the Board of the Foundation, Thomas Mitchell Preston, Sr. These funds were given to renovate the five-floor office building behind the stage. Part of the contribution established an endowment to keep open this drop-in center for the LGBTQ+ community, which specializes in services for transgender clients. It had been nearly a month since the events of Seed Blood, but the effects of his near escape with death were still apparent in how Hud moved, walked, and talked.

"In addition, I received communication from the Board this week that the position of Executive Director of the Murad Center will be funded in perpetuity by a personal gift from Mr. Preston himself."

What Hud did not say was that Thomas Preston had a few stipulations regarding this second gift. The Board of the Hadji Murad Life Center for Transgender Persons must seriously consider the application for Program Director of one, David Miller, aka Damon Santos. Mr. Miller would also have access to funds dedicated to completing his degree in Social Work. Also, Mr. Preston asked that the Center's board chair consider proposing Board membership to Ms. Raymonde Isaacson, assuring them that her fundraising obligation would be met annually for as long as she served the Foundation.

Hud stepped from the podium for a "grab and grin" in front of the giant check, shaking hands with the Murad Center's Board Chair, Ms. Cha Cha Rosette. The elegant Ms. Cha Cha lost her cool persona for a bit and hugged Hudson while cameras flashed.

I looked up again at poor Hud – one could still see vestiges of the terror of that night on the Museum's roof only three weeks ago in his eyes and wooden movements. He escaped the ordeal very shaken but with minor injuries. I noticed that Roy was nowhere to be seen, most likely by agreement.

Cha Cha walked to the podium while drying her eyes. She lowered the mic and looked up at the assembled guests. Omitting the *pro forma* remarks that usually acknowledge the community leaders on the dais, Cha Cha got to the heart of the matter in her typical fashion.

"One thing is true for all transgender persons, just as you discover your true self, everyone leaves you." She paused to let this sink in. The crowd was silent.

"The South Florida community is one of the largest LGBTQ+ communities in the world. More than half of our homeless children identify as LGBTQ. I was one of those."

Looking down, she said, "I am looking at the National Transgender Discrimination Survey, OK? It says that nineteen percent of transgender people were homeless at some point in their lives. Of those, twenty-nine percent said shelter officials turned them away."

She continued, "We know that fifty-five percent of trans people reported that one or more people in a homeless shelter sexually harassed them. Additionally, twenty-two percent said they were sexually assaulted, and twenty-five percent said they were physically assaulted."

She paused, raised her gaze to the crowd, and shouted with passionate conviction, "This shit... excuse me... this atrocity stops here!"

The crowd was on its feet with thunderous applause. Drag queens shouted, "Go, girl!" and "Pray it, Cha!"

"We are today, fulfilling a dream of our sister, Ms. Hadji Murad, the fabulous Gaye Dawn. It was her vision that in this town and rising from this earth, so sacred to the LGBTQ+ community, there would be a place of welcome and protection for all who are thrown out because of their choice to live an authentic life.

On behalf of the Board of Directors of the Hadji Murad Center for Transgender Persons, I want to thank the Preston Foundation, Mayor Michael Crawley, and all in this community who made her dream come true."

Seed Blood

As she stepped from the podium to cheers and applause, the DJ hit his music cue, and the entertainers from Club Masque strutted forward to perform a medley honoring their memorable star.

***

"So, explain it to me again because I have many questions." Davin Costa-Graves sat at one of the picnic tables set up on the lawn before the stage of the groundbreaking. Behind him, massaging his traps, was his very close buddy, Gints Bergovic, unconsciously claiming his new man. My Darling Kostas wrapped his arms around his "toga boy" from the gala, Tony Squires. The rest of us stood in various beautiful people poses, watching the crowd disperse.

From across the four caressing buddies, Rebecca shot me a mock surprised look that said. *Apparently, Greek satyrs don't care who they fuck.* She pulled closer to her gorgeous date, Mark. I remember thinking that I hoped that this one was exclusively straight. Guys and gals would easily be attracted to his manly charms, I wagered. Time will tell.

"You, Rebecca," Davin was asking, "How is it that you took him down? You are such a soft and delicate flower." Davin could not resist yanking a chain. I could hear Kayne's sharp intake of breath.

Here it comes.

Twisting around with a hand on one hip, she responded, "Your problem, my Darling, has always been that you underestimate me and my sex." She vamped a Wonder Woman pose, forearms crossed. There was not a person in our group who did not for a second understand the double meaning in that remark, even the sexually fluid boy toy, Davin.

Gints spoke up, "But, Big Doctor, how was it you took advantage of such bloody monster without Gints? He saw you coming, yes? How you know he was on roof?"

Striking a pose worthy of the protagonist of the Masterpiece Mystery's "Sherlock," Kayne shot his black forelock with his right hand, his left arm in a sling, and said, "Elementary, my dear Gints. The killer told us everything we needed to know that would end his rampage."

He continued to reconstruct the elements of his deduction for the case, ticking off each clue on the fingers of his uninjured hand while

259

explaining. Kayne reviewed the connection to the Abbey and the Portiuncula Center, the death-of-the-martyrs fantasy of the murderer, and the sexual attraction to his "mouthpiece." Ever the educator, he addressed the entire group, explaining his final analysis, which concluded with the horrible end of the killer.

"First, you will recall the presence of the FBI and the members of both police forces at the opening. It was inconceivable that the Palm Killer would pass up such a public stage as the opening of 'Seed Blood' for his final performance in his Theater of Blood. Yuric's denouement as it were."

Raymonde nudged me and mouthed Kayne's last word with a quizzical look. I whispered back, "It means 'ending.' He is being very cranial."

"For Yurick, the elaborate portrayals of sanctified torture and death in the exhibit were the aphrodisiac to continue his bloody rampage. He was drawn to it as he considered himself an ordained executioner who ripped salvation from the clutches of a monstrous deity.

"Finally, the killer's drama of staging his victims as Christian martyrs included many references to fire, especially in his communications to and attacks on Nick. Where in the Fritcher would he find the flames for his terrible execution? It is quite simple, really.

He was <u>on</u>, heroic, dramatic, intelligent, and fuckin' gorgeous.

"Also, in the video of Hudson Ch'en, the killer had crowned him with laurel. Mr. Ch'en was, in effect, 'laurelled.' In Latin, 'laurelled' is the literal meaning of the man's name, 'Laurentius' — Lawrence. The Roman Martyrology tells us that St. Lawrence was a third-century deacon of the Church who was roasted alive on a gridiron. It was easy from there to conclude that the fire pits on the roof of the Museum where the Seed Blood after-party was would feature the incinerated corpse of one, Hudson Ch'en."

I resisted the impulse to add, *And the flayed corpse of your favorite crime-fighting superhero, Nick Sechi* — a double murder of a bloodthirsty maniac. I still felt ice in my veins at the thought.

Kayne continued uninterruptedly, "I will admit that I came to this conclusion relatively late in the game. At the opening, I concentrated on keeping both Mr. Ch'en and Officer Sechi in my sights. They were ground zero in the bloody game, particularly Officer Sechi, the object of the killer's twisted sexual lust."

Making eye contact with his admiring audience, Kayn went on.

"When Hud and Nick disappeared from the banquet hall, the logical place to find them was on the roof of the Museum. Please note. The killer hacked the phones of both Officer Sechi and Mr. Ch'en, sending fake messages regarding a rendezvous on the roof.

"So, I left the celebration and proceeded to the service elevator, hoping to disguise my arrival at the scene of his next crime. The rest was the bloody confrontation resulting in the death of the murderer, the details of which I will spare you."

He ended with a "palms up" gesture, implying that his deductions were mere child's play to astonishing looks all around. A bright red and purple, toque-like bruise circling the whiteness of his neck was partially visible through his open shirt. A sling held his left arm.

Hudson quietly joined the group just as Kayne was discussing his attempted murder. The mention of the rooftop ordeal caused him to remember the fear that returned from time to time. He sagged and sat in one of the empty seats at the picnic table, his head in his hands. A friend who was most likely a new interest sidled up behind him, sat down next to him, and took his hand. I remember wondering how long it would take him or any of us to find some peace in all this.

Rebecca added to Kayne's account, "Actually, my arrival on the roof was completely serendipitous. I was checking to see that all was in place for the after-party. Thank God for sturdy women's designer shoes and a police officer with a steady arm." She pecked my cheek.

Laughs and cheers.

"If I may interrupt for a second?" Chief Robert Mays entered our group with Sheriff Dian Crawford, Special Agent Mary Chaffee, and the newly-elected Mayor of Wilton Manors, the Honorable Michael Crawley.

"Nick, with every intention of totally embarrassing you, I want to announce to you, your friends, and colleagues that the findings of the Internal Affairs Committee have completely exonerated you. All charges have been dismissed. We are fully reinstating you as a patrol officer in the Wilton Manors Police Department."

There were cheers, hugs, and kisses all around. Gints grabbed me in a bone crusher.

"You see that, Niko? Why you even worry, eh? Gints knew it would all turn out right. This America, not Latvia." Wagging a finger my way, "You should listen more to Gints."

Mays added as he turned to go, "Nick, I stand on my previous recommendation to take some time off. Been a hell of a two months."

Kayne embraced me with his one good arm and unashamedly kissed me. "Are we OK, bud?"

"Yes," I gulped, embracing his good side. Then, I whispered, "I hope better than OK...."

This was tough, but I went for it.

"Kayne, I've been thinking of a way to say this, but... well, I want to say...."

I stammered like a five-year-old caught with a fist full of cookies.

I placed my left hand on his chest and looked into his astonishing blue eyes and black shock of hair, partially covering the Mark of Cain on his forehead.

It's now or never, Nick. Go for it.

He put his index finger to my lips and drew closer.

As I opened my mouth to complete what I wanted to say, I found myself knocked out of his embrace and onto the ground. I was unable to stand due to a substantial weight on my back and legs. I rolled over to accept the frantic nuzzling and dog kisses of my "Beautiful Butterfly."

Shan, who had taken him for a walk, tried to call him to heel, but he would have none of it as if to say, "Learn Japanese, please. Then this Immortal Butterfly will obey."

I rolled and wrestled in the grass with my Chouko, to the delight of everyone.

Chapter Forty-One: His Last Call

Nick Sechi's Journal

"He is the Napoleon of Crime, Watson, the organizer of half that is evil, and nearly all that is undetected in this great city...."

"Easy, peasy. <u>The Final Problem.</u> One of Doyle's best." I announced.

We had been playing a game with "The Canon," shooting each other lines from Sherlock Holmes stories and guessing the cases of the Great Detective from iconic lines. The setting for our "literary research" was late-night martinis at Diogenes, Wilton Manors' hottest gay bar.

Kayne raised his Churchill in a salute. The flickering light from the fireplace in this very dark wood club, complete with a coffered ceiling, illuminated his vampire prince features and Asian-cast eyes. He was irresistible, handsome, strong, and intelligent.

Yeah, I had it bad. Totally hit by the lightning bolt. My thoughts wandered to some pretty romantic and frisky considerations.

I came back as Kayne remarked that the period décor of the bar reminded him of Mycroft Holmes' men's club in the Conan Doyle stories. Overstuffed leather chairs and tons of polished wood-- a very cool bar.

"Funny, I never thought I would be comfortable near a fire again."

"Yes, you've had your share of terror and flames." He tipped his glass towards mine. "Spirits help keep the nightmares away, I find anyway. Even superheroes fear something."

Recalling the papers that Brother Fintan showed us, I asked, "Kayne, did you know that Jonathan Yurick was...."

"Thomas Mitchell Preston, Jr."

He finished my sentence, paused, and, with eyes sparkling, paraphrased the Great Detective. "You know my methods, my dear student."

I was about to ask him for a further explanation when he executed what was becoming one of his favorite moves. He brought his index finger to lightly meet my lips, a gesture that always made me shudder with excitement and left me speechless.

He spread his hands and smiled. "Until I saw that document, Nick, my love...." He looked up at me, "Baby, I had no idea."

We both laughed.

The bar was mostly empty as the hour was late. Kayne introduced a new subject. "So, Nick, what are you going to do with your sabbatical year from the force?"

I thought for a moment, then, imitating his last response, I spread my hands and aped, "Baby, I have no idea."

"Fair dinkum, Mate." His Aussie slang was as mellow as his gin. After a beat, he added, "See here, do you snow ski?"

I grinned. "I'm a regular Gus Kenworthy, Mate."

"Rippa! Now that Olympian is one fine jock lad. Ski date with that bloke, and Bob's your uncle." He up-ended his glass. Before I could enter his last sentence into Google Translate on my mobile, clicking on Aussie Slang, he continued.

"I am thinking of a place near Aspen I often frequent. They have had exceptional ski weather this winter, and I think we may catch another month of it. I am off next semester, and my arm is coming along right proper. Might need to follow you along in a snowmobile, however. And then there is always *après ski*."

He sipped his drink and said, "What I am attempting to say is, would you be interested in getting snowbound with me for about a month? I am... well... frankly, despite our brief falling out, I am at a loss to tell you how much over these weeks, I...."

"Last call, gentlemen."

Kayne's words hung out there-- *Invitation from the Vampire*.

As I looked into the fire, I paused, and in my mind's eye, as if in a movie, I saw again all the characters who had filled our lives over the last few months: Rebecca, Hud, Gints, Hadji, Jared, Hell Boy, Damon, Kostas and the rest. The flames seemed to symbolize how our entwined lives had faced a ferocious struggle with evil fraught with danger and passion.

I wondered what terror was planted because of the spilled blood and death connected to *Seed Blood*. What would burst forth in our lives? Would any good come of all this?

As for Kayne and me, this thing really broke us– cut, bruised, and stabbed. That was only the physical effects. The emotional wreckage was hidden but close to the surface on both our parts,

We both needed to emerge whole from this. I needed to get my life back together again, on track, in balance. Kayne needed intellectual stimulation and a way back from his own terror, surely—the unspoken, the repressed.

Would it be wiser to get some distance and clear my head of the nightmares, the screaming, and the tortured dead? Despite our intense physical attraction, we hardly knew each other, having been thrown together in the recent chaos. Was another failed attempt at love fated for me in some fucked-up, star-crossed fashion?

I looked from the fire up to his expectant expression. At that moment, as I searched his handsome face, I realized I wanted more life, more light. I wanted....

Kayne sat back, suspecting I was about to give him the answer he did not want to hear. With a bit of desperation, he took my hand.

He spoke shining words.

"I cannot ignore everything that has happened to bring us together. But now, there is no fear, no hiding, no academic excuses or explanations. The past darkness is gone, Nick. The bloody battles toward the light bring the promise of life. The struggle brings faith and love. I am sure of it, Mate."

He paused for a moment and touched my lips with an index finger.

"Please be with me. We can drive away any new nightmares and reminders of death together, my love. Nick..."

Slowly, I reached over and brushed the hair from his forehead. I pulled his beautiful face to mine, kissing him with much pent-up passion.

Looking into his ice-blues, I said, "Can I bring my dog, Mister?"

Epilogue

At dawn, three days after the dedication of the Murad Center, Kayne and Nick stood side by side on a Fort Lauderdale Beach pier.

"He loved this place... always said it reminded him of the beaches near Perth. It's where I first found him. He was hiding beneath this pier, just below this spot. Living there, really."

They spoke no words for a long time, but the two men remained gazing at the relatively calm surf, glistening in the setting sun. Nick gently took Kayne's hand and stepped closer. They continued to stand in silence as Kayne looked down and slowly turned the object held in his other hand.

Nick followed his gaze to the metal urn and the lettering on the small plaque. He thought of how little the boy was.

Tears ran down Kayne's face as he let go of Nick's grasp. He turned and kissed Nick with ardor and heart-rending honesty. Moving off, he walked slowly back to the land end of the pier by himself.

He stopped, turned around, and brought the metal surface of the container to his lips for a second. With long, loping strides, he ran to the sea end of the structure while raising and rotating his right arm as if making a cricket pitch. The urn separated from his grasp, tumbled end over end while soaring high into the blaze of the rising sun, and vanished beneath the waves.

They remained watching the spot on the far-off sea surface. In the company of a few other youngsters, a young girl stood at the pier's rail, tossing flowers into the water. No one spoke.

Then Nick ran to bury his face against the back of Kayne's sobbing body, squeezing him with gentle desperation. At that moment, they were two souls with single grief, two hearts beating together.

The small plaque had read, "John Cochran Dawkins-Sorenson."

Hell Boy had found his champion, and Kayne had claimed the lost boy forever.

The End

A Note on Language

Language is a city to the building of which every human being brought a stone. -- Ralph Waldo Emerson.

The characters in the Sorenson Mysteries are diverse, reflecting the richness and dignity of the human family as it is now and has always been. I am convinced that exposure to the beauty of language magnifies the value of a multicultural approach to life and its potential to bring about understanding and peace.

I have attempted to use many backgrounds and languages as an artist might use shading to deepen and intensify the characters who fill these adventures within an intricate plot. My writing uses many foreign words, accents, slang, quotes, favorite phrases, and speaking styles to move the plot forward and create a visual and imagined auditory richness for the reader's exploration of the characters' minds. Words are the fingerprints and footprints of experience. It is the gifts and flavors of the many that wrest free goodness amid great malevolence, time after time.

Therefore, I hope that the languages of the cast will serve to expand the world of the Sorenson Mysteries. Some have said that books open the reader to new human spaces. The thought of sending a reader off in search of additional information is, frankly, quite satisfying. Scholarship is a good thing.

Also, I believe that one who speaks with an accent is not a liability but one who brings ages of rich cultural history and gifts to communication and, consequently, relationships. Understanding and acceptance come with increased knowledge.

Consequently, I intend that the context or the text of the stories will help the reader to understand the meaning of the speech of these unique folks. If confusion follows, it comes with my sincerest apologies and the hope that, within the twists and turns of the adventure, clarity will reign in the end.

A final thought on inappropriate language: Kayne J. Sorenson, Ph.D., his friends, colleagues, associates, and adversaries often use colorful and explicit language that some may find offensive. To that, concern the eminent Professor would respond, "Words are evocative. They often create what they express. Sometimes, the best word to use is raw in its expression because humans can be caught up in some very atrocious situations."

Never one to not challenge his students, Sorenson would broaden the perspective with, "And what then is truly obscene? A lascivious reference that connotes sexual behavior or those deprecatory words which through history have vilified, demonized, and enslaved individuals of different sexual orientations and faiths as well as whole races of the human family – these do more destruction than earthy language ever will."

I will not utter those offensive words and phrases in print, but I do challenge readers to seek them out, never use them and, above all, call out those who do. These words create a world of obscenity because they create discrimination, injustice, and death."

And to this, Kayne's dear friend Rebecca Quinto would add for the edification of the staunchly Puritanical, "Chillax, Darling. It's only sex."

Acknowledgments

Characters in *Seed Blood* have been inspired by a lifetime of reading, notably Sir Arthur Conan Doyle's Sherlock Holmes stories and the works of Charles Dickens, especially *Oliver Twist*. Educators, friends, and family provided inspiration for the twisted and profane, as well as the heroic and astonishing figures who come to life in the pages of this book, including the many pets who have rescued my heart and soul throughout my life.

I want to express my gratitude to the astonishing cast of friends who provided encouragement for the creation of *Seed Blood*. One needs a fan base — companions on the journey. I endeavor to deserve their respect and support.

Liza Wallner was the first to read my manuscripts and offered valuable advice and loving encouragement. I am humbled and grateful.

My dear friend, Joanne Mena, continues to inspire me regarding women's beauty, style, and intelligence. Her advice and perspectives have been critical in developing characters in my series. She is an accomplished businesswoman with a love of exceptional food, drink, political commentary, and fantastic dance moves. Does she party in fabulous designer shoes? Count on it.

The Fellowship of the Book is my name for our writers' group of three gifted authors, Michael Varga, Merrie Meyers, and Ned Skubic. I learn so much from you about writing and the creation of art. Thank you.

Mara LaLonde, the Principal Consultant for MSL Consulting, has been the go-to person for advice when nothing makes sense and my mind needs to be encouraged into creativity. You are inspiring, and I am grateful for your friendship.

I admire the entertainer, actress, and advocate, Tiffany Arieagas. Her years of dedicated work with those living with HIV/Aids and with members of the transgender community have transformed lives for decades. She is an inspiring example of living authentically and advancing inclusiveness. To know her is to understand integrity and beauty.

To others who have offered advice after reviewing my work, my dear friend, Irene Mendoza, and friends new and old. Thank you for not being put off by my mistakes and omissions. I benefited greatly from your patient endurance.

Finally, (Background music swells)

The very thought of you ...

My husband, Anton S. Wallner, Ph.D., is the man whose inspiration can only be captured in the following line in the text of *Seed Blood*:

"I was floored by the beauty found in his soulful stare. I felt an almost overpowering need to pull him into an embrace, climb into his back pocket, and stay there forever."

I have beheld so much wonder in your arms and am filled with the thankfulness that comes with loving an amazing person.

I am the luckiest person on the planet.

Afterword

Thanks for reading <u>Seed Blood.</u> I hope you enjoyed it. Please review it on Amazon.com and visit my website, www.tomseverino.com, to learn more about <u>The Kayne Sorenson Mysteries.</u>

Ready to get snowbound with Kayne and Nick in Aspen, Colorado? Keep reading for a preview of Book Two in the series <u>Tribal Blood, A Kayne Sorenson Mystery.</u>

Thomas Paul Severino

Tribal Blood

A Kayne Sorenson Mystery

by

Thomas Paul Severino

Prologue

The woman looked carefully at the severed flesh and bone.

Without removing her heavy gloves, she gently knocked a bit of the dried mud from its contours. It appeared to be human. Turning it over in the beam of her flashlight, she guessed it was part of a little finger. Carefully easing her find into a plastic zip-lock bag, she backed carefully out of the culvert.

White River barked excitedly as Susan Chipeta Walker emerged from the large drainage pipe. She had entered and climbed out against the direction of the minuscule water flow. Above, the western skies continued to darken with the promise of snow. A big storm was headed for the Richmond Ridge and surrounding territory. The bounty hunter could feel the changing atmospheric pressure in her bones. Time to head back. She called White River to her.

"Finally got something, pal," Susan said to her buddy. The big dog, aware of something important, barked again, circled her twice, and sat at her feet with frosty breath and tongue dripping. Her mistress adjusted the dog's harness vest with particular care.

Susan moved back to the other side of the drainage pipe, playing the light beam over the ground and the small icy flow that left the opening. She inspected the surrounding area on her hands and knees, careful not to disturb the terrain. She looked in the four compass directions for landmarks that would coordinate with this place on the mountain, speaking softly in the ancient tongue over the spot that yielded evidence of the dead.

Susan had spent many times with her grandfather and her younger brother on these mountains, learning the tracking skills that were a part of the tradition of her tribe. Together, they tracked both animals and men. Chief Arapeen was often asked by local law enforcement to trace the movement of criminals in the wilderness of Colorado, Nevada, and Utah. She remembered that just before he died, he spoke wise words of encouragement about their work together.

"You have mastered the tracking ways of our people, my children. You both have gone beyond even me in the art of listening to the voice of our Earth Mother and her brothers, the air, the water, and the sky. Use your skill only for good, my little braves."

Susan was 14, and her brother was 12 at the time of the great chief's death.

Pulling her heavy coat closer against the mountain chill, the bounty hunter headed back up the steep slope to her Jeep on the steep road above. White River ran ahead, making sure the way was clear and safe.

Susan Walker wanted to get off the mountain and back to the reservation before the storm hit. As she stepped into the vehicle, she looked up to see a light aircraft heading for the airstrip in the valley below. She thought, *They needed to head for cover like the rest of us.*

Susan slowly drove the Jeep further up the narrow mountain road to the turnaround. As she approached, a very large truck suddenly appeared behind her. *Too close*, she thought. *This could be trouble.* She opened the glove compartment and moved the Webley to her lap.

As she came to the turnaround, a broad space that swung out away from the mountain and high above the valley below, the truck rammed the back of the Jeep. The force sent her vehicle dangerously close to the low wall at the edge of the drop-off.

Susan stopped the forward motion of the Jeep, turned the wheels uphill, and set the brake. She jumped from the driver's seat, followed by the enraged White River. Behind her, the light aircraft descended to the landing strip.

"What's going on, asshole? Forget how to drive?" she addressed the two burly men who emerged from the truck aiming with her gun.

"No, I think we are doing just fine. Seems you've been poking your nose into places it don't belong."

"That so?"

As the dog waited for the signal to attack, Susan gestured to each man with the gun barrel. "Since I have my friend here aimed at your nuts," she said to the driver. Looking at his partner, she continued, "And can swing

278

over and take off yours before you can say 'deballed,' suppose you toss that ax handle this way, Bubba."

The larger of the two men dropped the club on the ground. Susan stepped closer and addressed her stalkers.

"Now, hands up, boys."

She reached into the coat of the smaller of the two to search for a weapon. The larger man, suddenly in motion, unleashed a black and silver blade from his belt and threw it into the side of the chest of the Native woman.

As Susan fell, dropping her gun, White River attacked, going for the arms of the would-be killer. Susan rolled onto her back and extracted the blade that had been partially stopped by the heavy padding of her coat.

Immediately, the smaller attacker raised the retrieved ax handle and delivered three sharp blows, first to her knife-wielding hand. The other two broke both of her legs at the thighs.

As Susan screamed, she managed to yell, "White River, find Red Cedar, go!"

The dog came off the grounded attacker, looked at his mistress, and took off down the road. Three shots hit the dirt to the side and behind the running dog. One came close to the left side of her hindquarters, kicking up gravel. White River continued to run on as the snowfall and lowering clouds obscured her escape. She sprinted off the road, taking an animal trail down the mountain.

The larger man staunched the blood on his arms and hands as best he could. Turning to his partner, he said, "Put up the gun before you cause an avalanche, shithead. Let's finish this thing, man. Then we'll go get that fucking dog."

www.ingramcontent.com/pod-product-compliance
Lightning Source LLC
Chambersburg PA
CBHW031705170626

46808CB00005B/1614